Endangered Species
Book 1:
"Diary of an Eco-Warrior"

by Vaulte Kamish

Published by
Shared Experience Art Machine

Survival is not a zero-sum game.

THE INVASION

I love London in the springtime. The women no longer wear weather-proof carpets and the city is opulent with flesh. Long-limbed sun seekers, languish on cafe sidewalks, reeking of chardonnay and erotic promise. Ripe diesel laces the verdant aroma of freshly cut grass, exciting the senses. This is a city of industry and infinite possibility, fecund with history, powered by dreams, greased by the industrious diaspora of Russian oligarchs, Indian industrialists, middle eastern oil magnates, and Chinese entrepreneurs. It is the birthplace of the Industrial Revolution and, quite possibly, the decline of Western civilisation.

Normally, I prowl the streets with great expectation. But not today. I had work to do. And I was feeling out of sorts. My neighbourhood had changed profoundly. It used to be filled with normal people - like DJs and prostitutes. Now, they'd become bankers.

My next door neighbour was the first to go. For several years, he'd been "Marty, the wonky-eyed widower". However, he was replaced by a fellow in a pin-stripe suit with a crimson lining, who introduced himself to me one morning as, 'Barry, fixed income.' He caught me by surprise, taking out the rubbish in my standard-issue, lay-about pyjamas.

'Steven, derivatives,' I countered, quickly. 'I've been dealing in Tokyo futures all night, hence the attire.' His eyes crackled with approval.

Actually, my name isn't Steven - it's Trevor. Not sure why I did that. Was I embarrassed? Force of habit. I gave false information whenever I worked a case. In fact, I enjoyed doing it all the time, even when I wasn't working. I liked being somebody else. Anybody else. International man of mystery. In his tatty pyjamas. That's me.

One-by-one, familiar establishments succumbed to a process of gentrification. My local boozer became a gastropub. Out went the McEwans and in came the Montrachet. The second-hand book shop - run by Carl, the dodgy ferret - became a pilates studio for trophy wives. Pity Carl couldn't stay to appreciate it; he would have loved ogling the punters in their skin-tight lycra.

The bookies became a Viennese patisserie, specialising in pretentious pastries that you could hold in two fingers and which cost more than a pint of petrol. The local butcher was replaced by an real-estate agent. They didn't wear overalls, perhaps, but they still ran a chop-shop, stripping out the dead flesh of rotten housing estates in order to make way for trendy restaurants and parking structures. Bijoux stores that sold only scented candles and greeting cards appeared. Poundstretchers was swept away by a boutique clothier for zero-sized women (no irony lost, there). The indian grocer held out as long as he could but, ultimately, capitulated. His shop was rendered to make way for "Channel for Baby".

I couldn't deny what was happening. Familiar faces were disappearing. They were replaced by horsey people with perfect teeth and blow-dried hair. Even the homeless had vanished into thin air, as if they'd been clamped and then carted off in the night for parking themselves illegally. People used to look out for one other, no matter how odd, or desperate (or, degenerate) they happened to be. We may have been a dysfunctional family, but we were family nonetheless. We got by on tolerance and charity. Until now. We became strangers to one another.

They say blood is thicker than water. But money is thicker than blood. Now, it was every man for himself.

It must be said, though, the streets did look a lot cleaner.

My girlfriend, Francesca, was posh and, for me, a kind of totem. She insulated me from tough, life-threatening decisions, such as where my next meal was coming from. And she got me into great parties. Plus, she was sexy as hell. That wasn't her only redeeming quality, however. At least not in the beginning. I enjoyed her spontaneity and her connectedness to others. In short, she had friends, whereas I had alibis. Sure, there were a few people I considered confidants, of a sort. But they had mental health issues. Francesca was different. Her friends were unencumbered by neuroses. They were public school boys and debutantes. They took life as it came. They could afford to take it all.

Francesca enjoyed talking to strangers. Not the way I did. She didn't do it to get something from them. She was innately curious. She used her real name and gave out her actual phone number when asked. It made me uneasy. Was I insecure? Probably. Yes, most definitely. I was a toy in her play-box. She wanted to rebel against the invasion and liked the fact that I was proletariat. For awhile, we were partners in crime, shocking the establishment.

She fancied us both starving artists. She worked with paint and I worked with words. She was enrolled in St Martins, but her art was terrible. If she had to make a living from it, we truly would be starving. As for my income, it was sporadic, to say the least. Thankfully, she had wealthy parents who didn't seem to care much about her whereabouts. They bought her a swank pad at One Hyde Park. Yet, she preferred mine, because it was more "authentic".

She paid my rent in return for sexual favours. At least that was our joke. A cruel one as it turned out, because they had been lacking lately. Things had been better in the beginning - back when we were friends with benefits. After she moved in, however, the benefits disappeared. And we realised that we hadn't really been friends, either. We were simply attracted to each other's "otherness". A holiday romance that should have remained on holiday.

She was starting to get on my nerves and I didn't like it. I didn't like the way I reacted to it, either. I should have been thankful, but I felt constricted, like a butterfly pinned under glass. She was also younger than me and didn't understand the importance of Man-Space. When she moved in, she was suddenly everywhere at once. My flat had become a nest of thongs, stuffed animals, toiletries, and dilapidated hair. It was too much home invasion. I had nowhere to hide.

Man-Space.

She wasn't bad at heart. Ponies and privilege hadn't corrupted her entirely, but her soul was under siege. She became bossier. She had a sense of entitlement that only money can buy. Sometimes it made her amusing - especially when she said precisely what was in her head, no matter how atrocious. Sometimes it made her cruel.

Lately, she'd become more cruel than usual. Our relationship did not give her bragging rights to her friends. I was treading water, while the rest of her world traded in success. She felt like an outsider to them and took it out on me. We'd become like a married couple - sexless friends who quarrel over trifles, but have too much shared history to leave. Thank goodness we didn't have children, or we'd be forced to think about someone other than ourselves.

It became painfully obvious that she had liked me for my roughness - not for the actual "me". I was no longer worthy of her patronage. I'd became an irritation, a stone inside her Jimmy Choo's. The novelty of mock-poverty was fading. Bit by bit, she become more like "one of them".

She stopped introducing me to her friends.

That's when I knew I had to get rid of her. There was no way this relationship was going to survive the honesty it required. Plus, I didn't like feeling small.

I began my campaign of disengagement by becoming as irritating as possible, so that breaking up would be her decision, not mine. I am a coward when it comes to break-ups.

Inevitably, they come to a messy end and I'm not good at mopping up the mess. I'm better at creating them.

At first, it seemed as if it was working, but Francesca proved tenacious. She must have made some private decision in regards to our relationship that didn't require my input. But that's how these things work. So, I ran away as much as possible, stayed out late, disappearing for days, coming home drunk. Gradually, I wore her down.

'Why do you always keep your passport in your back pocket?' she said, angrily. 'It's as if you can't wait to get away from me the first moment you get.'

'My work requires it.'

'What work?' she said, looking around my flat, scanning the detritus of my dissolute life. Her air of derision was inescapable.

'Can we please shag?' I said, bursting.

'No.'

'Why not?'

'I love you,' she said. 'But you disgust me.'

'Take pity on me, then. I have a medical condition. Blueball Introitus.'

'Which is why God gave you hands.'

I was going to miss Francesca. She was very convenient. Also, I liked her cat. He was good company. He didn't tell me what to wear, or ask me why I had used a certain tone of voice, or relate mundane stories about shopping with Kiki, DeeDee, or some other two-syllable companion who dressed from a Barbie catalog. That cat knew how to live amongst them without attracting attention. He was a survivor. Like me.

I went to my local coffee shop. I had an hour to kill before my rendezvous with Oz. The shop had been converted into an artisan, maison du chocolat. It still served coffee, but at five times the price - a calculated form of natural selection. I listened to the special language of the invaders and their elaborate code. By now, I knew that "Saint Barths" wasn't a Catholic icon, and that an "Aman-Junkie" was not a drug pusher. One-upmanship was important to status: better holidays, better cars, better bonuses. Despite their cool exterior, the competition for kudos was tooth-and-nail. These were Francesca's people. The men - brave knights, wielding briefcases and brollies, battling dragons on the stock market. The women - damsels in financial distress, who needed whopping overdrafts, and maintenance money. The men swapped paper: paper stocks, paper bonds, paper trophies, and paper money. Everything, bought and sold. Everyone, reduced to paper. When they went to the pub, they drank champagne instead of beer. They spoke too loudly, as if the world was desperate to hear what they had to say. My street overflowed with swaggering suits, like designer garbage, bellowing into bluetooth headsets, as if they had Tourette's. They also had a special way of walking - head held high, no shifty eyes - and no hoodies. They moved slower than the rest, like smug zombies, never hurried nor harassed. They actually stopped and waited for the lights to change before crossing the street! I tried to copy their behaviour for fear of being caught out.

It was the invasion of the "One-Percenters".

Well, perhaps not quite in my neighbourhood - they were the two-percenters. They couldn't afford (yet) to live in Chelsea, Knightsbridge, or Mayfair. But they still belonged to the privileged - the ones who owned over ninety percent of the country. And they were squeezing the rest of us out of it. We were becoming enslaved by the upper class.

'Where are you?' I asked into my smartphone, scanning the street.

'See if you can find me,' said Oz, jauntily. 'I'm incognito.'

The neighbourhood was tidy and affluent. Expensive cars. Flower boxes on the street lamps. Nothing out of the ordinary, except - 'Oz, please don't tell me you're in the van with the giant, inflatable cockroach on the roof?'

'Pretty cool, no? People'll think we're just exterminators, on an assignment.'

'We're supposed to be part of the catering crew. I think it

sends the wrong message.'

Oz leant out of the back of the van and grabbed my arm, 'Quick, get in!'

He was wearing a "We are Legion" hoodie, cinched up around his head. His arm was white and translucent, like a newborn worm. He recoiled from the sun, as if it was something dangerous. It struck me, then, that I'd never seen him outdoors. Normally, I'd visit him at his Council block - a penthouse bedsit - which he referred to as "The Citadel", since it was high up and packed to the gills with surveillance equipment. The more prosaic local authorities called it, "Lambeth Estates". Oz held camp there, hacking, jacking, and freaking any signal he could get his hands on. He was a one-man, rogue intelligence agency. I'd seen his roof once. It was littered with aerials and satellite dishes. Inside his bedsit, it was perpetual nighttime. He kept the curtains stapled shut to keep the glare off his computer monitors. Frankly, I was pleased not to have to go there today. The lift was always busted and you were forced to climb twenty-four flights of stairs. Perhaps Oz broke it on purpose to keep down the number of visitors.

I stumbled over the threshold, tripping over a pile of empty Nitro-Cola cans and Orange, Jaffa-cake boxes. Oz shuttered the doors, plunging us into darkness. I reached out wildly like a blind man, until my arm connected with an office chair. I wheeled it towards me, sat down, and waited for my eyes to grow accustomed to the gloom. Gradually, things came into focus. Oz massaged his keyboards in front of wall of LCD panels. He reminded me of those eighties rock musicians who played multiple synthesisers at once. Geek Macho.

It didn't matter how many times I saw him, it was always a shock. His nickname was Magua from, "The last of the Mohicans", on account of his hair, which he twisted upwards from all directions into a psychotic quiff, shaped like a scrub brush. If Lady Gaga and Marilyn Manson ever had a love child, it would probably look something like Oz. He was gangly, preening, and totally paranoid. His skin had an unhealthy sheen to it, as if mummified by cling-wrap, because he never went outside. I'd seen his feet once and wished I hadn't. He shed the skin from his soles like a snake, whenever he took his boots off. In fact, he never changed his socks until the weekend. He'd simply put one layer over the other, a new sock over the old one, until he peeled off all seven at the end of the week. He was a freak of nature. Nevertheless, I couldn't take my eyes off him. Watching him was like rubbernecking at the scene of a terrible, automobile accident. You knew you shouldn't look, but you couldn't help yourself.

'This van is hardly inconspicuous,' I said, rolling up beside him. 'People are going to remember it.'

'What will they remember?'

'A van with a cockroach on top.'

'Exactly! But, what kind of van? What colour? What license plate number?' he waited for me to say something, but I couldn't. 'You see. You can't remember anything, except the ornament.' He spun to face me. 'There was this geezer, yeah? A grifter. He'd ask people on the street for directions and pick their pockets at his leisure. He'd do it wearing a bright, orange plaster on the bridge of his nose. Later, when the police took the victim's statement, they couldn't remember anything about him. They'd been staring at his face for several minutes, but all they could remember was the plaster! Genius.'

'Why not pick their pockets from the shadows without ever being seen?'

'Sometimes it's better to hide in plain sight.' He swivelled back to his keyboard. 'Besides, I needed something to disguise the satellite dish.'

I heard a rustling beside me. It came from an empty aquarium. Down at the bottom, amongst food debris, I caught a glimpse of several cockroaches, foraging through the filth. It made me jump. I hated cockroaches. It was an irrational fear, but fear all the same. 'What the hell - '

'Stop it,' said Oz, 'you're freaking them out.'

'They're freaking *me* out!' I could see electrodes poking out of their heads. 'And what the hell have you done to them?!'

'Chillax. They're working with us tonight.' He gestured to his screens, which had surveillance video feeds from eight different cameras. It was then I noticed that the cameras were moving. 'They're running a reconnaissance mission.'

It was ingenious, but it made me nervous. These were important people. I didn't want to get rumbled just because Oz wanted to test out a new toy. 'I don't like it, Oz. Why don't we just stick to the original plan? All we need is the audio.'

'This is better. Look, I can control where they go.' He tapped some keys to make a point. One of the roach cameras suddenly changed direction. 'That's why I had to hack into their brains.'

'Couldn't you have picked some other creature? Roaches give me the creeps.'

'Roaches are best. They're more primitive. Hardier. They can go under floorboards, up walls, drainpipes, wherever. Plus, they don't need to be fed as often. I once put a roach into a sealed jar. No water, food, or air. How long do you think he lasted?'

'I have no idea.'

'Neither do I. I gave up after eight weeks.' He shook his head in admiration. 'You can't kill a cockroach. When armageddon comes, they'll outlast us all.'

I left him to play with his new friends, while I unpacked my kit. Mine was more modest: a flash disk recorder, some headphones, and a notepad. By contrast, Oz's van was filled with enough computing equipment to support a mission to the moon. I pushed the roach aquarium as far from me as possible. Unfortunately, I had trouble finding a workspace that wasn't crunchy. Every surface was covered in crumbs, electrical off-cuts, ransacked circuit boards, fungus, and nail clippings. Despite his lack of hygiene, Oz was an engineering wizard, which made him difficult to reproach. I bit my tongue and brushed aside whatever stuck to my jumper.

He offered me a cup of tea, which I graciously declined, more concerned of catching typhoid than out of decorum. Even in the dark, I was pretty sure that the tea bags had fur. He poured himself a mug of cola and dunked a Jaffa into it, sucking on it while inspecting his handy-work. He sounded like an old-aged pensioner without dentures, gumming on a wet sponge. I put on a pair of headphones to block it out.

Our mate, Barnaby, was already on the inside. He worked for an upscale catering company that handled most of the exclusive soirées around town. The kind of events where important people gathered, drank too much, and swapped gossip. A great place to be fly-on-the-wall. Naturally, I wasn't invited to such parties. In the world of journalism, I was a bottom-feeder. In fact, I could hardly call myself a journalist anymore. Nobody would knowingly tell me anything, so I had to scavenge any which way I can - which was where Barnaby came in.

We had a pretty good system. I would provide him with dainty and artistic looking champagne markers - designed by yours truly - that hid Oz's piezo, radio transmitters. They were suction-cupped to the foot of each glass. As far as the punters were concerned, they were decorative tags that helped them to identify which glass was theirs. What they didn't know was that the tags were pressure-sensitive pick-ups.

Glass is a great material for capturing reverberations. When you consider that people often hold a champagne glass by its stem, a short distance away from their mouths, it's as if they were holding a microphone and conducting an interview. Meanwhile, Oz and I would hunker down in a van parked outside the building, running a twenty-four track, audio recorder that received the wireless feeds, enabling us to record the conversations from all the glasses at once.

It was a bit of a scattergun approach, to be sure. You could never tell what you were going to get at the end of the day. However, tonight, we were at the house of a prominent MP, celebrating something private and exclusive, amongst a close coterie of friends, so I was hopeful. There would be a lot of post-processing work. Hours of recordings to sift through. Grunt work. I didn't do it for the kicks, though, I did it for the money.

In the past, it would have taken me days, but Oz had a better system. He'd cooked up some code that mapped the formant frequencies of all the speakers, analysed their speech patterns, and looked for "The Shift". This was a change in timbre, tone, or register that people often used when they were about to say something salacious. A bit like a person's "tell" in poker. His program would rip through the audio, neatly marking all the "shifts" and panning for gold, so we didn't have to.

Now, Oz had now added video to the mix. I wasn't entirely sure why. It probably was just an excuse to get some new gear into the field. He already had several of his "scouts" checking out the layout of the house, identifying where the motion-detectors for the alarm system were, looking for secret rooms, hidden drawers, and interesting tidbits of information.

'I'm going to fit them with a belly camera next,' said Oz, nonchalantly. 'By walking over a piece of paper, they'll be able to scan documents.'

Just then, a woman came out of the loo, saw the roach, shrieked, and stomped it with her heel. One of the LCD screens went dark.

'Crap! Man down!' said Oz, to nobody in particular. He sent "agent six" to go check out his fallen comrade, and make sure that nothing compromising was left behind.

'You were saying?' I said, ironically, stopping short of, "I told you so." Oz didn't reply. He was too busy with his evac operation to care.

The next few hours went by uneventfully. I began processing the audio, while Oz practiced deploying his army to ever farther recesses of the house. He lost three of his roaches before the night was out. Indeed, the party was dragging on, as a few stragglers refused to go home. Barnaby had long since packed up his kit and left. I could see that Oz was "in the zone" and didn't want to be interrupted, but I was getting bored.

'Shall we call it a night?' I said, hopefully.

'Look!' said Oz, excitedly. He tapped panel four. I pulled up next to him. On the screen, we could see that the MP had fallen into bed with one of his guests. They were going at it like jack-rabbits.

'That's not his wife,' I said.

'Damn right, it's not,' replied Oz. 'This is the icing on the cake!' He herded some of the other roaches to the room. They took up different positions, so he had several angles on the action. 'I wish we had audio in there.'

'I don't think we need audio, Oz. It's pretty obvious what's going on.'

'Pillow talk, mate. That's when the best-kept secrets get un-kept. I'll have to redesign the camera pack, though, to accommodate a microphone. It's going to add extra bulk and weight.'

As unsavoury as it was, this was going to be a scoop. The tabloids would pay a pretty penny for it.

And so would the MP.

We celebrated later with a doner kebab. The owner of the establishment asked us to leave, however, as he didn't want our van parked outside, scaring away the customers. We shifted it further down the block and went to work, editing the rest of our spoils. I worked through the night, compiling the audio. Most of the guests were bitching about taxes. A bonus of forty million was really only twenty at the end of the day, unless you spun a complex web of offshore accounts. And reliable nannies in London were in desperately short supply.

Their natter was irritating. Politics had become about personalities and image management, not principles. I did get some dirt on a few dignitaries, and the MP's sex tape would be a gold mine. Thank God for that, because I had a razor-blade heart-burn from all the kebabs I'd eaten.

I looked over at Oz and saw him playing with some elaborate computer model of a globe, covered in an infra-red heat map of some kind. 'What's that? Global warming?'

'Global discontent,' he said, cryptically. He invited me over. 'This is how humanity is feeling, right now.' He pointed out the different colours, 'Yellow, happy. Blue, sad.'

'And, red?'

'Angry.'

I could see a lot of red over North America.

'If you break it down by geography,' Oz continued, 'the most miserable people in the world live in the most advanced countries. Except, Asia.' He pointed to blobs of orange in the Far East.

'How are you getting all this?'

'I modified one of the Google bots to crawl its own database. It searches terms that match emotional buzz words and linguistic patterns, using some proprietary algorithms I cooked up over breakfast,' he said, draining a can of Nitro Cola.

'Is that breakfast?' I said, looking at the can he'd discarded.

'Watch what happens when I step back fifteen years and roll forward,' he said, ignoring me. The map abruptly changed to happier colours, then stepped forward through shades of blue over the years, while the continents in the West grew progressively red. He tapped the Western Hemisphere, 'Looks like we're on the brink of anarchy, mate.'

'Why?'

He folded his arms and spun round to face me, 'That's the million dollar question.' His breath made my eyes water. It smelled like caffeinated toe cheese, with a hint of citrus. 'I've been running regressions for the past few hours, trying to find the correlation.'

'What does that mean in English?'

'I think I've found the reason for all the misery.'

'What is it?'

'Guess.'

I knew what was coming. Oz was a conspiracy theorist extraordinaire. No doubt, he had provocative and elaborate explanation all worked out.

'Maybe it's because we spend too much time alone, on our computers, sitting in darkened rooms all day, eating chemicals, and living vicariously?' I said.

Oz didn't get me. He'd been diagnosed once as a highly functional, autistic. It gave him an ability to see patterns out of the ordinary, but didn't endow him with a sense of irony.

'Guess again.'

'Economic depression.'

'Close, but no cigar.'

'The weather?'

'No.'

'Plastic surgery?'

'You're getting off base, mate. Shall I tell you?'

'Please. Not that I don't enjoy this game, but I think we'll be here all day.'

'Wankers,' he said, smiling, 'and their bonuses.' He tapped his keyboard, exploding graphs, and drilling down into the data. 'In the eighties, performance pay became the norm. Look. Here's the baseline for the working population. Then, here's the one for the financial services. See? Banker's bonuses went ballistic, outstripping every other industry year on year. And the more the banker's bonuses grew, yeah, the more miserable the rest of the population became.'

'Alright, so there's a correlation,' I said, playing devil's advocate. 'Doesn't prove cause and effect.'

'Why not? They live in a gated community.'

'Meaning?'

'Think about it,' said Oz, throwing his hands about like a windmill. 'Bankers don't contribute to the general economy. They don't create anything. They're parasites. They deploy other people's capital, while siphoning off fees. They off-shore their earnings and avoid taxes. Then, they bankrupt the people whose money they've borrowed and spend it on themselves - buying yachts, private jets, and expensive holidays that nobody else can afford. They've created their own, global economy for the superclass.'

'Cockroaches,' I said.

'Damn right,' nodded Oz, enthusiastically.

'Or, lobsters.'

'Come again?'

'Lobsters are expensive, considered a luxury, despite the fact that they're bottom feeders. Cockroaches of the sea.'

Oz stopped moving, then looked at me, unsure of how to continue our conversation. I think he found the eye contact a bit overstimulating, because he went back to his graphs. 'Check it,' he said, pointing at the data. 'It all started with Reagan in the eighties. Just look at that hockey stick to the stars, mate. The investment banks crawled so far up his backside that he became the ass-puppet of Wall Street. He embedded their cronies at the Treasury and let them pull the strings of power. Every president since has been their ring-piece. Even Obama, the prodigal son, can't get rid of them. And, because they're multinationals, they've spread their disease across the globe. The Bank of England is Barclays' bitch. Markets manipulated, countries destabilised, and governments grifted.'

'This has been going on for decades, Oz. Why should things be any different now?'

'The difference is perception, my friend. The public didn't mind bending over, so long as they got scraps from the table. They got their pension plans, their forty-two inch plasmas, and their MTV. The middle class got bigger. Everyone felt better off. But it was a house of cards. They were leveraged to the hilt. Then, the wankers got greedy. After raiding the larder, they nicked the silverware and fleeced the staff. Everything collapsed. They caused the recession, but gave themselves bonuses. And, then, while the rest of us were on our knees, they stopped lending, dropped savings interest to nought percent, and pushed up credit cards to fifty percent a-p-r?! Fifty percent! That's loan-sharking, mate, no doubt about it. And government endorsed loan-sharking to boot! They squeezed both ends of the tube, the silly sods. Now, the middle class is working class. They lost everything. Their gains, obliterated. They finally woke up and realised they were wearing the emperor's new clothes. They're back to where they started, but poorer. And angry. Even caviar tastes like dog shit, when you lick it off a boot. Get my meaning? '

Oz was not your regular political anarchist. He was smart and capable - a dangerous mind.

'Normally, in a recession, the happiness quotient rises,' he continued. 'People muck in together, figure they're in the same boat. They spend time with family, re-evaluate their lives, help the community. Not this time. This time they can see where their money went. To the knobs in Hello magazine. Celebrity cribs on reality TV. Pimp my Maybach. You can't cross the street in central London without tripping over an Aston Martin. Did you see what happened at Harrods last year? The new owners parked their Lamborghinis on double-yellow and got clamped. What did they do? Absolutely nothing. They left them behind and bought a couple more, because it was easier to spend a million quid to get the dealer to deliver than pay a visit to the pound. They couldn't be bothered. They might as well have stuck two fingers up to the rest of us.'

'If it's a global phenomena,' I ventured, 'then why is the US worse off ?'

'Because, they bought the bullshit of the American Dream. And now they feel entitled to it. Whereas, the British are too busy whinging to be that idealistic.'

'A black man became president,' I said. 'Dreams can come true.'

'You can't sell a lie without a few poster children. People have to win the lottery from time to time. But the cat's out of the bag, mate. Check out the "inequality of opportunity index". Social mobility is a fiction. Envy fuelled the capitalist economy. With everyone trying to outdo their neighbours, they worked harder. It was good for GDP. But, in the end, capitalism destroyed democracy. Special interest groups help the entitled to game the system. For two hundred years, the super-rich have gotten richer at everyone else's expense. Passed it down the generations. And, now, thanks to the market collapse, they can truly spend it! Everything's so ridiculously cheap to them right now - land, corporations - countries, even! It's a bargain basement sale. The middle-class worked their guts out, just to get behind. There is no equal opportunity. It's America's dirty little secret.'

'Let them eat cake,' I said, ironically.

'Let them eat lobster.' Oz smiled. 'That's where we come in, sunshine. We're the real Robin Hood.'

Whatever it was he said made me feel better about myself. Until the heartburn doused my throat in stomach acid. Death by kebabicide.

'Here's what I owe you for tonight,' I said, changing the subject.

He shook his head. 'I'm an artist. I don't do it for the money.'

'I know, Oz. But you need to eat. Preferably, something that wasn't made in a laboratory. Better yet, hire a cleaner.'

Oz gave me the shoulder and went back to his business. 'Bringing down the establishment. That's payment enough for me, mate.'

I tried to traverse the van without tripping over his "lifestyle".

'Thanks, Oz. See you soon.' I popped the door handle and stepped out into the light.

When I got home, Francesca was not happy. She had stayed up for me - even though I'd expressly told her not to. Suddenly, it became my fault. I was accused of being callous and contributing to her insomnia by making her worry. I could see that my frequent disappearances were finally getting to her.

You might hate me for saying this, but I must be honest. I love women to bits. But they are infuriating. They change the goal posts on a daily basis. You say it's not fair, but, for them, it's standard operating procedure. They test your commitment. No matter how many times you say you love them, they try to trip you up. Rarely content with the way things are, they push, prod, cajole, threaten - counter and caress. It's exhausting. And, quite frankly, after listening to ten hours of the uber-elite discussing hedge funds, political imbroglios, and country estates - I wanted to sit down with a beer, watch the telly, and turn off my brain.

But that wasn't what Francesca had in mind. There was something else brewing - I just didn't know what.

We ended up watching "Invasion of the Bodysnatchers". Not the original, mind you, but the one with Donald Sutherland. It was a scary movie - all the more so, after what I'd seen happening in my own backyard. Plus, I couldn't help brooding on Oz's "happiness quotient" and the lobsters. Perhaps, it was a latent response to all the people of privilege kicking around my echoic memory. Whatever it was, I couldn't help thinking, "Society is making me redundant".

Francesca chose that moment to take my hand and tell me that she loved me. She'd never done that before.

It scared me more than the movie.

Where the hell did that come from? At first, I pretended not to hear. But her eyes watered with a warning: the tidal wave was about to hit the barrier.

To be frank, I was surprised by the strength of her emotion. She had always been such a shallow person. It's cruel of me to say, I know, but she would have said so, herself. When we first slept together, I had been a bit too earnest for her liking. I had to dial it back. The liquor lowered my guard. That was my excuse, anyway. She laughed at my schoolboy sincerity and made it clear that this was to be a light-hearted affair. I took her advice and kept my emotional distance. Plus, my recent, calculated absences were meant to accelerate her departure. But, now, something had clearly… gone wrong.

She looked into my eyes, searching for an answer.

'Thank you,' I replied.

That wasn't the answer she was looking for. She pulled her hand away. Then, hit me with an ashtray.

I feigned innocence, but knew better. Besides, the movie was reaching its climax. I wanted to see if everyone had been turned into pod people, or if a spark of humanity would triumph. I felt my life depended on it.

She didn't stay to watch it with me, but stomped off to bed in a huff. Clearly, she wasn't a happy bunny.

'You despise me, then?' she stood on my doorstep in the rain. It would have been dramatic, had her chauffeur not been by her side, holding an umbrella over her head, and cradling her cat. He pretended not to earwig on our conversation.

'I don't despise you,' I said, 'that's not the problem.'

'It's because I won't sleep with you!'

'I'm sorry, can you repeat that? I'm not sure they heard that in Manchester.'

'Then, what IS the problem?' her voice was stern, but her eyes were pleading, as if to say, "Don't make me go back there to - to them."

I took time to formulate my answer - not because I had something thoughtful to say - but because she was wearing a hot miniskirt, and I wanted to linger on her legs awhile. 'We just spent too much time together.'

I closed the door.

I heard her high heels click angrily down the steps, like a demented tap dancer. The truth was I despised myself. And she was a constant reminder of it.

I took my first breath as a free man and surveyed my domain, now that sanity was restored. But my flat now seemed oppressive and quiet, like a sarcophagus. A bedsit caked in kitty litter and sadness.

I ripped a large trash bag from the roll and began binning her stuff. I did this with ruthless efficiency, until I reached the bedroom and saw her depression on the pillow. The scent of her perfumed skin lingered with regret. It was the smell of sweat and rain, honeysuckle thighs, and nether must.

I sat down in a funk, imagined her getting into the car and telling the driver to take her for some serious retail therapy. She would need a complete makeover to cleanse her of folly - a detox to shake the last eight months of what amounted to a bad field trip. She'd gather her friends around the campfire at Cecconi's and frighten them with tales from the dark side of the tracks, over blinis and martinis.

But what about me? Where was my exit strategy?

I was stuck where I began.

I didn't say a proper goodbye, because I didn't want to. But now, looking at her pillow, it made me feel sadder than when she'd left the room.

I slept on the sofa.

I was fooling myself when I said I wouldn't miss her. It's easy to focus on someone's negative qualities whenever they're around. Absence makes the heart grow fonder.

I went on a three-day bender and woke up in a strange flat, belonging to a girl I'd met in a pub. I didn't remember her name, but she had lilac hair extensions and breasts like water balloons. I felt as if I was body-surfing on gelatine, when we had intercourse. It was a bad, out-of-body experience. I floated above her, instead of being in the same bed together. It was the first time I'd ever thought sex could be silly and pointless, which only exacerbated my feeling of detachment. Besides, balloons are for children. I went back home and slapped on the washing-up gloves. It was time to complete the Francesca removal operation, once and for all.

Despite my best efforts, her presence remained - especially her hair. Everyday, I found more and more of it around - on the furniture, on the bath mat, even on my clothes that were folded up in the cupboard. She had shed over everything. I burnt it - but, it kept multiplying. I was afraid to fall asleep in case the hair would cocoon itself around me in the night, suffocating me in a chrysalis. I might wake up the next morning, looking exactly the same, but harbouring an inexplicable desire to work at a bank, have a family of four, and get a golf club membership.

I struggled to preserve my independence, but she invaded my dreams. I thought of her standing outside my door, sometimes with laughing eyes, eager with anticipation. Sometimes, sad and in need of comfort. Her eyes were voluminous and caught the moonlight, floating towards me in the dark, like a jack-o-lantern, or one of those "Sad Eyes" portraits of children by Margaret Keane. Enormous globes of reproach. But there were good times, too. She could fart comfortably in my presence. That was a significant milestone. She had been more charitable then. I hoarded those happy memories. It was unhealthy.

A few weeks later, I ran into her in the street. She was walking to her car and had to cross in front of me. I was about to smile and say something, when I realised that she didn't recognise me - or, rather, pretended not to. She had the same haughty, head-held-high expression as all the others.

I felt a pit in my stomach.

Just then, I heard a plummy, male voice from someone waiting in her car, "Come on Poppit, we're going to be late for the opening."

She had been turned.

Best to pretend we feel no emotion - at least not show it in public. That's how the invasion works. Your compassion is your weakness. It singles you out as the underclass. We brushed past one another - as strangers.

I had lost her forever.

I spent the rest of the day in the park, lying on my back, and anaesthetising myself with cheap vodka. Summer was in full bloom and I sheltered in its warm embrace. Just then, my phone rang. I picked it up on impulse, wanting to hear Francesca's voice, but I hit myself in the eye. My hands were no longer my own, but the vodka's. I felt I was on a grass travelator, moving backwards, while the sky spun round around me like a pinwheel.

I don't know what I said, only that I said it with conviction. Soon after, I realised I'd said too much. Then I learnt that the lady on the other end of the phone was not Francesca. Thank God for that! But, now, I had embarrassed myself to someone else.

Her name was Lucy Keller. She wanted to discuss an assignment. I tried to commit the address to memory, but the ground kept leaping up at me. I managed to coral my senses and ride the carousel. In retrospect, this was a wake-up call. Lucy gave me a new lease of life that night. I owe her for that one.

But she owes me many times over for all that's happened since.

THE SILVER SPOON

Lucy Keller had arranged to meet me at a cafe called, "The Silver Spoon". As soon as I entered, I felt conspicuous. It was very hoity-toity. Miniature cupcakes, crochet doilies, and silver tea sets, that kind of thing. I had entered a Chelsea girl's dollhouse wearing soiled jeans and stubble.

There weren't many other customers, so I picked her out immediately. Unlike me, she was immaculately coiffed, as if she'd walked off the cover of a woman's fashion magazine. Her skin was a cocoa, buttery brown. Not from the sun. Definitely in the DNA. Mediterranean looking. She had green eyes and rich, black hair. White teeth, too, but not from a dentistry kit. These had the natural shine of someone who spends a lot of time outdoors, living off the land, chewing nuts and berries. Her jewellery wasn't ostentatious, but tasteful - and reassuringly expensive. My fear of running a fool's errand subsided.

'Are you feeling better from yesterday?' she said.

'Sure,' I replied, nonchalantly, shimmying into her booth, but I gouged my groin on the corner of the table, upsetting her tea service, and pinching a gonad. Not the entrance I had in mind.

The crockery commotion brought the waiter over. 'Good,' she said pleasantly, 'I've been trying to get his attention for the past five minutes'.

Apparently, he was from the French School of Waitering. The ones who scan the room with a studious look, without managing to look anybody in the eye, least of all those who require their service. He clucked with a supercilious air, mopped up my mess, and deliberately placed my menu out of reach.

Lucy dotted some errant drops on the table with her napkin, then neatly refolded it beside her saucer. Disaster averted. 'Want some coffee?'

'Only if it's Irish.' I needed something to numb my senses, but keep me awake. Trust the Irish to invent something so contradictory. The waiter raised an eyebrow at me, then disappeared.

Lucy narrowed her eyes and stared at my shoulder. Then, reached over and touched me. It seemed an unusually intimate gesture for a first time meeting. 'Sorry, but you have a long, reddish hair, on your sweater,' she said, plucking it off, and placing it in a spare napkin, as might a forensic investigator. 'It was distracting.'

'Irish Setter,' I replied. 'Dog-sitting for a friend.'

'She has beautiful hair.'

'*He*. He's a show dog, you know. Got a grooming award from Crufts and everything.'

'Indeed.'

I don't think she found me the least bit charming, or amusing. Clearly, I was off my game.

When our drinks arrived, she poured herself a spot of tea with clinical precision. I could see that she had a particular way of doing things. Ritualistic. A specific order. The spoon was delicately shaken and put to the side, just so.

As for me, I tried in vain to circumnavigate the dollop of whipped cream that was floating on my drink, but ended up wearing it on my nose. I'd lost my napkin to the floor, so I used my sleeve. I could feel the heat of disapproval from her eyes. She waited for the waiter to leave us, before continuing our conversation.

She'd read an article I'd written some years ago for a wildlife magazine. It was an eyewitness account of Brazilian deforestation - how it was eradicating valuable medicinal plants that could benefit humanity and, also, threatening the sloth population. She was quite taken with it.

In truth, I wrote it from the library. I never went to Brazil. And I couldn't care less about the sloths. I was strapped for cash, so I fabricated a bunch of receipts, including a dodgy airline ticket, and pocketed the expenses.

I didn't feel guilty about this. The commissioning editor had it coming to him. He made my life a living hell. His mouth was a angry shower of saliva and vitriol, especially when he called my name. I nicknamed him, "MSA", for "Mister Spitting Apoplectic". He tugged on his tie all the time, as if it was strangling him. He carried a hand exerciser, which he pumped frenetically throughout the day. It had been given to him by an anger management therapist under court order. He was supposed to squeeze it instead of assaulting his staff.

He squeezed it a lot whenever I was around.

'Do you have the goddamn copy, yet? Where's my copy? Are you listening to me? Or, is there nothing behind those ears except cotton wool and sunshine?' His breath smelled of Jack Daniels and rotting possum. Which came as no surprise, since he spent most of his days getting sozzled by lunchtime. I avoided the office in the mornings and waited until "Happy Hour", before attempting any meaningful conversation with him, although he rarely remembered anything about it afterwards. He was a merry drunk.

Sometimes, for my own amusement, I'd ask him for a raise. He never paid me a penny, though. It was early in my career and I needed the byline. Also, his daughter was a minx. That's really why I stayed. Although, she wouldn't have sex with me unless I was dressed up as a schoolgirl, in tights and a pleated skirt. That was really weird. I pretended to be turned on, but, actually, I found it disturbing. It made me feel vulnerable.

Anyways, her father eventually went down the captain of a sinking ship, when the magazine folded. He died shortly after. I was called in a month later to collect my personal affects. It was late at night. The corridors were empty, lit by spooky shadows from rain-spattered windows. I was busying loading computer equipment into a hold-all. I figured that I needed it more than they did. After all, they were going out of business. I wasn't. That's when I heard it - a rhythmic squeaking of a hand exerciser, echoing in the corridors, drawing nearer, as if the ghost of Apoplectic was lost wandering the halls. It made the hairs on my neck stand on end. I left everything behind and got the hell out of there.

In any event, Lucy liked my piece, because it had the voice of authority and conviction - back in the day when I was relatively earnest. Since then, I had mastered the art of false sincerity. I don't regret this. I get far more work now than I did then. Paying the bills is an occupational hazard.

She had Googled my past, knew about my stint at Rolling Stone, and that investigative stuff I did back when I called myself a journalist, before I lost one of my testicles to Bosnian terrorists. Actually, I lost it on my way to see them by falling down the stairs with my Sat phone in my pocket. I literally got my knickers in a twist. The pain was excruciating beyond words, but I desperately needed the pay, so I swallowed my pride and carried out the interview through clenched teeth. They mistook my demeanour for aggression and ended up answering most of my questions without protest. Turned out to be a great interview, but at too high a price. I had literally worked my balls off for that assignment. The truth wasn't heroic. It was far more impressive put another other way. I told the paper I'd been tortured and got hardship pay.

Lucy pushed a newspaper she'd been reading across the table and tapped the cover story. 'Another Internet billionaire is born.' It had a photo of a pre-pubescent boy, dressed in jeans and a t-shirt, smirking with self-satisfaction.

'What's this one done?'

'He's created an App for the gamification of friendship,' she said.

'He's definitely on to something. I heard that Yale University has a masterclass to teach students how to talk to other people - in person.'

'Well, now, you can earn points for it,' she said, sipping her tea. 'Did you know that the term "Billionaire" is a recent one?

There simply weren't any of significant number, until now.'

'A billion is the new million, I suppose.'

She didn't appreciate the interruption. Class was in session.

'The gap between the have and have-nots is widening, despite the fact that people at the top are getting richer - richer than ever before.'

'You're preaching to the converted, Miss Keller. They've already invaded my neighbourhood. I know what they're capable of.'

'Those aren't the real rich. You won't ever see the real rich. What you're seeing are the wannabes.'

"Perhaps, she's an anarchist?" I thought to myself.

'What do people, who have more money than God, do to celebrate their status?' she asked.

'Spend it,' I said.

'Yes, but they look for things that money can't buy, taboos to break. When you have a billion in the bank, you are above the law. Other people do whatever you want, because they want what you have. You feel entitled. You've earned the right, to do what you please, because you're better than everyone else. Now, imagine that feeling of unbridled wealth and power,' she tapped the newspaper article again, 'in the hands of a child. Do you think he has a moral compass? He hasn't even finished puberty.'

'Well, at least he isn't Hitler.'

'Hardly much comfort,' she said, sipping her tea. 'The balance of power is shifting. For centuries it was carefully controlled by dynastic families, the status quo. Now, it's in the hands of the disrupters. These are people who think that all change is good, and the faster the better. Does that not terrify you?'

'Isn't it a step in the right direction?'

'It's an acceleration.'

'An acceleration of what?'

Her eyes opened wide and she fixed me with an intensity I found unnerving. 'Mass extinction.'

This conversation forced a series of rapid mental calculations: the happiness quotient, the transformation of my neighbourhood, the tyranny of the one-percenters… all of it was whizzing around and around in my brain, but it wasn't properly in gear. There was a spark of truth, something that connected all these inter-related pieces, but I couldn't figure out what. The pilot light of my brain was struggling to fire up the neurons. The Irish coffee wasn't helping, either.

She could see that I was grappling with the magnitude of it all, so she pressed further. 'There have been five mass extinctions, since time began. We are now entering our sixth.'

'I know there's been a bit of global warming and all, but… mass extinction? Isn't that a bit, dramatic?'

Lucy shook her head. 'The last one wiped out the dinosaurs. Lucky for us, we weren't alive then. New life forms appeared and the planet rebounded. Biodiversity flourished, relatively unmolested - until now. Over the last one hundred years, thanks to aggressive industrialisation, deforestation, aggro-farming, strip mining, and the like, mankind has undone all of mother nature's hard work. We've consumed the fruits of her labour in the blink of an eye. That's sixty five million years of evolution down the toilet. In the last sixty years alone, the fishing industry has decimated ninety percent of the large fish population. Gone forever. None of these species are coming back. Ever again. Do you find this too dramatic?'

'I see your point.'

'Do you know the definition of "mass extinction"?' She waited for me to dutifully shake my head. 'It's when a long-term stress meets with a short-term shock. In our case, the long-term stress is the rapid depletion of biodiversity, accelerated by human consumption. All we need now is a short-term shock to tip the balance. Say, for example, a sudden correction caused by global warming. The more significant the stress, which we have in abundance, the less significant the shock needs to be to cause a meltdown. We are precipitously close to the destruction of our planet.'

She opened a satchel that she had on the seat beside her, and pulled out a freshly bound document, setting it on the table. 'Here. This is the endangered species list. Every few years, various agencies and non-profit institutions consult one another to compile it. This is the latest version.'

I thumbed through the document. It was an impressive list. Beside each animal's name was an estimated number of survivors. For the top twenty, the numbers weren't good. Not good at all.

'Unfortunately,' she continued, 'this list doesn't improve their chances of survival. Quite the opposite. It sets off an avalanche of poaching. In fact, it has created a whole new marketplace.'

'For what?'

'Private zoos, for the discerning billionaire. They hunt down and collect endangered species, just because they can. Oftentimes, they have no idea how to keep them in captivity, so they invent party games. You've heard of cock fights, I presume?'

'Yes.'

'Well, picture the same thing with a pair of Komodo Dragons,' she said, taking back the list. 'Our planet has become their plaything. They pillage for profit and amusement. Their arrogance will destroy our entire ecological system, as well as ourselves.'

Maybe, she was Marxist? Or, worse, an animal rights nutter. They can be particularly volatile. I tried to recall if I'd given her my address. No, thank goodness. I was probably over-reacting. Besides, she was too beautiful to be one of those. She wore close-fitting clothes and make-up. Plus, she liked my work. And she'd heard I was "affordable" - which means "cheap".

Frankly, I was desperate. Like many writers in my profession, I was freelance. A work-for-hire. A word whore. And she could probably smell it a mile away. It piqued my curiosity.

'So, what's this got to do with me?'

'I want you to write a biography.'

'Yours?'

'No,' she said impatiently, then glanced furtively around the room. 'Have you heard of Chuck Collins?'

Who hadn't? He was probably the only other guy worse off than myself. 'Yeah, he's the one that had that crocodile -'

'Please, keep your voice down,' she said, cutting me short. 'Besides, we don't talk about that. Especially, not in front of him.'

Okay, some skeletons in the closet, I see. The incident in question had been a YouTube sensation. Before it aired, Collins had worked in relative obscurity as a naturalist anchor on an animal wildlife program for kids. He was very committed, I recall. He was trying to save the planet, but nobody cared. Not until the crocodile attacked him. That made him an instant celebrity.

Of course, you could never air something that grisly on television. But on the Internet - anything goes. His ratings shot through the roof. He was given a TV series, merchandising, educational books – the works. Things were really good for awhile and, then, something happened.

'Sure, I know Collins. He was a wildlife expert.'

'Not was. IS!' she said, defensively. 'And a tracker. The best in the business.'

I felt we were starting off on the wrong foot. She was clearly protective of him for some reason. Had they been an item once?

'What is it you want me to do?' I asked.

'I want you to shadow him on his expedition, chronicle his exploits, become his ghostwriter.'

'What, exactly, is this expedition?'

Lucy leaned back in her seat and pushed back a lock of hair. She was clearly contemplating how to sell me on this. 'Can I trust you?'

'Sure.'

'No,' she said, with more intensity, 'can I trust you? Completely? Because, what I'm about to tell you is highly confidential.'

I waited the requisite amount of time to illustrate my sincerity. 'Yes.'

'Chuck and I tried to get people to care. We made countless programmes. They didn't work. Nobody wants to hear about mass extinction. They'd rather watch cats playing piano.'

'People spend a lifetime ignoring the inevitability of their own death. How can you expect them to care about the death of the planet?'

'Yes,' she said, distracted. 'It's an abstract concept. We need to make the crisis less abstract. We need to make it personal. People need to be outraged by what's happening, and they need to know who's responsible.'

'The one-percenters.'

'Exactly.'

'If your plan is to shame the rich, you've got your work cut out for you.'

'Shame isn't exactly what I had in mind. I'm thinking more of a threat.'

'Blackmail?'

'I prefer to think of it as a charitable donation towards the preservation of our future.'

'How do you intend to do this?'

'Chuck and I noticed that our programmes actually endangered the very species we'd been trying to protect, not unlike the what was happening with the endangered species list, except that ours was more, how shall I say, "glossy", and the response to them more predictable. Poachers were using the show as a catalogue, offering to deliver up the animals to the highest bidder. We were culpable. Chuck and I felt terrible about it. Then, I wondered what might happen if we used the show as bait? If there was a way to follow the trail of the animals from the wild into captivity, directly to the wealthy individuals who'd commissioned the poachers, then we could connect the dots, and establish responsibility. It would require significant research, preparation, and some investigative reporting. And we would need to be in the right place at the right time.

'A set-up.'

'Yes.'

'Then what? You ask them to write you a cheque?'

'We ask them to make a donation to our wildlife preservation fund, or risk public exposure.'

'What makes you think they'd even care?'

'The one percent rely upon the remaining ninety-nine percent for their status. You can't live like a lord without vassals. If the common man knew that the people who robbed them in the present were also robbing them of their future, it could lead to a peasant revolt. It's far better to appear philanthropic than opportunist. Besides, philanthropy is a tax-efficient way of showing off. Ever since Buffet gave half his billions to charity, it's become a fashionable way to money-launder ill-got gains for a cleaner conscience, while getting a hefty tax rebate. Philanthro-capitalism confers social acceptance in addition to a sense of immortality. It's a win-win scenario.'

'Not to be a killjoy, or anything, but I'm just a freelance journalist. Hardly, an animal specialist. Wouldn't you be better off talking to one of the wildlife preservation foundations? They could provide coverage and sponsorship at the same time, without the need for blackmail.'

She shook her head. 'They have a conflict of interest. Look at the list. Every one they've ever written has left out more than sixty percent of the world's truly, most endangered species.'

'Why would they do that?'

'Because non-profit doesn't mean, "no-profit". The licensing deals alone generate millions of dollars a year - calendars, colouring books, plush toys, posters. People go to zoos, buy the merchandise, and sponsor animals in the wild. Corporations make massive donations, so long as it buys credibility with the public. They make a lot of money. Too much, in fact, for their own good. But only if the animals are cute. If you were given the choice between a white, fluffy seal, with puppy-dog eyes, or a self-mutilating Axiotl, which do you think would get the sympathy vote, and earn the most licensing revenue?'

'Fair enough.'

'They don't want the public to know about the ugly ducklings. It's bad for business. Yet, those animals are fighting for survival, too. And they're just as important to our ecosystem. They deserve our protection.'

'Alright, let's assume for a moment that your plan to

blackmail the rich even works, which I have my doubts about, what do you intend to do with the money?'

She leaned in closer. 'Have you heard of Animal Land?'

'Sure,' I said, 'it was an amusement park and petting zoo of some kind. Didn't it burn down, or something?'

I was being coy. I knew of the Animal Land disaster. It was the final nail in the coffin of Collins' career. It had been a huge, utopian experiment to put animals and humans side-by-side in an ecologically sound, self-sufficient, safari-cum-amusement park. They built a massive complex of domes to rival the Eden Project. They harnessed energy from the sun, wind, and geothermal. They even recycled the public toilet waste for fuel and fresh water - which they served in the cafeteria. There was a hotel, water slides, adventure activities - you name it. But the animals didn't get with the program. They went on a rampage – actually, attacked a school bus of preschoolers on a field trip. Some tourists were mauled, while others fled in terror. In the end, all the animals had to be put down. Hunters from around the world eagerly got to work shooting all the livestock that Collins had painstakingly transported to the park over the years. When the hunters ran out of ammo, they called in the fire department to burn everything to the ground, and ensure that none of the more exotic species got away.

'Well, as you probably know,' she said, 'Animal Land was closed. On account of a particular, incident.'

"Greek Tragedy, more like", I thought to myself.

'What you don't know is that it was a set-up. Sabotage!' she said, punctuating her words by stabbing her tea cup with her finger.

This was getting more interesting. 'By whom?'

She sat back and crossed her arms. 'Let's not get ahead of ourselves. Are you interested in the job, or not?'

She was a consummate professional, I must admit. Her pitch was delivered with fabulous theatricality - the furtive glances, the umbrage, the intimacy of danger, the rousing call to action… then, pulling back at the last moment to let the worm squirm on the hook.

I was the worm, by the way. I knew that. Not that it mattered, now. I was already in way over my head. Smitten by her exquisite perfume. She was magnificent. Intoxicating to be around. But I'd learnt the hard way never to come across as too eager. Especially, with a beautiful woman. It wreaks havoc with your self-respect and invites other people to take advantage.

On the other hand, desperation has a louder voice than caution.

'I'm in.'

'Good. Here's what I need. The autobiography is your cover. Chuck is very suspicious of outsiders, but he has a large ego. But his writing is infantile. If he thinks you are writing about him, he won't ask too many questions. What I really need is for you to do some investigative reporting, for me.'

'You want me to find out who burned down the park?'

She smiled. 'Amongst other things.'

Her smile made me uneasy. What was really going on behind those eyes? As if I'd ever know.

'We want to rebuild the park, yes,' she said. 'But this time, we'll have an insurance policy. Our biggest donors will have the greatest incentive to prevent our destruction, since they have the most to hide.'

'Okay. So, when do I meet Collins, my subject and celebrity?'

'That depends,' she said coyly. 'It's entirely up to you.'

'I don't follow.'

'I don't know where he is.' She paused to take a sip of tea. 'I was hoping you could find him.'

CHUCK COLLINS

Lucy planned to put me on retainer for a few weeks and see what I could turn up. The money wasn't bad. It wasn't great, either. But some is better than none.

She took me back to her flat to do some research. I needed to understand Collins in order to find him, apparently. I don't want to crow but I'm actually very good at tracking people down, especially the ones that don't want to be found. I've had years of personal experience.

I may not be much of a journalist, but I have a knack for the investigative part. It suits my lazy disposition. Rather than scouring the world, racking up fees in endless pursuit - I like to sit in cafes with a laptop and cellphone, conducting investigations, and "Photoshopping" my fees to justify my retainer.

Tracking a tracker, however, would prove challenging. If Collins wanted to drop off the radar, then he'd be tough to find. This meant I'd probably have to get off my butt and actually go somewhere.

This didn't bother me, though. I needed a radical change. I wanted to get out of town and reinvent myself. People can hide, but they rarely change. They retain certain idiosyncrasies. They might have a penchant for porn, or a certain type of cigar, or use an inordinate amount of hand-sanitizer - that kind of thing. I'd go hunting for clues. And there would be witnesses. People leave behind "droppings" like a bear in the woods.

Lucy didn't disappoint. As Collins' principal producer, she

had kept ten years worth of everything - showreels, programmes, clippings, interviews, transcripts. It was a one-woman fan club. She had discovered him, a diamond in the rough, when he got his first commission for the BBC. They were inseparable ever since.

'Sorry about the mess,' she said, as we entered her immaculate flat. 'I spend most of my time in LA and don't have a cleaner.'

It was a showroom apartment. Not a crumb out of place. I tried to imagine her having Oz for a roommate. That made me laugh.

She had a cat. It sidled up to me and rubbed its back against my leg in a friendly manner. Made me miss Francesca's even more. I reached down to give him a proper scratching, but Lucy whisked him away.

'Careful,' she said. 'My cat's bipolar.'

She set him down before a small bowl and took out a blister pack of pills.

'Best steer clear until he's had his medication,' she said, opening a tin of food. She slipped her fingers into the mystery meat, pushing a pill deep into its centre.

The cat's name was Nemesis.

I sifted through Lucy's clippings. Collins had a troubled childhood. He grew up in Zimbabwe, but was of British origin. His parents had financial troubles, possibly political ones as well, because they left under the cover of darkness. Unfortunately, they forgot to take their son, who was out collecting beetles at the time (his zoological interests blossomed early).

They also forgot to tell him where they'd gone, or send someone to collect him. He returned that fateful night to an empty house, which was promptly repossessed by the government, and exchanged for an orphanage – where he spent the next few years. When he was asked about this incident in an interview, he said that his parents probably had a lot on their mind at the time. Hmmm. A strange form of denial. Surely, it would be hard to forget that you had a son? But, as I was soon to discover, Collins had a fecund imagination - a powerful, reality distortion field - that created the world as he wanted it to be, rather than the way it really was. As far as I am aware, he never saw his parents ever again.

He was adopted by a local park ranger who needed help chasing poachers from the wildlife preservation. He found an eager assistant in the young boy, who enjoyed taking pot shots at them with a sniper rifle. He may have enjoyed this a little too much, as he spent weeks on end, following them through the bush, tracking them in camouflage, or pretending to be the animal they were targeting, just waiting for the perfect moment - to shoot them in the ass.

That was his calling card. To this day, many of the poachers from the region cannot sit down comfortably. It is often mistaken by their employers as a sign of pride when, in fact, it is a medical condition.

The ranger had adopted another surrogate son – a South African, by the name of De Konig, who was only a couple of years older than Collins. There is very little information on him. All we know is that he was a crack shot and a lone wolf. He and Collins left the park at the same time, after their adopted father perished tragically in an elephant stampede.

Collins spoke of his time at the wildlife preserve as idyllic, but there was an undercurrent of sadness. I got the impression that he was hiding something.

He began his career as a tracker in Africa, then travelled to Australia, and on to New Zealand. He was good at it, too, but often got into spats with his clients. It wasn't unusual for someone with his skills to guide amateur hunters, but the work was distasteful to him. According to one police transcript, he actually gagged and trussed up a client as a pig, and put them into one of their own wild boar hunts. Luckily, their fellow hunters realised this just before the kill.

It was a close call and Collins was stripped of his credentials. He dealt with it in his usual way – by going somewhere else and starting over. He was amazingly resilient, perhaps on account of all his previous misfortune.

He did a stint for the BBC as a wildlife consultant and this is where he met Lucy. It was there he got the bug to be in front of the camera. This proved to be short-lived, however, as his reporting style was somewhat inflammatory and politically incorrect - even by BBC standards. Some of the titles of the episodes from his children's wildlife programme are particularly revealing: "Happy Feet: The Secret Lives of Gay Penguins", "Preying Mantis: Coitus Interruptus", and "Hippo Poop". Also, there were unfavourable reports of him endangering the crew on account of being more interested in helping animals than other people.

Not long after, he reinvented himself again as a naturalist, and hosted an amateur wildlife program on a local cable channel in America. This was eventually parlayed into a television series that very few people saw but, nonetheless, kept going. The series ran for several years, as Collins scoured the globe for animals and plants in peril.

Wherever he went, Lucy was sure to go with him. I saw pictures of her building camp fires, cooking meals, and generally mucking in wherever she could. She clearly loved the outdoors. Yet, she was incongruous to it. After months of living in the bush, she still looked like a supermodel who had been helicoptered in for a fashion shoot, while the rest of her crew looked like cadavers at the morgue.

Lucy had handpicked her highlights, yet I must have watched over six hours of Collins in action. It was hard not to like the guy. In his early years, he came across as a babe lost in the woods, excited by everything he saw. There was something infectious and endearing, yet hapless about him. He seemed genuinely shocked when the animals refused to cooperate. After all, he was there to help them.

He had a tremendous knack for getting in the soup. Each episode brought new confrontations and successive injuries. In one episode he upset a bee hive, which came to a sticky and painful end. Then, he was charged by a buffalo, accosted by a

Koala, pecked by an angry Emu, decked by a panda, swarmed by red ants, face-slapped by a Portugese Man-o-war, assaulted by a psychotic beaver, crushed by a cow, heckled by dolphins, and body-checked by a moose. And that was just the first season.

But the guy definitely had charisma. When he spoke to camera, it felt as if he was speaking directly to you and no one else. He rallied you to his cause. Then, as he matured, a hardness set in. He became scared - literally and figuratively. The hazards of the job were taking their toll. He became irascible, his tirades legendary. He took fantastic risks. Only the most stalwart of his crew remained. In fact, a few boom operators even died on location.

In the end, he became embittered. I felt he was constantly seeking approval from the public, but became disillusioned by the silence at the other end. Even after skyrocketing to glory from the YouTube video, he seemed frustrated by the public's insincerity. He wanted them to care as deeply as he did about what really mattered to him. But, ultimately, it was a one-way conversation.

If television was too small for Collins, then Animal Land gave him a new lease on life. It was big - really big. It was to be his capping glory. He had a renewed sense of purpose and an urgency about him, as he set to evangelising his greatest achievement. He became the beneficiary of an anonymous donor, and no expenses were spared. It was to be the greatest show on earth.

Like many of his previous assignments, he took to it with a zeal that was commendable in its ardour, if not somewhat out of place with reality. Let's face it, Animal Land was a tourist trap. You could sense the investors salivating at the merchandising opportunities. But Collins, to his credit, seemed utterly oblivious to the crass commercialism of it all. In his mind, he was creating a utopia for both man and beast.

Children came in droves, delighted by the exotic llamas, the prancing antelopes, and the rhinoceros park. But their squeals of delight could not mask the ill-fated premise: Wild animals are wild. Even more so when not behind bars. It was a teddy-bear picnic just waiting to happen. And the tourists weren't there to commune with nature. They wanted to gawk at the animal circus, bask in their own superiority, and, then, buy corn-dogs and plush toys at the concession stand.

It was a tragedy from the start.

As I watched the last episode of his television program, I couldn't help but feel a certain sadness. Collins didn't deserve what had happened to him. I realised that now. Obviously, he felt the same way. Otherwise, he wouldn't have disappeared from the limelight and abandoned the cause he held so dearly, no matter what the trials had been. The disaster at Animal Land had been so catastrophic that nobody could have expected otherwise.

He was probably in some far-flung corner of the world, licking his wounds, punishing himself for what he perceived to be his most momentous failure. And now, Lucy raised the possibility that he wasn't to blame. Was this wishful thinking, or had higher powers had it in for Collins from the start? I knew what it was like to be the underdog, the guy who kept bashing his face against the wall, hoping that somebody would notice. He touched a nerve.

I looked at my watch. Lucy hadn't returned from running her errand and that was over two hours ago. Should I be concerned? More important, I needed to find a toilet. I had drunk five cups of coffee and my bladder was a watermelon.

I went to the hallway and saw two doors. I figured that the bathroom was the first one I came to, but then I saw that the other door, at the end of the hallway, was open. Probably, her bedroom.

I couldn't resist. It's not that I was perving. I was just curious, so I slipped inside.

Her room was neat, her bed unmade. The bed faced a small, but tidy writing desk. All the items on it were neatly arranged: writing paper, pens, paper clips, envelopes, and a pack of Russian, gold-tipped cigarettes. I sniffed the packet. Very heady, very exotic. There were only a couple missing. No ashtray, either. Not the sign of a compulsive smoker, but one who partakes occasionally - a guilty indulgence.

My eye caught some movement. The door was now opening, very, very slowly.

Crap!

I froze. This wouldn't look good. I had to fashion a good excuse.

It was the cat.

He stopped and stared at me with unblinking eyes. Thank God for that. Still, his saucer gaze was unsettling and a bit hostile.

'Hey there, Nemesis, buddy - how you doing?' I stepped forward, but he hissed. His back hairs shot up and he arched something frightful. I spoke to him in dulcet tones. What happened next was a blur.

He launched himself at my face. I couldn't see a damn thing, but I could feel his sharp claws digging into my neck. Then, he bit me. I may have over-reacted a little. I grabbed his fury face and flung him across the room. He ricocheted off a lamp, but landed on his feet. Kitty was pissed.

I hotfooted it out of there, but he leapt onto my back, before I made it to the hallway. Now, he was harder to reach.

I body-checked him against the wall. He squealed - not a pleasant sound - but wouldn't let go. I dropped to the ground and did a fireman's roll. Each time my weight bore down on him, he made a horrible squelching sound, but didn't stop clawing up a fury. When I saw my own blood on my hands, I realised I had to take things up a notch.

I scrabbled into the bathroom and dove into the tub, getting myself ensnared in the shower curtain. I thrashed around, while Nemesis chewed on my earlobes, setting my nerves on fire. I yelped like a baby and grabbed the flexible hose. 'I'll teach you to mess with me, you friggin' fur-ball from hell!'

I blasted kitty and he didn't like it. Not one bit. He tried to escape, but I held him there as punishment. Not very mature, I know, but I was running on adrenaline.

Satisfied that he'd had enough, I pitched him out onto the bath mat. He stood there like a drowned rat. I could see the anger and hurt in his eyes.

We had come to an understanding – for now.

He skulked away.

I caught my reflection in the mirror. Christ! I'd had a cheese-grater facial. There was nothing to swab my fresh wounds with, except beautiful, fluffy cream towels. Or, toilet paper.

I chose the latter.

I don't put much store in fate, or bad luck for that matter. But I hadn't had a lucky break for months. I had long since spent the money I got for the MP video. Then, Lucy came along. I thought it was a sign of something good, but now I wasn't so sure. If I had trouble fighting off a house cat, how was I going to survive an expedition with Chuck Collins? We weren't hiking into Hyde Park. No, we'd be going places where no man had gone before.

Lucy showed up a short while later. She didn't remark that her cat was wet - only that it had carefully eaten around its medicine, leaving the pills behind. She saw my face, however, and put two-and-two together.

She sighed. There didn't seem to be time enough for her to say what she really wanted. 'We need to go to LA. How soon can you be ready?'

'Right now,' I said, pulling out my passport from my back pocket. It was damp, but legible. 'I never travel anywhere without it.'

Lucy was impressed. 'What about clothes and things?'

'I'll get what I need on the road, prefer to travel light. Look - I've even taken a shower, so I'm good to go.' I smiled, dislodging the torn pieces of toilet paper that were stuck to my facial wounds. They fluttered down to the beige carpet, like petals from a red rose.

'Fine. We'll take Nemesis to the cat hotel and head to the airport.'

'They have a hotel for cats?'

She was confused by my question. 'Of course. He can't stay here on his own.'

I looked at Nemesis, now purring sweetly in her arms. I'm sure if she left a window open, he could happily live off the pigeon population in our absence. He'd be just fine on his own. In fact, he was probably the only one likely to be left alive at the end of it all. But I didn't know that then.

Ignorance is bliss.

DOUBLE-EDGED SWORD

I was feeling better now that we were on the plane to somewhere else. And it was nice to be flying business class, for once.

Not my money, mind you. I could get used to this lifestyle. Up till now, I had always flown cattle-class, where the seats were instruments of torture. First, I'd try to get my feet as far under the seat in front of me as I could, before the other person put their's back and kneecapped me. Then, I'd stake my claim to at least one arm-rest, unless my neighbour's love-handles got there first. Then, I'd carefully stow and lock my tray table, so it wouldn't puncture my lungs, or break a rib, when we hit turbulence. Eating meals, too, was hazardous. Scalding plates had to be juggled, liquids capped, and silverware secured.

Thanks to Lucy, though, I could leave this struggle far behind. We actually got to know each other better on the flight. Perhaps, the shock of comfort left me vulnerable to her questions. She asked about Francesca, having heard a lot more over the phone that fateful afternoon in the park, than I had figured.

'So, you like dating little girls?" she said, looking down at me through her Nana Mouskouri glasses. They made her look like a schoolteacher. A very hot schoolteacher. 'Because you find them easier to manipulate?'

I felt like a tit.

'So, how did you get a name like Keller?' I said, changing the subject. 'You don't look like a Keller.'

'What do I look like?'

'It's a Scottish name, isn't it? You don't look Scottish.' I knew that because my father was Scottish and, like many Scotsmen, he spent money as if he was passing a gall-stone. My mother, on the other hand, was Venezuelan. And she liked to spend it. She was also a skilled lier, which gave him no end of grief. But she did it with such panache that it was hard to fault her. How they ended up together, I'll never know. I guess I got the best of both.

'I was adopted,' she said. 'My mother was Black Irish.'

'An interesting coin of phrase, don't you think?'

She failed to see the irony. 'How so?'

I struggled to think of an analogy. 'We have something in common, you and I. Opposite worlds colliding in a single uterus.'

That came out badly.

She went back to reading her copy of "The Economist". I went back to my Bloody Mary.

This was the second time I'd gotten off to a bad start. Here's hoping, third time's a charm.

At the end of the day, results mattered. I had to justify my per-diem. I didn't have to seduce her. Not that I didn't want to, mind you, but - still. I could be professional, so long as I was getting paid.

I recalled from my research that Collins had been adopted, too. That was something they had in common. I was going to be the third wheel. Not the ideal scenario.

Nevertheless, Lucy came across as an outsider, like me. She was confident, but uncomfortable. Something didn't fit right. She had money, but preferred discretion. She liked the finer things in life, but didn't collect icons. She was intelligent and wasn't one to suffer fools, but often kept this to herself. She moved easily between cultures, but didn't belong to any. All told, I suspected that she had the funds to mount this operation on her own, yet we were headed to the Animal Channel's headquarters to pitch her project. Why?

In many ways, she struck me as a Trustafarian. She was well-educated, international, good-looking, and not wanting. And what about her father? She had only mentioned her mother. The name Keller rang a bell, but I couldn't place it. It was sloppy of me not to investigate my employer, but I didn't have the time. I was so eager to get a fresh start that I was in danger of jumping out the frying pan and into the fire. Slash and burn. The story of my life.

I had this friend many years ago. His name was Roger. A good name, as it turned out, because he roger'd everything in sight. When we roomed together at university, he would proposition every woman he met. Every one. Without fail. He'd march up to a total stranger and ask her to do something lewd with him. The law of averages meant that only one in one hundred would actually be crazy enough to say, "yes". So, he asked a hundred women a day. And he had crazy sex all the time. He found he could improve his odds at certain venues: university socials, hen parties, funerals, and quilting seminars. He had no shame. None, whatsoever.

After university, though, he perfected his technique and hunted his quarry with greater efficiency. He could tell at an instant who in the room was the most likely candidate for debauchery and single them out from the start. To his credit, however, he wasn't a cad. Not in the least. He became a serial monogamist and a consummate gentleman. Whomever he dated, he doted on. He gave them everything they wanted. But he had a policy. The moment they said they loved him… he left.

He was very disciplined in this regard, which I greatly admired, given that he dated some of the most impressive women I'd ever seen. I wanted to understand why, so I asked him one afternoon. He was staying with me at the time, lounging around in a silk bathrobe, which ended in hand-stitched slippers. I don't think I'd seen him wearing anything else the entire week. It had become his uniform.

'When a woman says they love you,' he explained, 'they don't really want *you*. They want something else. Something you don't have. It's the beginning of the end.'

This struck me as strange. Was this not a self-fulfilling prophecy? He denied them nothing else. Why, then did it come to this?

My own amorous entanglements did not end well. Clearly, I had a lot to learn from Roger. The girls I dated came with excess baggage: daddy complexes, eating disorders, and psychotic ex-boyfriends. I found them fascinating at first, then neurotic, and, finally, annoying. They, too, liked my independence, the fact that I wasn't trying to please people all the time. At least, they liked this in the beginning. Then, they'd accuse me of being selfish and emotionally detached. Perhaps, they thought I would be their salvation. Bad idea. I wasn't a pope-on-a-rope that could wash them clean. I found their honesty frightening. They'd relate the most terrible stories of things they'd done and were ashamed of. I'd become their confessional. I heard things I shouldn't have. Maybe, I had inadvertently made promises that were impossible to keep. I promised them something more than myself and, yet, that was all I had to give. We ended up disappointing one another.

Those were the early days.

I'm sure most people project a better version of themselves in the beginning: a calculated appearance, fit body, intrepid intellect, world savviness, silk slippers... Until, one day, you come home and find your significant other in their boxer shorts, eating cereal from the box, playing video games, and shouting at the television set. There comes a time when we no longer feel bothered to impress. Or, we've come to terms with our own, inevitable mortality.

Yup. Sad, but true. I had fallen into the same trap. I had appealed to these women's imaginations - that I might, someday, become a better version of myself. But that day never came.

I adopted Roger's strategy. After all, he was happy and care-free. And I wasn't. I wanted that feeling.

I began to benefit, almost immediately. Things became less complicated. I no longer had to spend countless hours, standing in doorways, sitting in parked cars, loitering in cloak rooms long after the party had ended - asking, 'What's wrong?' - to which came the reply, "Nothing" - when, in fact, this was clearly far from the truth. I simply dispensed with diplomacy and pursued my own self-interests.

Despite all the attention we get in our lives, is it not true - that we die as we are born - all alone? As children, we are driven to independence. We cannot wait to be the masters of our own universe. As teenagers, we hate to be told what we can and cannot do. Then, for the rest of our lives, we compete for everything - in school, in love, in work, in friendship. Yet, at some point, we are forced to make a terrible decision. Either we suppress our competitive nature, make the sacrifice and become subservient to others, or we pursue our own agenda at all costs and let our egos run rampant. For many of us, it is a choice between excellence and mediocrity. Do I settle down with "Mister Safer-but-Average", or run off into the sunset with the charismatic devil on his Harley Davidson? Do I become a good corporate soldier, or take over the corporation? Do I give my heart, or take someone else's?

I made my choice. Winner takes all. It was *my* life to live.

The only problem was - it wasn't working. I wasn't happy. Everyone I'd ever cared about was left behind.

There was at least another eight hours before our plane landed in L.A. I hadn't brought any reading material, so I flipped idly through the in-flight magazine. I came across an article in which a medical anthropologist (don't ask me, either) studied a group of Italian immigrants in New York city who lived well into their nineties - far beyond the rest of the population. At first, he studied their diet. Then, their DNA. He found nothing unusual. In the end, he concluded that it was the strength of their community that resulted in their longevity. They had such a rich network of family and friends that they were never alone, or wanting, even when they were sick, or had fallen on hard times. Nobody left the community. Nobody was left behind, either.

I have heard it said that married couples, too, live longer.

Supposedly, they are more content from their commitment to one another. Yet, this didn't ring true. All the married couples I knew fought constantly. It seemed more like a death sentence than a stay of execution. They paid lip-service to matrimony, extolled the virtues of having children - said it was beautiful, fulfilling, and holy - only to bitch about school fees, dental plans, and the agonies of parenthood. Spousal estrangement was common. There was no passion, only pathos.

A few years ago, I tried to contact Roger, hoping for some spiritual guidance. I was in a miserable place and thought he could help. We had drifted apart after moving continents, eventually trading broken promises. Finally, I decided to take the initiative, but discovered that he'd died several years prior in a car crash. Apparently, he was driving too fast in a Ferrari, with a hooker riding shot-gun.

I'd like to believe he died with a smile on his face.

To be perfectly frank, I don't think he would have helped me much anyway. He was kind of an asshole. But he was a lot of fun to be around. I think he could afford to be generous, so long as it was self-serving. And, if you factored into his plans, you were golden. At the end of the day, we all rode shot-gun in Roger's life. We did whatever he wanted. The rest of us were just cheerleaders, along for the ride.

I suppose that what Roger did was nothing more than a protection mechanism. He kept his emotional distance, because he understood the paradox of love better than most. To give ourselves is to negate ourselves. By giving everything we have, except our hearts, we get what we want, without losing ourselves in the process.

The fact of the matter is, love is a double-edged sword. The moment it's realised, it cuts both ways.

ENDANGEROUS

In Los Angeles, people spend more time in their cars than in their homes. Which is probably why they drive Hummers, SUVs, and mongo pick-up trucks. They're simply taking their homes with them, out on the road. It was refreshing to see so many people benefit from the War in Iraq without troubling themselves with niggly little things, like introspection - or, doubt.

Lucy, on the other hand, had rented a Prius. A worrywart's car. Very sensible and eco-friendly, yes, except that it felt as if we were cruising around in a small, styrofoam box. I would have preferred the Ford Mustang that we saw on the lot. That was my kind of automobile. But she had the credit card with credit, so she made the call.

I had been to Los Angeles before, so I was wary. I knew from experience how dangerously seductive it could be. You arrive feeling King of the Hill, feeling cocky and supercharged, thinking of all the great things you're going to accomplish in the city of angels. The streets are big. The houses are big. The girls are big, especially the joggers on San Vincente, with their gravity-defying body parts. All of humanity is at your disposal. Then, four months later, you get into a funk worrying about where you're going to get your next skinny latte, as opposed to something more primal. Perhaps, it's because you spend half the day brain-baked in your car. Or, maybe, living here is just too easy. Sometimes, you need the struggle to remind you what it's like to be alive.

We stopped along the way at a convenience store, so I could go to the bathroom.

'For a grown man, you certainly have a tiny bladder,' said Lucy.

'They super-sized my Cola at the airport. It's not my fault I asked for a medium and they gave me a bucket.'

'No one forced you to drink it all.'

'Don't worry, I won't take long. I'm tiny, remember.'

That didn't come out very well, either.

Truth be told, America did make me feel small. Everything here was bigger - the cars, the roads, the people. On the flip-side, there was definitely an underclass of the overweight. They were often found in amusement parks and shopping mausoleums, wheeling themselves around on motorised fat-cycles. Yet, they were made to feel welcome. Not only was there a solidarity in numbers, but an XL shirt in America would have been a XXXL anywhere else. Which came as no surprise, since food was cheap, plentiful, and served on horse platters. Sometimes, it was sold by the pound, instead of by the portion. Consumerism was not only rampant - it was celebrated. And without irony. One restaurant advertised, "All you can eat surf and turf for $9.99!" While, across the street, I saw something more sinister - "Fat-Free Liposuction services. Toddlers welcome."

Inside the convenience store, I couldn't help stopping to look and wonder. There were so many colours, so much variety - so many things I didn't need. They were fun to look at, stretching from mile to endless aisle. They made me feel important. Here were all these brands, backed by captains of industry, that competed for my attention. Mine. I was the all-important consumer and they didn't want me to forget it.

I felt sorry for the poor hunter-gatherer in his cave. He must have had a pretty gruelling life. Imagine if he could have driven down to the local convenience store, instead of fighting the wooly mammoth for his dinner? Everyone in the clan would be equal. People could take turns running errands and school runs. They'd no longer have to hunt. They could spend more leisure time with their families. Instead of fighting all the time, they could make necklaces, write poetry, or build community centres. Of course, they'd have to take care of those with special needs, now that they weren't left to die in the wild, so they'd have to build ramps and separate cubicles in the washrooms. Health and safety would mandate that children shouldn't be allowed to participate in games that might result in scrapes and bruises, so mental activities would take on greater importance than physical activity. People would live closer together, offering greater economies of scale, so they would need bigger buildings, with elevators. Not everyone, though, would be of equal intelligence. Some people would have a harder time finding purpose, especially the ones who used to be great hunters, but not so great at mental arithmetic. Not all of them, of course. Some would find their way into professional sports. But they'd be the lucky few, the ones paid to entertain the rest of us in the arena. Whereas the unlucky ones would have to attend self-help seminars and support groups. Other, more capable people, would rise in importance and take care of everyone else - possibly, on a pan-tribal scale. They'd create a welfare system to enable them to take care of others who they didn't even know, while they were away on business. Then, they'd build better roads and faster vehicles to help themselves move around, so they could maximise their efficiency and help even more people on welfare. They would be called the "gurus" and would be fêted with more food and sex than the others. Meanwhile, the non-gurus would get so fat from doing nothing that they'd need to use the ramps that they'd originally built for the less capable people, which they themselves had now become.

You know… maybe the hunter-gatherers had it better than I thought.

'Feeling better?' Lucy propped the car door for me, as I

exited the store.

'Yes, except the toilet looked like it was inside out.'

'I hope you washed your hands.'

'Sure,' I said, before shoving a fluorescent, shiny pink thing under her nose. 'Fancy one?'

'What is it?'

'I don't know. I had to buy something in order to use the washroom.' I looked at the list of ingredients. 'It seems to be a foodstuff made without any actual food.'

'No, thank you,' she said, starting the silent engine. It took me awhile to realise we were actually driving.

I took a nibble off the end of it to see what it was like. 'Wow! Better living through chemistry. I feel turbo charged already!' Maybe this is what kept Los Angeles going?

Lucy didn't seem the least bit curious. Her body was a temple, I could tell. She wore big shades and a thin cotton dress that teased me with her figure. She had a habit of curling her tongue around her front teeth when she was concentrating. I saw her doing it now, while she looked both ways, and turned the steering wheel.

'Where are we going?' I asked, enjoying the rush of sugar.

'We need to pitch the show to the network. Technically, they're footing your bill, not me.' She was flustered by the traffic, scanning for her opportunity to enter.

'Today? Right now? Was I supposed to prepare something?'

'No. You just come as you are.'

'Don't I always?'

That made her smile. Made me feel good.

Animal Channel was doing well, judging by the size of their office. Everything was shiny and corporate - all concrete and glass. There was a giant, stuffed bear in the lobby, poised for the kill in a hideous snarl. A plaque at its feet proclaimed that it had been felled by the head of the network, Percy Hemming, while threatening his crew, but Lucy's account was less heroic. Apparently, it had been shot in the ass, while trying to run away.

We were the first to be seated in a large, glass goldfish bowl of a boardroom in the middle of an open-plan office. I felt naked, because I couldn't lurk unseen in the corner, as was my modus operandi.

An intern with black, nicotine-stained teeth asked me if I wanted coffee, killing any desire I may have had for having one.

Lucy was nervous. I hadn't seen this side of her. She was fussing with the AV equipment and whispering to herself, presumably perfecting her pitch. Or, cursing the television Gods.

Percy swept in with a flourish, bookended by four minions. He was short, bald, and fat. Yet, his presence engulfed the room - as did his cigar, which he kept glued to his lips, even while speaking. Or, broadcasting, more like. He spoke as if he had a New Jersey megaphone buried in his larynx.

Percy pointed a finger at me. 'Who's this guy?'

'He's a journalist,' said Lucy, making Percy self-conscious. 'Part of my research team.'

'What happened to his face?'

'Terminal acne,' I replied, hoping to shut down further discussion. No one needed to know about Nemesis.

Percy sat down warily and and kept me in his sights, like a mongoose watching a snake. It didn't take long, though, before he was back on form, making pleasantries that were highly unpleasant. He bragged about bagging a young intern the night before. On this very table in fact. Nice.

He was faux jocular and intimidating, the sort of man used to getting his way all the time, preferably at a disadvantage to others. He seemed bemused, yet grumpy by Lucy's presence. He complained about other important matters to attend to, 'So this had better be good.'

Unfazed, Lucy began her presentation by rolling tape.

A British narrator decried the fragile state of our earth's ecosystem. Images paraded across the screen of burning rainforest, gridlocked highways, mobile phone land fills, and indigent people picking through mountains of steaming garbage.

"The Western world accounts for only a quarter of the world's population, yet consumes three quarters of its resources," proclaimed the narrator. "Soon, there will be nothing left to go around. And what of our cousins in the animal kingdom? Who will protect them when all else is forsaken?"

Ecological horrors flashed across the screen: melting ice floes, exhausted polar bears drowning in the ocean, schools of bloated fish, floating in vast oil slicks, piles of dead antelopes bulldozed into an open, mass grave...

Percy fidgeted in his seat. 'This is seriously depressing,' he said, in a stage whisper.

"There's only one man who can answer the call of the wild!" cried our narrator, as an image of Chuck Collins filled the screen with the title, "Endangered Species".

'Jesus Christ,' exclaimed Percy, 'kill me now!'

Someone hit the lights, forcing Lucy to pause the video. Percy was poised to strike, but she was unfazed. 'Let me play the rest. You'll like where this is going.'

Percy wasn't placated. 'I already know where it's going. In the toilet, where it belongs.'

'Please, Percy, hear me out.'

'I'd rather have a hydrochloric enema than sit through any more of this crappy-sappy, hippy-dippy, save the planet love-fest. Chuck Collins is a washed-up, has-been loser.'

'No, Percy. He has vision. And a heart. Two things you never had.'

'Don't shovel a shoveler, missy. Remember, I know you. Inside and out.' Lucy squirmed, recalling an unpleasant memory. 'You hitched your ride to a falling star. Don't say I didn't warn you.' He had clearly hit his stride. 'We both know why people watched his program. It's not about the animals. They can see animals at the zoo. No, they watched because they wanted to see Collins get his ass kicked. It made good television. And you know why? Because deep down, we know. *We are the animals.* All of us. This was just another gladiator show. We wanted blood, but Collins got soft. His head got too big for the box. And he forgot who put him there, just like you!' Percy pointed his cigar at her like a red hot poker. 'Don't bite the hand that feeds you, capische?'

He was about as Italian as a Cornetto, but that didn't stop him from peppering his speech with stuff he'd lifted from "The Sopranos".

Lucy stood her ground. 'You owe me.'

'I don't owe you a dime! I lost thirty million backing that cockamamie venture. Animal Land was an unmitigated disaster from start to finish.'

'All of which was repaid by insurance,' chimed Lucy.

'Nevertheless, he dumped me in a maelstrom of a P-R shit storm from which I am only now just recovering from. And you want me to re-open that canker, so it can fester all over my precious primetime?! I would rather see Collins hung, drawn, and quartered. Now, that would be a show worth watching!' He stood up. 'Okay, is that all you got? Because I've got a two o'clock with my masseuse. And I think it's going to be a happy ending.'

Lucy ignored him and hit play, letting the heavy metal soundtrack drown out the brown-nosed chuckling from Percy's posse. The screen projected rapid cuts of Collins under attack from various animals, followed by the full title, "Endangered & Dangerous: Extreme Edition!"

Percy's eyes lit up.

The words on the screen merged into, "Endangerous!"

Lucy killed the video. She knew Percy had taken the bait and now it was time to yank the rod. She threw down a heavy document onto the table in front of him.

He kept a poker face. 'I'm listening.'

'It's the World Wildlife Foundation's list of endangered species. You'll see that I've underlined the most dangerous ones. Collins is going to get up close and personal. Too close. That's the show.' Lucy leaned back and folded her arms.

Percy broke into a broad grin. 'Keller! There you are,' he laughed. 'You're back! For a moment, I thought you were a pussy. But now - you're a producer!'

'I learnt from the master.'

'Don't blow smoke up my ass, unless you're a Thai hooker and I'm paying for it. Even then, I'd ask for a discount. What's it going to cost me?'

Lucy chewed her lip. 'We'll do the pilot for a quarter'.

Percy chewed his cigar. 'Dream on, baby. You give me a taste. I like what I see, I'll commission some more. One-fifty.'

'Two hundred,' countered Lucy, without batting an eyelid. 'Plus, my quote. The last one. Before everything went to shit.'

'Alright, missy,' said Percy. 'Endangerous. I like it.' He took a puff of his cigar, satisfied. 'Now get it on tape.' He left with a chuckle, followed by his entourage.

Lucy said nothing to me, while gathering her materials. I'd been a voyeur to something dirty. Her silence underlined the moral precariousness of it all. She was going to risk Collins' life for a shot at a commission. And she had trundled me along for the ride.

I may have been desperate, but I wasn't foolhardy. The world's most dangerous species. "Endangerous", even. Hmm. That sounded like a Malatov cocktail of bad idea. First off, I didn't like the sound of dangerous animals. That's generally a euphemism for deadly and I rather do enjoy being alive. Second, I know from experience that these animals tend to live in horribly inhospitable places. Places where staying alive is a daily assault course. And, finally, Collins was a disaster magnet. The sad irony was that animals hated him. He'd devoted his whole life to helping them, yet they couldn't wait to tear him apart.

She must have been aggravated by my silence, because she looked up at me. 'Is there a problem?'

'I thought you said you were giving him a second chance. This sounds like a suicide mission.'

'Don't worry about Chuck. He's very hard to kill.'

'You think? Because he doesn't have much of a track record with lady luck.'

'You're not the first to underestimate him. He heals quickly.'

'Does he know about this plan of yours?'

'Not exactly. Not yet.'

'And if he doesn't cooperate?'

'He will. Our mission is righteous,' she said, vindictive and resolute. 'He knows what's at stake. Failure is not an option.'

'Just don't sell him a lie that you might regret.'

Her eyes narrowed, something like a cross between a kitten and a viper. 'That's pretty rich, coming from you. You're not exactly a paragon of truth, or purity.' I stared at her, blankly. But she wasn't giving up. 'I've done my homework. I know that you did some of your past research - off the reservation. Why do you think I hired you in the first place?'

'What, exactly, are you implying, Lucy?' I blinked, innocently.

'That there are certain government institutions, shall we say, that use freelance journalists for extra-curricular intelligence activities. Is that clear enough for you?'

Now, I get it. She had probably read that piece I did for the leftist rag, "The Muted Scream". I pretended to be an operative working for the CIA and did a kiss-and-tell piece. Not a bad article, if I may say so myself, but it was a complete fabrication.

'I can neither confirm, nor deny that allegation,' I said, with a straight face.

'I wasn't born yesterday. I've seen your kind before. I am guessing that you had special training? That you have some useful contacts who could help us?' I returned her stare without a word. She gathered up her things.

We walked in silence, until we reached the car park. This time, she spoke conspiratorially. 'Look, Trevor, I'll level with you. This is not how I want to do this, but needs must. Collins was working on something just before Animal Land was destroyed. He was investigating the trafficking of a rare species of turtle that were being used in underground death matches.'

'Must have been a slow night.'

'He hoped to rehabilitate them at Animal Land,' she said, ignoring my comment. 'It was an expensive operation, but the success of Animal Land allowed him to bankroll it.'

'So, you think someone wanted to cut off his air supply?'

'He was onto something big.'

'And Collins got too close.'

'There's too much coincidence in the timing. There are only a handful of trackers that can find and capture rare species like these. It's a small community. And Collins isn't one to play ball.' She looked around to make sure we were alone. 'Somebody doesn't want him back on the beat. Which is all the more reason why I'm determined to find out who and why.'

'Alright, then,' I said, 'what happens now?'

She came down a notch and whispered. 'The turtles are shipped to China. We tried to track them back to source, but the lead went cold in the Ukraine. I need you to pick up where the last guy left off.'

'What happened to the last guy?'

'Best case scenario, he took the money and ran.'

'Worst case scenario?'

'He found the source.'

'If you think that I'm some kind of Special Forces action-man, than you're sorely mistaken,' I said, hoping to set expectations.

'You've survived this long, haven't you? That's good enough for me.'

Yes, I suppose she was right. I was good at staying alive. So far, anyway.

I thought of the bear standing in the lobby. Maybe I, too, was destined to become a trophy in Percy's office. Perhaps, he could give me a symmetrical package.

'But we haven't much time to work it out,' she said. 'Percy's generosity is specious.'

CUORA TRIFASCIATA

For the next few weeks, I stretched my per diem as far as it would go. Thankfully, I was in Southeast Asia where life comes cheap.

I was doing background research for the show. That was the ruse to Animal Channel, anyway. My first line of enquiry was to pick up where my unfortunate predecessor had left off. I didn't intend to get too close to whatever it was, as he was probably now feeding the fish at the bottom of a Ukranian tide-pool. Nevertheless, he had found something worth getting killed over.

Collins had been on the trail of a turtle farming operation that criss-crossed the globe. It was a pet project of his. Not because there is anything inherently wrong in turtle farming, although it is rather cruel how they bleed them alive and use their body parts for medicinal purposes. No, he was enraged by the trafficking of a far rarer breed: the Cuora Trifasciata. It's meat may have tasted like the sole of a shoe, but its parts were considered a cure for a variety of ills. The highest potency of its kind. And part of the reason why it was heading toward endangered status.

Regular soft-shell turtles fetch a pittance, but the Cuora Trifasciata go for nearly $2,000 a turtle. That's serious money in this part of the world. However, they are notoriously hard to farm and their livelihood was threatened. The farms themselves were predominantly in Thailand and China, but someone had recently put most of them out of business, and was doing it from somewhere else. I hadn't yet discovered where, but they had an export hub located in Vietnam, which is where I was now.

I pretended to be a tourist. A clumsy cover, I know, but I had little else at my disposal. This was a bare bones operation. Luckily, I found an American divorcee at my hotel, Nancy, who was only to happy to accompany me on my reconnaissance. I thought it would look better if we appeared to be a couple on our Summer vacation. If anybody asked, I would say I was a schoolteacher with a passion for photography.

I told her that I was recently bereaved - a partial truth, perhaps. Playing the sympathy card always helps. She took a shine to me, but (thankfully) kept a respectful distance. I didn't want her to get too close. It's not that she wasn't attractive. She had a healthy exuberance and a fit body, but I didn't want to get embroiled in a holiday romance, when danger was in the air.

We spent an hour at the docks one afternoon, watching the ships come in and unload their cargo. She found my maritime obsession odd, especially my passion for snapping countless photos of cranes, until I explained that my father had been a longshoreman. Eventually, I saw what I came for. A fairly nondescript barge arrived fully loaded. I took Nancy with me to get a closer look.

'Is there a reason why we're playing hide and seek?' she said, as we ducked down between the crates.

'People don't act natural when they see a camera,' I explained. 'I want authenticity.'

We waited for the cargo to be unloaded and parked inside the warehouse. Convinced that the coast was clear, we crept over to where the containers had been deposited. I pulled out a pair of bolt-cutters from my trousers. Asking her to hold my camera, I broke the lock.

'Hang on a minute,' she drawled, 'are you some kind of spy?'
'If I told you, I'd have to kill you,' I said, demurely.
She giggled. 'How exciting.'
We pried open the door and slipped inside. I used my

keyring flashlight to get a better look. The turtles were in slatted cages. They popped their heads back inside their shells, when struck by my torch-light. There, amongst the mottled lettuce and defecation, I saw them - 'The Cuora Trifasciata!'

'Say what?' laughed Nancy.

I hastily snapped some photos, and swept the beam across the cage. There was a label, "Kuromizu Enterprises".

'Here, strike a pose.' I positioned Nancy in front of the cages. She put her hand up, like she was holding a platter just under the label. She flicked her hair back and gave me a toothy grin. I snapped a couple more for good measure.

'Perfect! Great!' I grabbed her hand. 'Now, let's go!'

We made our getaway.

Unfortunately, we ran into some dockworkers loitering by the exit. They stopped talking when they saw us and took an unhealthy interest. They hadn't been speaking Vietnamese, either. It sounded more like Korean. One of them asked me in broken English if I had a light. I said 'no' and kept on walking, but I could feel their eyes boring into my back.

'That was fun,' said Nancy, when we finally flagged a rickshaw. 'What's next?'

It was then, I realised. She'd been carrying a tote bag from the hotel with its name clearly emblazoned on it. No point in going back there now.

'How about some dinner?' I suggested.

Dinner was painful. Nancy drank - and spoke - too much. She told me about her work at an orthodontist's office, which - I apologise in advance to any orthodontists reading this - has to be one of the most mind-numbingly, boring professions on the planet. I learned more than I can take about kids braces and retainers.

When I felt her toes climbing up my leg, I knew it was time to go. I had my passport in my back pocket, as per usual. Time to fast-forward. I propped her up, while I searched for a rickshaw driver.

Ho Chi Minh City has always been a pleasure to walk at

night. Things never seem to slow down, even after sunset. Bare bulbs hung from ceilings in the open-air shop houses. Neighbours gathered to chew the fat, or share a meal. It was a simple, honest life. Even though people struggled to make a living, they didn't do it at one another's expense. There was camaraderie here, something that I envied. It was a reminder that survival was not a zero-sum game. In fact, quite the opposite. It relied upon a close community.

I watched a stream of bicycles move effortlessly through the streets, like a school of syncopated fish. Perfumed girls, in neatly pressed white dresses, sat side-saddle on their boyfriends' bicycles. Under normal circumstances, I would have indulged the senses, maybe even flirted with Nancy, who now had her head on my shoulder, but I became aware of someone following us. If I wasn't mistaken, it was the boys from the dock.

I thanked Nancy for helping me save the world and deposited her in a cycle rickshaw.

'Wait, where are you going?'

'You go on ahead.' I said. 'I have to do some night shooting.'

She winked knowingly and collapsed in the back. I paid the driver and waved him on.

Now, I had to get to the airport.

But first, I had to lose the boys.

I walked along the streets, snapping random photos, looking for an opportunity to run and shake my tail. But the boys stuck to me like glue. After forty minutes, I arrived at a more chic area, which was what I wanted. I identified the most expensive restaurant that I could, targeting tourists and rich locals, figuring they wouldn't dare follow me inside.

I made my way up the stairs, sneaking a look over my shoulder. The ploy seemed to work. They waited across the street.

Sitting comfortably in the dining room, I ordered a starter and a main, then asked for directions to the washroom, praying that there would be a window of some kind.

Indeed, there was, but it was going to be a tight squeeze. I did my best to fit through, but got stuck half-way.

Someone cleared their throat behind me. 'Can I help you?' A British gentleman, by the sound of the accent.

'Um, yes. I just need a little push,' I said.

Luckily for me, the fellow obliged. 'Don't normally see people exiting this way. I hope you didn't forget to pay your bill?'

'No, nothing like that,' I laughed. 'I was spying on my wife and her new lover.'

'I see,' said the gentleman. 'Your secret's safe with me.'

He gave me a good push and I landed on a metal balustrade. I thanked him over my shoulder and looked for a way to scale the building. I couldn't help but attract attention. People across the street had drifted to their windows, to watch the funny foreigner hanging off the building. I managed to scramble to the roof. But when I stood up to run to the other side, I lost my shoe.

'Dammit!'

I had worn slip-ons to keep my feet cool. Not the best shoe for scaling rooftops. It slid down the tiles and stopped at the gutter. I stretched my foot out gingerly, testing my balance. I managed to get close enough to dip my toe into the errant shoe. Slowly, carefully, I hooked it, and lifted it upwards. Then, I slipped and lost my balance. Scrambling to gain traction, I lost *both* shoes over the side.

'Shit.'

I heard them plop to the ground. The boys spat out their cigarette butts and sprung into action. I ran back up along the roof, crouched low, and hurdled myself from one eave to the next. Soon, I ran out of roof. I could see the boys running alongside, tracking me down in the street. Quickly, I double-backed to where I'd seen a skylight. Luckily, it popped open easily, and I jumped down.

A pottery sculpture broke my fall. I was inside an art gallery. The crash took the inhabitants by surprise, which enabled me to brush past them, and down the stairs. I could hear someone shouting expletives behind me, as I jumped three steps at time.

I missed the last flight and rolled out into the street. I shot up and ran in the direction of an alleyway up ahead.

I could hear a commotion clamouring behind me and snuck a quick peek, trying not to slow myself down. The boys from the dock were in hot pursuit, as was the waiter from the restaurant, carrying a tray with the food I ordered.

I ran like the clappers. I know what happens in places like these. They fashion you a Vietnamese bow-tie - from your own tongue. I felt something wet and sticky hit my back. At first, I thought it was blood, but it turned out to be sauce. In frustration, the waiter had hurled my food at me, like a missile, coating me in sweet chilli.

After twenty minutes of pure panic, I stopped. I couldn't go on. My feet were a mess and I was drenched in sweat. Plus, I was attracting looks from other pedestrians. At least, I didn't see anyone following me and that's all that mattered. I slicked back my wet hair, dislodging a noodle, and tucked in my shirt. That was a close call. Never again.

At the airport, I found a flight to anywhere but here.

It wasn't due to leave for an hour, so I sat down at one of the bars. An American was nursing a drink and chewing the ear off the barman. He couldn't help noticing that I was barefoot.

'Customs,' I said, by way of explanation.

He commiserated, as if he'd seen it all before. 'Bloodsuckers!'

I ordered a gin martini.

'Gin??' He cried. 'Don't drink perfume! Have a man's drink - Bourbon.' He jostled his glass to make a point.

'I may only be half the man I used to be,' I said. 'But, why not? Bourbon it is.'

He wasn't bad company. In fact, I'd go so far as to say he was the best company I'd had in a long, long while.

When my flight was called, I thanked him profusely for his company, and lifted his wallet. I checked the contents when I was clear. None to shabby. My spoils would last me another couple of weeks, if I was prudent.

TRACKING A TRACKER

I kept moving, not stopping more than a day in any one destination. I travelled with multi-currency cash cards. As soon as they were spent, I threw them away. I switched SIM cards every twelve hours and removed the battery to my phone when not in use.

This may seem paranoid, but I had learnt my lesson the hard way. It wasn't just on account of my Vietnamese incident. Early in my so-called career, I worked a case on a multi-national corporation. I narrowly escaped getting kneecapped by their "legal affairs" department. They cornered me in a Howard Johnsons. Not a good place to die. I managed to outsmart them and made my getaway in an Amish horse and carriage. But that's a story for another time.

I wasn't a particularly good fighter. I knew a few moves, but fighting wasn't my thing. Some guys love to fight. They ache for an opportunity to dive into the thick of it. That's not my style. I like to slip away, out the back door. Let someone else get the exercise. Besides, I've never seen anything good come from a head-on confrontation. I like to use my brain - and my legs - to get out of a bad situation.

From now on, I had to be more careful. I didn't want to risk researching Kuromizu Enterprises just yet. If they had alerted me to their operation, I'd also alerted them that I was snooping. That was sloppy on my part. It was going to catch up to me somewhere, sometime. I figured it was best to focus on finding Collins. That was my immediate concern. He was going to be in danger, too.

Collins had covered his tracks. But he had trouble blending in on account of his notoriety. Apparently, the network had sold his show at bargain basement prices, because re-runs were everywhere. Even in Borneo, if you can believe it.

I often came across Animal Land t-shirts for sale, despite - or, perhaps, because of - what had happened to it. One of them even had a hand-drawn picture of a giraffe on fire.

In the end, I figured he'd hide out in a large city. Somewhere he could get lost in the crush of humanity.

I got lucky two weeks later.

I popped in a new SIM card and a fully juiced battery, before placing a call to Lucy in LA. 'I've found him.'

'Where are you?'

I shifted the receiver to the other ear, so I wouldn't accidentally make eye contact with the elderly, bald guy who was doing the funky chicken in a pair of soiled diapers. 'The Philippines.'

'I'll catch the next flight out.'

'I don't think that's a good idea,' I said, looking around at the assortment of humanity scattered round the bar. 'This isn't exactly a holiday resort.'

'I can take care of myself. Text me your location,' she said, before hanging up on me.

I crumpled the flyer with Chuck's picture on it and shoved it into my pocket. If Lucy arrived tomorrow, then she'd be just in time for the show. This gave me a day to kill.

There was no point in going outside. The heat was too oppressive. Even my sweat was sweating. I'd have to find somewhere to hold up for awhile. I'd have to find another bar. Preferably, somewhere I wouldn't catch syphilis from the sanitary-ware.

I flagged down a taxi and asked the driver to recommend a place, but soon regretted it. His cab smelled of armpit and he drove like a granny on amphetamines, tapping the brakes every five seconds, or whenever anything appeared within fifty feet of us. He lurched painfully through traffic, smacking me around like a pinball in back. He'd even welded the seat belts to the floor, so they wouldn't get in the way of my safety.

I had rented my own car earlier, but, quite frankly, it was a piece of shit on wheels. The rental agent assured me it was the latest model, which might have been true back in the '70s. It even had an 8-track, tape player. I rest my case. Besides, I've had a phobia about tape players in cars, ever since my incident in Tripoli. My informant at the time insisted on playing his latest "AHA" album. As it turned out, the boy band became our background music, while we were chased by a bunch of thugs in a blacked-out Mercedes Sedan. They ran us off the road and over a cliff.

Luckily, we hit a tree trunk that was growing out of the hillside, so we didn't end up in the ravine. Unluckily for my informant, he went through the windshield. Even worse, his damn cassette wouldn't stop playing. I was pinned down with a broken arm and couldn't reach it. The friggin' thing was stuck on auto-reverse, so I had to listen to the same album for five hours before the paramedics arrived. The pain in my arm wasn't as excruciating as listening to the mind-numbing falsetto of, "Take On Me".

What the hell does that even mean, anyway? Take on me? Couldn't somebody have taught those guys English, or at least proof read their lyrics, before they went global?

My cab driver pulled up in front of a dilapidated shop window, emblazoned with a logo of a decapitated chicken, dancing on a frying pan.

'This is the place.'

'Are you kidding?'

'You want air-conditioning, right? This has air-conditioning.' The shop front killed my curiosity. The cabbie read my mind. 'You go downstairs. Karaoke bar. Downstairs.'

I paid the fare and made my descent into hell.

The place was called "The Blue Niel". I figured it was a typo for "Nile", until I met the proprietor, Niel. He wore a tiara, evening dress, and heels. His makeup ran rivers from some kind of exertion, so at first I thought he was a burn victim. Instead, he'd been singing the blues all night.

His punters were lucky to get the microphone to themselves, however, since Niel wanted to sing every number himself. But they didn't seem to mind. Niel had his groupies - in particular, a gang of drunk Taiwanese businessmen, who were swaying and clapping along to, "Close To You", while wearing tissue-paper, birthday hats. Never mind that it wasn't anybody's birthday.

I settled into a comfortably dark booth. The pleather seats were a little cracked and crusty. Otherwise, this would be a better place to spend the night than a roach motel. There were drinks on tap, unusual entertainment and - as the cabbie had said - working air-conditioning. I was going to be just fine.

I didn't have to worry about my belongings, either. The nice thing about travelling in the Philippines is that you return with less baggage than you arrive, excluding any emotional scars, of course. Not only will the airline do the courtesy of losing everything in transit, but people like to take whatever you've got left as bribes - like my watch, camera, belt, t-shirt. Some guy even asked me for my purple, Superdry cargo shorts. I was sad to let them go. But I was better for it. They made me look stupid anyway, and guys often hit on me when I wore them. Not that it made any difference now.

Perhaps, this was why Collins had come here. It was far, far away from the past. Although, I had long since learned that you can never run away from a painful memory. Still, here was a place where you could really let go - of everything. A place where everyone was only too happy to take it from you. All of it.

It was liberating. In fact, I hadn't felt this incomplete in years and I was loving it. That was, until I found my wallet missing.

I laughed to myself. It was all too ridiculous. I was penniless in a place probably run by low-rent gangsters, managed by a transvestite, who was now singing, "Blue Velvet", with a lisp. Niel laughed, too, although I think he mistook my miniature nervous-breakdown for appreciation of his warble.

Yes, it was going to be an interesting night. I had found Collins. That's all that mattered. I would be vindicated in Lucy's eyes. See - I wasn't such a cock-up, after all. I had justified my per-diem without Photoshopping anything. No, tonight was a night of quiet celebration.

What was it that Prufrock said? "Go gently into the night like a patient anaesthetised upon a table...?" That's how I was going to go into this night and hang the consequences in the morning.

SHOOTBOXING

The crowd was whipped into a frenzy and they wanted blood.

The air was thick with booze and sweat. Bookies jammed fists of cash into their shirt pockets, while the audience heckled the fighters in the cage. I gripped Lucy's arm tight and pulled her close, as the nicotine soup swirled around us. There was more action, here, in the bleachers than there was in the ring. At least that's how it felt in the beginning.

Lucy gasped when she saw Collins. He was a celebrity alright - in the Thai Boxing circuit - but this wasn't like any Shootboxing I'd ever seen.

He was bare-chested and wore flowing, silk pyjama-pants. I thought he was channelling Bruce Lee, until he sailed across the ring and used his face to break his fall. He hit a metal post the way a rotten lemon connects with a baseball bat. His body became entangled in the ropes, his head hung low. The bell rang.

End of round seven.

A pair of gnarled, brown hands grabbed Collins and dragged him back to his corner, while his opponent – a large Australian Kangaroo – bashed its gloves together for dramatic effect. The crowd went wild and the bookies opened up a new round of betting.

Collins' wizened Thai trainer shouted above the din. 'You've got to try harder, Chuck. I told you, watch his left hook! He's making mince meat outta you. If I don't know better, I'd say you were enjoying it.'

Chuck smiled through bloodstained teeth. He tried to spit, but got spittle down his chin. He looked up at the jeering faces around him, then back at the Kangaroo, who now had a feedbag strapped around its ears, while its handlers wrapped fresh tape around its fore-paws.

Chuck's trainer slapped his cheek to get his attention. 'Look at this crowd, Chuck. This crowd is angry. If you don't finish this, they finish you.' He was dead serious.

The bell rang for round eight.

The handlers put the gloves back on the marsupial. Freshly fed and watered, the Kangaroo came out cocky. It bounced lazily from one foot to the other. Its face an expressionless mask. Collins raised himself into a fighter's stance, defying the odds. His body had been pummelled blue as a grape, but he was determined to see it through to the end, and damper the agony of defeat. This wasn't going to be a long fight.

The kangaroo narrowed its eyes, then hopped over to him. It stopped short and tilted his head.

Collins stood his ground.

The kangaroo sprang backwards, balanced on its tail, and kicked Collins in the gut. Collins cartwheeled backwards, head over heels, and landed in a heap at the perimeter of the cage. He stood up like a broken bicycle and raised his gloves again. The crowd heckled and threw anything they could at him, but it bounced off the cage.

The kangaroo flicked its ears, loped across the mat in three bounds, and round-housed Collins with its tail. Collins hit the chain link mesh with a splash, and slid into a puddle of his own sweat and blood.

The crowd booed. They felt cheated. Collins wasn't fighting back.

'Go home Yankee!' shouted someone next to me. He'd already thrown his beer bottle, so he looked for something else to hurl. His only choice was between a midget and a mangy dog. The dog lost. It yelped when it crashed into the cage, rousing Collins from his stupor.

The referee tried to keep the kangaroo away, while he gave

Collins the count. But the kangaroo fed off the fury of the crowd. It body-checked the Ref, before closing in for the kill.

Lucy shut her eyes. 'I can't take any more of this. It's a train wreck.'

The kangaroo used its hind legs to dribble Collins' head across the mat, like a rubber-banded, ball-on-a-bat. Collins put up a hand in a gesture of futility. He couldn't see straight. Everything had multiplied. The referee tried to wedge himself between Collins and the kangaroo, but got caught up in the melee. The crowd cheered, as the kangaroo flung the referee high into the air, smacking him against the chain-link.

It was every man - and marsupial - for himself.

A horn blew loudly. The show was over. Beer bottles and betting slips rained down on the cage, as Chuck's trainer and crew pounced into the ring to pull him to safety. They would be lucky to get out of there alive.

After the show, Lucy and I found Collins in his dressing room, sprawled out prostrate on a bench, both his hands in ice buckets. His body looked as if it'd been hit by a bus. One eye was swollen shut; his lips were puffy and distended, like a samurai duck. He looked terrible. Mickey Rourke on a bad hair day. But up close and personal, I could see he was a powerful man. Escaping death many times over had obviously kept him in good shape.

His torso was covered in all sorts of scars and exotic tattoos, Chinese and Tibetan characters - Sanskrit slogans, even. Later, I would be told that these had been inscribed on him to ward off evil, that he wanted to protect himself from the animals that he was trying to save, and reverse whatever terrible curse had been so cruelly manifested upon him. I think he should have asked for his money back.

His trainer was in a corner, arguing over an envelope of cash with the Philippine promoter. Clearly he wasn't pleased. He split the money and dumped Chuck's cut onto Chuck's back. 'You were supposed to go down in the fifth,' he said, angrily. 'Not the eighth.' He tut-tutted. 'Why you never learn?'

'I pud om a goob show, dimit I?' said Collins, semi-coherently. 'Thads all dad really madders ad de end ob de day.'

I checked out one of the show posters on the wall. It had a picture of a panda wearing bloody boxing gloves, in a logo for the WWWF - "The World Wildlife Wrestling Foundation". Cute, if not a little crude.

Lucy tenderly laid her hand on Collins' shoulder, prompting him to recoil in pain, 'Owww.'

'Sorry, Chuck. It's me, Lucy.'

'Looby?' Chuck turned his one good eye to face her. 'Dib you catch duh show?'

'Freak show, more like.'

'Thass show business, baby,' he spat out something small, pulpy, and white. 'At least it pays well.' He looked at the cash scattered around him. 'Most of the time, anyway.'

'We need to get you out of here,' said Lucy, showing genuine concern.

'What's the rush?'

'Did you see the crowd out there?' I said. 'I don't think they got their money's worth.'

Collins fixed me with his one good eye. 'Who are you?'

'Never mind him,' said Lucy, 'I have a proposition to make.'

'I doubted this was a social call.'

'What's that supposed to mean?' she said, testily.

Chuck feigned indifference. 'I'm all ears.'

Lucy leaned forward. 'I've got you a show.'

He puffed himself up. 'I have a show.'

'You're a circus performer. You fight kangaroos.'

'Only on Wednesdays. I'm boxing a Baboon come Friday.'

'The rate you're going, you won't make it to Friday.'

'Look, I appreciate your concern, Lucy. I really do. But, let's face it, animals hate me. At least this way they get what they want and I get a buzz from the crowd. Plus, I make money to build an animal shelter.' He wiped the blood and vaseline from his face with a towel. 'I should've done live performance long ago. The money's good and the perks aren't bad, know what I mean?' He tried to wink with his one good eye, but it came out creepy.

Lucy was visibly irritated. She'd heard this excuse before. 'Animals don't hate you Chuck. They just don't understand what's at stake. And why should they? They won't know they're extinct, until they are. You said so yourself.'

'I'm cursed, Lucy. You know it. I know it. So, let's stop kidding ourselves.'

I had known Lucy long enough to know that she was scared, but she covered it well. Seeing Chuck like this, broken and alone, defeated – it wasn't how she'd remembered him. It wasn't the memory she wanted to part with, either.

'Go ahead, feel sorry for yourself. Out there, animals are dying. Rare species are going extinct. You're the only one who can help them. Yet, here you are. Sitting on your butt in some godforsaken circus, feeling sorry for yourself, and letting the world laugh at you.'

'They were always laughing, Lucy.'

'Well, I'm not laughing.' A single tear slid down her cheek. She brushed it quickly away.

This seemed to hurt Chuck more than the pummelling he'd got in the ring. He reached out to touch her face, but she batted his hand away. 'I'm tired,' she said. 'I've just come off a long haul flight. And I'm premenstrual. So, don't let it go to your head.'

'No, you're not.'

'Not what?'

'Premenstrual,' he said. 'I could always smell your cycle.'

Before Lucy could react, the door flew open, and a small seedy-looking gentleman stepped in, wearing earrings, and dressed like a gay pirate. He was flanked by a couple of heavies.

'Chucky, my friend. Why you no call?' he said, in a high-pitched, sing-song voice.

The friendly atmosphere was clearly bogus, but Collins kept things congenial. 'Jack. How nice of you to come.'

Jack whinnied like a pony. 'You have been a naughty boy, Chucky. You remember our arrangement?'

'Refresh my memory.'

Jack drew closer with a sinister smile. 'This my country. You fight, you pay. Remember?'

Collins spoke as if remembering for the first time. 'Oh, you want a cut of my money?'

Jack giggled. 'My money, Chucky. My money.'

Collins considered this a moment. 'Why?'

A cloud passed over Jack's face. He whipped out a Balisong blade with a flourish. 'No cut - I cut. You wanna playtime?'

One of the heavies cracked his fingers, before fitting a knuckle-duster.

Collins smiled.

Jack smiled.

Lucy smiled, like someone falling down the stairs.

I could feel my smile cracking the corners of my face.

Collins broke the tension. 'Sure, Jack. Sure.' He carefully picked up the bills that had fallen down around him. 'Take whatever you want.' Jack held out his hand, expectingly. 'Hang on just a sec,' said Collins, casually, as he used the bills to mop the sweat from his pecks. Then, he wiped his armpits. Finally, he bent over and gave his butt crack a good rub with the wad of notes, before handing them over. 'Here.'

Jack winced, as if he'd eaten a mouldy soursop.

The doctor finished dressing Chuck's new wounds back at Lucy's hotel room.

'How do I look?' said Collins, remarkably cheerful. Now, he had two black eyes, both swollen shut, with a bandage around his head, and his arm in a sling.

Lucy's answer was her silence. She thanked the doctor and paid him off at the door.

'You look like the invisible man,' I said.

Chuck didn't get it, so I pointed at his head bandages.

He wasn't amused. 'Who are you, anyway?'

'I'm your ghostwriter.'

'You certainly were a ghost back there in the fight,' he said, reaching for the glass and straw that Lucy had placed in front of him. 'What happened to your face?'

'I was attacked,' I said, casually.

'By what? A blunt razor?'

'No. Something else.' I didn't want to admit it was Nemesis.

Chuck attempted, unsuccessfully, to get the straw into his mouth. Lucy helped him with it. He took a drag, then spat. 'What the hell is this?'

'Juice,' said Lucy.

'Are you trying to kill me?' he spluttered. 'Get me some whiskey!'

Lucy begrudgingly obliged with a bottle from the minibar.

Chuck's jolliness returned, if not somewhat sedated. 'So, what is this show all about? I might as well hear your pitch, since you've come all this way.'

Lucy sat down and took Chuck's hand. It was a tender gesture. I felt I was intruding, so I retired to the sofa. She gave him the whole rundown, but conveniently left out the crux of her pitch to Percy. Chuck listened quietly, taking it all in.

'You know what this means,' said Lucy. 'Open season on every endangered animal on the list. A poacher's paradise. We've lost valuable time already.'

'When did the Velocarabbit make the list?'

Lucy expressed dismay. 'A lot has happened while you've had your head in the sand, Chuck. These animals are depending upon you. They're the last of their kind. Nobody else cares.'

'I guess that's something I know a little about,' he said, sadly.

'And your fans,' said Lucy, 'they've been calling and calling. Percy's got huge sacks of fan mail clogging the halls. Isn't that right?' she turned to me and gave a wink.

'Bucket loads,' I said, dutifully.

'Really?' Collins drained his fifth whiskey miniature and let out a sigh. 'Well, can't let my fans down, can I?'

'That would be a travesty,' I added.

Lucy gave me a look not to over-egg the pudding.

Collins stretched back in his chair. 'We owe nothing in this life and we're owed nothing in return...'

There was a dramatic pause.

We waited in anticipation.

His bottle slipped from his hand and bounced off the carpet. He began to snore.

THE INVISIBLE MAN

I helped dump Collins' body onto Lucy's bed. It wasn't easy. He weighed over two hundred pounds. Lucy peeled back the covers and removed his shoes. Then, she tucked him in. She sat down at the edge of the bed and watched him sleep. Very tender, almost maternal.

There was history here. I could see that. I could fill in the blanks with my imagination. Having spent years together out on the range, under a canopy of stars, without family, without the usual obligations that keep two people apart, something must have happened. I was definitely the third wheel.

I went into the living room area and settled back into the sofa. The cushions were a bit on the poofy side, but it was going to be luxury compared to the booth at the "Blue Niel". I had come to an arrangement with Niel over my missing wallet. He was surprisingly accommodating, actually. In return, I had to listen to his cringeworthy rendition of Broadway show-tunes all night. And, yes, alright - truth be told - there was a little fondling involved. Just enough to stroke his ego. I'm neither ashamed, nor apologetic about this. Men who pretend to be women — transexuals in particular — can be oddly compelling to be around. They have the uncanny ability to be disturbingly sexy. The good ones, anyway. They know just which buttons to push and what fantasies to engage. They know how heterosexual men think. They titillate. Smoke and mirrors. They know how to sell an illusion to a man with whom nothing will be consummated. Go too far and you break the illusion.

They were outsiders who understood the system. I suspect that many of those stories you here about, the ones where Western men get "unwittingly" involved with Asian bar boys, have more to do with self-enforced denial than guile. There is a tacit understanding in the importance of maintaining the illusion, even if some people take it further than others.

My musings were interrupted by the feeling I was being watched. I sensed Lucy standing over me. The lights were out, but I felt the electricity of having her nearby.

She spoke quietly. 'You're one of life's observers.'

'What do you mean?'

'Always in the background, never in the fore.'

'I'm a journalist. That's what I do.'

'You're not a journalist,' she said, 'you're a ghost.' She lay down on the sofa with me.

I felt awkward. Normally, I would have relished this moment. She was a beautiful woman. But the situation had been thrust upon me without any guidelines, and I felt at a disadvantage. What should I do with my arm - use it to pull her closer?

'Don't get any ideas,' she said. 'I just need some company. Do you mind, if I lie here?'

I told her I didn't when, in reality, it was an exquisite form of torture.

We lay still, quietly breathing together, and spooning.

Eventually, she spoke. 'It's hard seeing him like this. This isn't him. He used to be so much larger than life.'

'He still is.'

'Not like he was,' she sighed. 'I'd never met anyone like him. Strong and confident.'

I felt a knife in my chest. Jealousy? Why? I'd only known Lucy for a short while. This was unbecoming.

'In the beginning,' she said, 'we used to kid around a lot. He called me "Jane" and I called him "Tarzan". We thought we were invincible. But then…' She tailed off.

Her hair was soft and fragrant. She used a conditioner from Shiseido. I know, because I had seen it in her dop-kit, amongst other things, when I went to take a leak. Her body was warm and close. Darn. I felt a boner building. Hopefully, it would only be a half-stiffy. Otherwise, things could get awkward. I tried to think of something horrible to bring it down. Like, rotten fruit. Ice cold underpants. Mouldy dentures floating in a glass. Tax returns. Dammnit! It wasn't working. The force was strong with this one. I'd have to think of something more extreme. Masturbation with a blender! There! Yes, it shrank instantly. But, now, I couldn't get the thought out of my head. Oh, God, that was too horrible. Images of Bobbitt and his wife's scissors flooded my subconscious. Christ, that must have been terrible! Shit. Now, I'd always think of this at exactly the wrong moment! I would never be able to have sex ever again.

Lucy broke my runaway train of thought. 'The crocodile was a close call. But Chuck was stronger for it, more determined. Fearless. I was proud of him then. Now, he seems - so broken.' She turned to face me. I could feel her hot, sweet breath on my face. It smelled of vanilla beans. Why? Had she eaten a yogurt? Now, I was hungry, as well as aroused. I wasn't sure what to do. My arm had gone numb from where she lay on it, and I felt pins and needles kicking in. It seemed like the right moment to make a move, so I closed the gap to kiss her. No. She turned away before I could make contact.

But she didn't leave.

It might be strange to hear me say this, but I found myself missing Niel's forthrightness. At least with him you knew exactly where you stood and what was expected of you. There were definite rules of engagement. Not with this one.

Women are very complicated. And Lucy was more complicated than most. But, then, I guess I'm a sucker for complicated.

The next morning, I woke up in a cold sweat. Not from fear. Not at first. The air conditioning had turned my room into a meat locker. That was part of it.

I panicked when I tried to get off the sofa. I was in a box without an opening. That's how it seemed. There were walls where there shouldn't have been. I didn't know which way was up or down. No way out.

I gasped.

Stop. Get a grip. I know this feeling. It's happened before. Take your time. Take… your… time.

I was on the floor. That was all. I'd fallen off the sofa and rolled under the glass coffee table. Normality was restored. This has happened to me many times over the years. I wake up in a strange bed and find walls where I don't expect them. It comes from jet lag and drinking. It comes from being in a thousand unfamiliar hotel rooms. It comes from being perpetually adrift in the world.

The Japanese have another explanation for this feeling. According to their folklore, there is a female demon sitting on your chest. Your mind wakes up before your brain is engaged, but your body is still asleep, so you're unable to move. If you were able to open your eyes, you'd see her floating over you - her long, sinewy black hair snaking up towards the ceiling like tendrils of incense smoke, while she stares back at you with vacant, albino eyes. It's a hideous thought. That's why I always open up my eyes very, very slowly - just in case.

This time, there wasn't any demon lady. Nor was there Lucy, either. Instead, I found a note. She and Chuck had gone down to the hotel restaurant for some lunch. I looked at my watch. One o'clock. Crap! I'd slept over twelve hours.

I found Chuck and Lucy huddled around a dining table, giggling excitedly over a bunch of drawings and maps. Even though Lucy had shared the couch with me, she and Collins shared something that I could never come close to.

I watched them from a distance, hiding behind a potted plant. I saw how she was with him, touching his arm, her body posture, the eye contact. She was a juicy fruit, ripe for the picking. Low-hanging fruit.

Enough. This was stupid. I was acting like a child. I composed myself and sauntered over.

Chuck was a new man. Twelve hours of sleep had rejuvenated him. He greeted me warmly, 'It lives!' His eyes had gone purple, but he could see through them now. Mr Magoo without his glasses. He turned to Lucy, 'Do you mind?'

'Sorry?' she said, confused.

'I'd like a private word with my ghost, if I may?'

'Sure,' she said, awkwardly. 'Um, I'll just go to the washroom.'

When Lucy had left, Collins turned to me conspiratorially. 'She's something, isn't she?'

'Yes, she is.'

'I'm sorry she had to see me like that, back there. You, too. Not my finest hour.'

'I understand.'

'Do you?'

'Do I?'

'Understand?' his eyes bored into me.

'I don't follow.'

'Look,' he said, 'I don't know how this works. I've never had a ghost before.'

'Trevor. You can call me Trevor.'

'Call me Chuck.'

'Chuck.'

'Trevor.'

'We're off to a good start,' I said.

'Good. Let's start the biography from today, shall we, and leave out all the other bits, from before?'

'Sure, Chuck.'

'What's your angle?' he said, brusquely. 'Why are you here?'

'Lucy invited me.'

'On what basis?'

'She pays me to write. About you.'

'Good,' he seemed satisfied. Then, suddenly - 'And what else?'

'What else is there?'

'What about the couch?'

'That?' I tossed off a chuckle in an off-handed manner.

'Yes, that.' He wasn't laughing.

'You had the bed. It was a matter of convenience. Nothing else.'

'Nothing?'

'Nothing at all.'

'Good. Let's keep it that way. Lucy's a sensitive woman. I'd hate to see her get hurt.' He clapped his hand on my shoulder in a manly gesture. 'Okay?'

'Sure, Chuck, sure.'

'Great. I think we're getting somewhere.'

'Yes, we most certainly are.'

'Because I don't like misunderstandings. I like to keep things simple.'

'Simple is my middle name.'

'Is it?'

'No.'

'Of course not.' He smiled. 'Please, have some breakfast. We've got a busy day ahead of us.'

'Thank you.' I was relieved to change topic.

Lucy returned to her seat. She could see that the air had somehow been cleared, so she went back to making notes and drawings, while consulting the endangered species list. 'There was a sighting earlier in the year of the abominable snow crab, so I've put it back on the roster.'

'They're far more resourceful than people think,' said Collins.

'And the urban sewer squid is propagating nicely in Brazil,' she said, excitedly. 'I have a contact in São Paulo who managed to breed them in captivity.'

'I'd love to get some footage.'

'No problemo! It'll be great to reunite the team, don't you think?' Lucy was genuinely thrilled. 'They're dying to get back on the road. I can probably assemble the old crew, with a few replacements, of course.'

'Of course,' said Collins. He seemed to be letting her steer the rudder for now. 'But I'll need to consult with Swami Krishnamurdu first.'

Lucy was caught off guard, 'Who?'

'He's my spiritual adviser,' said Collins. 'I spent six months in an ashram in Goa. He taught me the power of psychic management.'

'By suggesting you let yourself get pummelled in the ring by wild animals?'

'Yes. It was part of my training. He helped me expose my Id, while channeling the ego chakra into my sola-plexus for safe-keeping.'

Lucy detected something. It smelled like horsehit. The self-servicing kind.

'Um, okay,' she said, not entirely sure what to make of this. She flashed me a furtive glance that telegraphed anxiety. 'Perhaps we should start small and work our way up? What about... the hemaphroditic boil worm?'

Collins chuckled. 'I think we can take off the training wheels, Lucy. I'm a third-level ascetic.' He put his hands together and touched the tips of his fingers to his chin. 'No, we're going for the big one. The trophy prize.'

Lucy exchanged a knowing look with me. It made me feel a bit better, like I was part of the team.

'If Collins is coming back,' said Collins pretentiously, 'he's coming back with a bang!' He clapped his hands on both our shoulders. 'Are you ready for the big one?'

We looked eagerly into his eyes, searching for a sign.

'Better saddle up the rainforest gear,' said Collins, mischievously.

Lucy smiled. I did, too, even though I had no idea what was going on.

'We're going after the Razor Eagle!'

RAZOR EAGLE

The Amazon rainforest is 1.4 billion acres and we were in the thick of it. Machete blades glistened, wet with vegetation, as they hacked away at the relentless terrain.

Seen from the air, the jungle looks majestic and tranquil. Down on the ground, though, it's humid and horrible. And loud. With nearly half the world's animal species living under one canopy, it's a cacophony of twerps, whoops, screeches, and buzzings.

Our motley crew chopped their way through the tangled bush. Collins was on point, practically bounding forward with the exuberance of a school boy on a field trip. This was despite the fact that he'd already had several run-ins with the wildlife. Whatever the "curse" was that he feared, it remained firmly in effect.

Behind him, Roger, the camo-clad, Australian cameraman, humped his equipment with a mercenary air. Part time war photographer and survival freak, he enjoyed fashioning gourds and other pieces of equipment from whatever raw materials he found in the wild. Quite ingenious, actually. He even made me a river grass day pack.

Then came the sound guy, Bunny, who looked as if he'd stumbled off the "Magic Roundabout" and was high on cocoa leaves most of the time. He collected mushrooms and other rare hallucinogenic substances from around the world for his personal, mail order business, especially the ones that had not yet been discovered (or, banned by the authorities). He had eyes like the Alice in Wonderland rabbit and a brain steeped in herbicides. One scary hippy. But, also, one of the most accommodating characters you'll ever meet. And good to have in time of crisis. Nothing phased him, not even when we were bum-rushed by an ocelot. In fact, I think he yawned at the time.

There was also a local guide whose name I didn't know. I don't think anybody else did either, because everyone just called him "Guide".

I was next. My feet were killing me. They were rubbed raw from my boots, precipitated by the moisture. Everything was damp. I hadn't been dry in weeks. Even worse, I was coated in termite jelly. It was the most effective mosquito repellant in the jungle, apparently. We had to crush them up periodically and lather up at least three times a day, or we'd be sucked dry.

Then came Lucy, who, like Chuck, was clearly in her element. Bizarrely immaculate, she barely broke a sweat. Plus, she was one of the few of us that the insects didn't feast on.

The same couldn't be said, however, of Marcus - the network spy. He was covered in welts. He waved his machete angrily in the air at anything that was airborne, instead of working the bush. I took a few steps backwards to avoid decapitation.

'Goddammnit! Why don't they leave me alone? I've got nothing more to give!' he said, exasperated.

At least the insects liked Marcus, because nobody else did. Percy had sent him to keep an eye on us. Marcus was the money-man and he took his role far too seriously. He actually had the cash strapped around his body with duct tape and made us beg him for it, as if he was removing a pound of flesh each time we needed our per-diem. Collins made him a sound assistant and boom operator, so he could do something useful in return for freeloading.

His one saving grace was his satellite phone, although he guarded it jealously. Nobody was allowed to use it for more than a minute - if that. It wasn't long before we realised that it wasn't for emergencies. It had a GPS tracking device that kept corporate HQ regularly updated on our exact location. That's why we called him the spy. He hadn't stopped whinging, either.

From the moment we left camp, he exhaled a steady stream of verbal diarrhoea that we had long since learned to ignore.

'How do we even know they're here? This could be a circle jerk. Three weeks and all you've got to show for it is footage of flowers and fauna. Hours and hours of mating insects! Not to mention exotic diseases. I haven't peed in three days. Three days! Do you know what that feels like?'

'At least you won't dehydrate,' offered Chuck, over his shoulder.

'My testicles are as big as pomegranates!' whined Marcus, as he shifted his gait to move his maracas to the other side.

'I told you not to swim in that river,' said Chuck, cooly. 'But you thought you knew best.'

'I needed to relieve my hives.'

'The river's full of parasites. They're like heat seeking missiles - only they're attracted to pee. You didn't pee in the river, did you?'

'What? Oh my God. What do I do? I've got a parasite in my penis! How the hell do I get rid of it?'

'You tell me,' deadpanned Collins, 'I've got one of my own.'

Marcus quit whining and went back to bile. 'Just you wait, mister. You'll get yours. Just you wait and see.' Collins returned to his bushwhacking with a grin. But Marcus had only just got the wind back in his sails. 'We're way over budget, you know. And we haven't even got the goods. Percy's going to be pissed. He's only funding this Podunk operation of yours out of morbid curiosity.'

That caught Collins' attention. 'Then, why is he funding this operation, exactly?'

Marcus flashed a look at Lucy, conscious that he may have said too much already, but Lucy's face was a mask.

Collins pressed further. 'What are you looking at her for?'

Marcus deflected. 'Who gives a shit about these endangerous species anyways? They're freakin' nasty. Maybe they should go extinct. Do us all a favour!'

Collins spoke slowly and amicably, as if to a retarded child. 'Marcus, please. You are releasing lots of negative energy into our beautiful surroundings. You are inviting bad karma. You see this man, here,' he pointed to Roger. 'He would like nothing more than to crack your skull open like a tiny, little coconut. He can do this. I've seen him. Then, he will use it as a canteen. The human head can hold a surprisingly large amount of water, once it's hollowed out. And if we retain the scalp, it keeps the contents very cool and well-insulated.' He shared a chuckle with Roger, 'Just like in Papua New Guinea, no?' He turned back to Marcus. 'However, this would be regrettable. Why? Because we are all creatures of the cosmos. Even you, Marcus, even you. We are all part of one, precious ecosystem. Which means, we are all in this together. If we let your body die, because you are missing your head, we create dissonance. Just as, if we let these species die, because we didn't care - we create catastrophe. We do not wish to upset the biodiversity of our planet by crippling the harmonious balance that nature has put before us. So, please, shut up before we use your head as a thermos.'

Marcus took a step back. He was only five-five, so Collins towered over him. 'You're not the big man you think you are,' he said. 'So, if I were you - ' He slipped and fell backwards into the foliage. Collins was about to say something, when he was struck silent by what he saw. Marcus had landed in a mushy, brown pile that looked like a giant cow patty - 'What the hell...?'

'Shhhhh,' hissed Collins. 'Don't move.'

Marcus froze.

Collins held up his hand for silence. He looked around furtively, then bent down and examined the yuck that Marcus was lying in. It resembled black porridge, mixed with refried beans, after a heavy flow of Montezuma's Revenge.

Collins called over Guide. They huddled and spoke in hushed tones. Roger took the opportunity to run tape and get their conference on camera. He squatted down with the camera between his legs and swivelled the eyepiece upwards. Collins checked the surrounding brush for tell-tale signs. He looked at Guide, before plunging a finger into the gooey doo-doo. He rolled it over the tips of his fingers like cornmeal and held it up to his nose. It smelled like the inside of a donkey's ass.

Guide did the same. Together they sniffed their fingers and exchanged glances.

Collins popped his finger into his mouth.

Marcus wretched. His involuntary reflex caused his boom to twitch, smacking Roger in the head. 'Oi, watch it, mate!'

Collins savoured his swallow, before making his pronouncement to camera. 'That's Razor Eagle poo alright. Their digestive systems are very primitive. That's eighty-percent food matter, twenty-percent waste. And I can taste the gaw-gaw root, which is their favourite food.' He put his hand on the patty. 'Still warm. We must be close.'

He stood up and went into action-man mode. Roger did the same, crouching low and hugging the camera close to him. Marcus trailed behind them, reluctantly, until his boom got tangled in the bush. For a moment, I thought he looked like a lost fisherman, cussing his tackle. He managed to hit Roger again, in the back of the neck.

'For Chrissake!' Roger dropped his camera, grabbed Marcus' rod, and wrestled it from him. 'You do that one more time and I'm going to shove this thing so far up your pecker you'll forget all about that goddamn parasite! Understand me?'

Lucy interceded. 'Come on, boys, the prize is just around the corner. Let's not fall apart now.' She put her hand soothingly on Roger. He responded to her gentle touch and backed off.

'Here,' said Lucy, 'why don't we run some tape?' Then to Collins, 'Chuck, give us an intro. Hot on the trail. Okay?'

Roger let go of Marcus' boom and picked up his camera.

'Thanks,' said Marcus to Lucy. 'That guy's got a screw loose.' Lucy gave him a look not to push it.

Collins took his stance in front of camera.

'Remember,' said Lucy, '"Endangerous". Perhaps you can give us a tag to camera this time?'

'I'd rather not say it,' replied Collins.

'Chuck, it's the name of the show.'

'I worry that it sends the wrong message. It's very aggressive.'

'Fine,' sighed Lucy, 'we'll do it in post.'

'I have final cut,' countered Collins.

'Not any more, you don't,' interjected Marcus. 'I do.'

Collins glared at Lucy. 'What?'

'That's right,' said Marcus. 'Time you showed me some respect. It's my show now. You got it?' He pulled up his britches. 'So here's what you're going to do,' he said with a swagger. 'You're going to say the name of the show. Capische?' He was Percy's "Mini-Me". 'Plus,' said Marcus, 'you need to mention Samsung's 52 inch LCD technology. They're a sponsor.'

Collins regarded him in silence, then turned slowly around and continued on his way.

'Hey, you. Come back here!' shouted Marcus.

But nobody was listening. One-by-one we followed suit, until Marcus was forced to fall in.

That was the end of his moment of authority.

About a half hour later, Collins examined some scratchings at a nearby tree and nodded to Guide. He beckoned Lucy over and showed her the signs. She hurried back to us to share the news, brimming with excitement. 'Chuck thinks its mating season!'

From that point forward, Collins stopped whacking, but crept quietly forwards. We all did the same. Even Marcus had finally stopped yapping. After a few minutes, we came across more razor eagle patties, glistening and fetid. Collins told everyone to stop and stay put. He was going to go on ahead to investigate.

'We don't want to catch them by surprise,' he whispered. 'It could get nasty.' He scooped up gobs of poo and rubbed it all over his face, neck and shoulders. Marcus and I were dumbfounded. But the others behaved as if they'd seen it all before.

I looked to Lucy. 'What's up with that?'

'To mask his scent. Razor eagles have a very keen sense of smell, especially during mating season,' she said.

Chuck finished applying his diarrhoea mask, then disappeared into the thicket, alone.

'Aren't you going?' I said, to Guide.

'No. Angry Birds,' said Guide. 'Best be here.'

We waited on edge, thick with adrenaline. All except Bunny, who sat cross-legged on the ground and made circles with his head. It had taken us several weeks to get to this moment and most of us were running on fumes. The tension made me realise just how tired I actually was. My limbs felt like sandbags, my throat like sandpaper when I swallowed. Guide had a nervous tick in the corner of his mouth. It kept twitching, as if attached to a string pulled by an invisible force. Marcus grimaced and put his hand in his pocket, discreetly shifting the elastic of his underpants to reseat his aching balls. Roger passed the time by checking his equipment. He liked to go over everything in the same order, like a pilot before take-off: tools, flash drives, rechargeable batteries, knives, shoelaces, eyeball… Yuck! He polished his glass eye with a handkerchief, before popping it back into its socket. Only when he was content all was in working order, did he start whittling. He was pretty good, too. He'd already made a wooden butterfly the last time we stopped. I caught Lucy staring at me, her eyes wide with excitement. Under other circumstances, one might confuse it with arousal. She had clearly missed the adventure of a Chuck Collins expedition.

Marcus finally found his voice again. 'So, what's the big deal?' Lucy shushed him, but he didn't care. 'They're eagles, right? Why is everyone so excited?'

Lucy pivoted on her heel. 'Do you know how razor eagles protect their eggs?' Marcus shook his head. She crept closer to him. 'They find a large animal. About your size.' She put her finger on his belly button, seductively, and traced slowly upwards.

He smiled. 'That tickles!'

'Then, they rip open its belly and place the eggs inside its entrails to keep them warm, while they go off to hunt.' Marcus winced. 'Do you want to become a baby eagle incubator?' said Lucy, provocatively. Marcus shook his head. She took her hand away. 'Good. So, stop drawing attention to yourself.' She stepped back and smiled. Marcus gulped and kept his mouth shut.

Ten minutes later, the bushes came alive, as Collins crept back in amongst us. He, too, had the same wild-eyed look as Lucy. Now that the poo had dried, he resembled a crazed aborigine. 'There are six of them. Get ready! Let's go!'

He motioned Roger to follow him first. Roger immediately caked himself in poo. Bunny, Lucy, and Guide followed suit. I figured I had nothing to lose, so I did the same.

'Is this really necessary?' said Marcus. 'I've already got this shit all over my ass.'

'Suit yourself,' smiled Lucy.

We fell-in single file and slipped gingerly into the unknown.

FACHON

We moved as silently as we could. The going got easier as the jungle thinned. Before long, we reached a large clearing. There, right in the middle of it, was a hideously ugly bird, squatting on a nest of eggs. This was the female. Five males walked a perimeter, on guard duty.

When I'd first heard about the razor eagle, I imagined something the size of a falcon. Something that could sit on your arm. These stood six feet tall and had ferocious, sharp talons that could shred a buffalo. Their heads were pale blue, like a turkey, and the birds themselves gave off a rank odour - a heady mix of crotch and hops. It was even worse than the eagle poo we had smothered ourselves in. I had to breath through my mouth, so as not to gag.

We clustered in three teams, hugging the terrain, so as not to be seen. Or, smelt. Roughly thirty feet from the perimeter of the clearing, Roger gripped my shoulder and pulled me to a halt. I looked at him for advice, but he was looking over my left shoulder with a finger to his lips. I glanced quickly over my shoulder, but saw nothing there. Then, I remembered - I had been looking at his glass eye. That eye often looked over your shoulder, even when the other was looking straight at you. Whenever we had a long conversation - which wasn't often, mind you - I found it disconcerting. It made me feel as if he was watching someone behind my back. He had meant for me to stop.

Collins nodded to Roger, who hefted the camera onto his

shoulder. Bunny primed the audio recorder and gave a thumbs up. Marcus was quivering and refused to lower the boom into position. Instead, he clung onto the pole as if it was a life-saver.

Bunny crept over to him and whispered. 'Dude, you need to bring the boom.'

'I can't,' said Marcus, genuinely scared. 'I don't have enough shit on me. I'll be a sitting duck. I don't want to become an incubator.'

'We're all sitting ducks, if we don't get the shot, man.' He pulled out a root from his top pocket and popped it in Marcus' mouth, before he could protest. 'Here,' he said, 'chew on this.' Marcus wanted to say something, but Bunny was firm. 'Chew.'

After a moment, Marcus relaxed. He took a deep breath, then nodded. Bunny backed away and Marcus lowered the boom mic into position. Crisis averted.

Collins crept under the boom and Roger crouched opposite him. Collins spoke quietly and earnestly to camera. 'There are believed to be only six razor eagles in existence and it looks like they're all here. We've missed the mating cycle, but eggs have been laid. No one has ever captured these magnificent birds on camera, let alone witnessed a birth. A world first right here on "Endangerous!"'

Marcus let out a long, nasal laugh, breaking cover. 'You said it! Endangerous! Sweet!' Collins looked horrified and beckoned for him to be quiet, but Marcus was oblivious. 'Wow! Hot damn. I feel so - alive!' Marcus flapped his arms, then wrapped them around himself like a blanket.

The male razor eagles swivelled their heads in unison towards us. The largest one extended its wings and shook them menacingly, as might a peacock, while letting out an ear-piercing, guttural wail. It was a horrible sound - the sound of someone sodomising a baby moose. It went through our bowls, up our throats, and tickled our teeth.

Marcus pointed at the eagle and laughed. 'Big Bird!'

'It's not Big Bird, Marcus, get down!' hissed Collins.

The rest of us crouched low and backed away, giving Marcus a wide berth. The birds let out another, ear-blasting squeal. One of the males skittered towards Marcus, stopping a few feet away. It looked around from one of us to the next with beady, reptilian eyes, wondering who posed the biggest threat.

'I want to pet him,' said Marcus.

'Don't pet him,' said Collins. 'He won't like it.'

The razor eagle was confused. It looked at Marcus and cocked its head.

'But I want to,' said Marcus, petulantly. 'He's my birdy. Go get your own.' He stuck out his hand.

Everything went quiet. I could hear the blood rushing in my ears.

The razor eagle jolted.

Marcus' arm came off at the shoulder and dropped to the floor.

'Hey,' complained Marcus. 'What did you do that for?' He seemed more confused than upset. Blood pumped from his empty shoulder socket. He bent down to pick up his arm, but it was now slippery and difficult to handle. 'Shit. Does anybody have a bandaid, or something?'

Collins turned to Bunny. 'What the hell did you give him?'

Bunny shrugged. 'I usually have one of those for breakfast. Just to take the edge off, you know?'

'You're a bad birdy. Bad!' said Marcus, to the bird, without much conviction. He was losing lots of blood. It squirted at regular intervals onto the foliage, like red wine from a spigot. 'I don't feel so good,' he said, teetering on his feet. 'Maybe we can stay in tonight? Just order room service, or something.' He collapsed and sat, cross-legged on the ground. His face had turned the colour of bone. He put his severed arm in his lap, and closed his eyes. The bird screeched, setting off the others. It opened its wings to their full, sixteen foot diameter, then grabbed Marcus by the leg, before lifting him high up into the air, and flew away.

'Holy crap,' I said. 'What the hell?'

'There goes pay day,' said Roger.

'Don't worry,' said Collins. 'The eagle will probably drop him from a height to pulverise the bones and make him easier to eat. He still has a chance.' We watched the eagle circle the clearing, then drop his cargo. Collins nodded, 'Yep, there he goes.'

Marcus plummeted down, shouting gleefully. 'Weeeeeeeeeeeee!' But then, he hit some branches with his neck. It made the sound of freshly snapped broccoli.

'Maybe not,' thought Collins, out loud.

Marcus' body lay in a heap, his arms and legs twisted backwards, at odd angles, like a discarded doll at a daycare centre. He was most definitely dead.

'We've got the Sat phone, though,' said Lucy, retrieving it from the ground. 'At least that's in one piece.'

The other eagles were getting ancy now. They edged towards us, flapping their enormous wings. Another one of the males ventured forth.

I shouted above the din. 'We've got to get out of here!'

Too late. The other male returned from his attempt to tenderise Marcus and had us trapped between him and the others.

'Stand perfectly still,' shouted Collins. 'Their sight works better on moving targets. Freeze and we'll blend in.'

Everybody froze as best they could.

It was hard to be still under the circumstances. My legs were shaking and my forehead sweat was washing off my poo camouflage. I looked to the others for comfort. Lucy and Collins were lying on the ground in a foetal position, protecting their head and privates. Roger was down on one knee, cradling the camera on his lap, still recording. Bunny appeared to be taking a nap. And Guide? Where was Guide? I had no idea. He was even better than I was at disappearing in a crisis. I hugged the trunk of a tree. Not the best place to be, I thought, but too late now.

The two male eagles sniffed around us. The ploy seemed to be working. They wandered in circles, even stepped on Collins a couple of times, but were confused by the sudden stillness. One of them came right up to me and sniffed my neck. I nearly shat my pants.

"Please, God," I thought to myself, "this was not the way I was meant to go. Please don't let me die by an angry bird in the Amazon." But, then, it backed off.

The birds returned to their nest. Their screeching died down. You could hear the collective sigh of relief. We were in the clear - for the time being, away.

Collins uncoiled himself and told us to stay where we were. We'd have to wait until nightfall. They'd be on high alert, watching us like, well, razor eagles.

In the meantime, Collins told Roger that he wanted to try to set up the camera closer to the nest and trigger it via remote. He was hoping to get a shot of the eggs hatching, if we were lucky enough to still be alive when it happened.

Roger wanted to go, too, but Collins refused, 'Too dangerous.' Collins put the camera on his back and crawled on his belly towards the nest. It was an agonising to watch. He moved ever so slowly. Finally, he found the cover of a small bush and cautiously set up the camera, so that only the lens would peek out from between the leaves. When he'd finished his prep, he turned and gave us the thumbs up.

Just then, we heard a whooping sound.

I couldn't tell where it was coming from, but it grew louder. A huge gust of wind ruffled the eagles' feathers, sending them into a panic.

A big black helicopter hovered over the clearing and jettisoned several small canisters.

'Smoke grenades!' shouted Roger, above the mayhem, as he dove for cover.

The canisters exploded when they hit the ground, spewing out thick, white smoke. Several mercenaries jumped from the chopper and abseiled to the ground. They opened fire on the eagles with automatic weapons. One bird took flight, while the others launched themselves at the soldiers. It was difficult to see what was going on through the maelstrom of bullets and smoke. But one thing's for sure - we were caught in the crossfire, like fish in a barrel.

Roger went into soldier-of-fortune mode. He dove into a roll from one tree to the next, his knife gripped firmly between his teeth. Lucy kept close to Chuck - leaving me with Bunny, who was carefully coiling his iPod cable without paying much attention to the firefight.

'Bunny, we've got to get out of here!' I shouted.

'It's okay, man. Want some root?'

'No, Bunny. This is bad. We need to keep moving.'

Bunny shook his head. 'They might mistake you for a bird, man. Better lay low.'

I gave up arguing with him. I ran over to Chuck and Lucy instead.

'Goddamn poachers,' spat Chuck. 'They ruined my shot.'

These didn't strike me as ordinary poachers, though. They were well armed and fully loaded. This was a private army.

The female razor eagle launched itself at the helicopter. It pecked and scratched at the cockpit glass, but kept slipping off the bonnet. The pilot took advantage and rocked the copter forwards, nose down, sending the bird into the rotor blades. The end was instant. Down below, we were showered in feathers and blood.

The mercenaries worked in a semi-circle, firing short bursts, ripping the remaining eagles to pieces. They had significant fire-power, but the eagles were crafty. This was their home turf and they had eggs to protect. They weaved their talons back and forth like scythes, cutting through the forest like butter. Occasionally, one of their talons connected with a mercenary. In fact, one of them was knee-capped right in front of me. He left his legs behind and went down in a torrent of blood and spinovial fluid. I froze, not sure what to do. I thought of helping the poor guy, or, at least, borrowing his gun for my own protection, but he was yanked up into the sky, and flung into a tree, where he was skewered on some branches.

'I've got to get the camera,' shouted Chuck, as he ran for it.

Lucy hesitated, so I grabbed her arm. 'No, let him go.'

'But it's suicide,' she yelled.

'That's what you wanted, isn't it?' I replied. She looked at me reproachfully, then pushed away, and ran after Chuck.

I felt angry. She had made her choice. The smoke was clearing now, presenting fewer opportunities to hide.

Chuck reached the camera, but an eagle plopped down in front of him. 'Shoo, birdy,' he said.

The eagle wasn't listening. It plunged its talon into his leg. To my surprise, Chuck didn't react, but clung onto the camera instead, trying to protect the equipment. The bird twisted violently, ripping off his leg, and went airborne.

Chuck shouted after it. 'Hey - give it back!'

The bird was just as confused as I was. It had expected to take Chuck with him. It was then that I realised - Chuck's leg was a prosthetic. I recall, now, that he lost it to the crocodile attack, the one which launched his career on YouTube. Lucky call. If the bird had grabbed the other leg, things would have gone badly.

The eagle dropped Chuck's leg and came back round for another pass, but it was hit by a volley of gunfire by one of the mercenaries, saving Chuck's life. Chuck wasn't grateful, though. In fact, he was angry.

He hopped on one leg and whacked the soldier with his prosthetic.

The soldier shrugged him off and spoke into a headpiece. 'Perimeter nearly secure sir. Just two more to go.'

The shooting was sporadic now. It struck me as odd that poachers would slaughter the animals they'd come to collect. Just then, a second helicopter arrived.

A small man, wearing a blue Nehru jacket with buttons up the sides, poked his head out from the open bay. 'Ze eggs! Mon dieu. Be careful of ze eggs!' He hastily threw down a zip line and clambered, unskilfully, from the chopper. He couldn't wait to hit the ground, which he did with a thump, after becoming tangled at the end of his line. 'Merde!' He fumbled with his release, then leapt up onto his feet, and ran towards the nest. A large and muscular, senior mercenary scaled down after him, and kept watch over his boss.

The frenchman cradled two eggs protectively in his arms, 'We must protect them, or we have nothing. Nothing!'

The last of the razor eagles hit the dirt and twitched violently, before going still.

I looked around. The carnage was complete.

Lucy strode up to the Frenchman without a hint of fear. 'Who the hell are you?' she demanded. The leader of the mercenaries grabbed her from behind and held her fast, protecting his boss. The Frenchman blinked at her. Even caked in eagle shit, she was still a paragon of beauty.

'I am Henri Fachon,' he smiled, coquettishly. 'And who might you be - my little angel of the forest?'

BUSH BROTHERS

They had us trussed up, cross-legged on the ground, and tied to one another to make it harder to escape. Guide had gone missing. Now that Marcus was dead, we were down to five: Collins, Lucy, Roger, Bunny, and myself.

Collins was unusually quiet. He watched the mercenaries closely, the commander in particular - a man who stood tall and erect, more at ease in his skin than the others. Perhaps he have less to prove, than the rest of his crew. He didn't return Collins' stare, as if on purpose.

After flirting unsuccessfully with Lucy, Fachon seemed more interested in his albumen. He transferred his precious eggs to an airtight, military grade equipment case, and accompanied the case back to his helicopter. The mercenary commander ordered his men to leave the dead and collect the wounded. The sun set on the aftermath of the battle. The smoke had cleared. All that was left were feathers, yolk, and blood.

Finally, the commander strode up to Collins and spoke to him in an Afrikaans accent. 'That's the second time I've saved your life. There won't be a third.'

'You know him?' piped Lucy.

'We are bush brothers,' said the leader, smiling insincerely.

Collins didn't return the smile. 'Lucy, meet De Konig. We grew up together in Zimbabwe. That was a long time ago. Long before he became a lackey to the poachers and their private petting zoos.' This was said without irony.

'Don't act so high and mighty,' said De Konig. 'I helped stock your Animal Land adventure park, remember?'

'My purpose was pure,' said Collins. 'I am but a lone shepherd.'

De Konig wasn't buying. 'So what is this shepherd doing on my mountain?'

'Cosmic fate has brought us back together, brother.'

'I don't believe in fate,' said De Konig. One of the mercenaries brought him an unbroken egg that had been lost in the skirmish. 'Make a fire,' he ordered. 'I could use the protein.' Collins was horrified and De Konig knew it. De Konig pulled out a foldable spork and made a big show of scrambling the egg right under his nose. He inhaled deeply. 'Such a sweet aroma from such an ugly bird.' He scooped up some of the egg and shoved it towards Collins' mouth. Collins clenched his teeth. This scrambled egg was all that remained of an extremely rare species. The last of the Razor Eagles had been slaughtered and God only knew what Fachon was going to do with his.

I knew it was wrong, but I wished De Konig had offered me the egg. After I'd gone through all of my freeze-dried rations in the first two weeks - which, incidentally, tasted of flavoured cardboard - I was forced to live off the land. For the longest time, I had no idea what I was eating. Guide and Lucy would disappear into the forest and return with earthy tasting salads and barbecued mystery-meat. It didn't taste terrible, but I was pretty sure I didn't want to know how the sausage was made. One day, I chanced upon them by accident and saw the preparations. The salad was made from tree bark - the soft, inner part, closest to the core. The dressing was made from pulverised white termites and other assorted creepy-crawlies. The "fries" were fried caterpillars, and the barbecued meat came from the occasional tapir. A fried egg - Razor Eagle, or otherwise - sounded like heaven on a plate.

Collins refused to eat it. De Konig laughed and ate the egg himself. He even licked the spork clean. 'Who's the frog?' said Collins, after a fashion.

'The less you know the better,' replied De Konig.

'Better for who?'

'Better for everyone.'

De Konig barked at his men, until the mop-up was complete. One-by-one, they mounted the chopper. When De Konig was the last on the ground, he pulled out a huge, saw-toothed blade and approached Collins with it. His expression put me on edge.

He cut Collins' bonds. 'Here, you might need this.' He turned the blade around, passing Collins the handle. 'I'd advise you to make tracks before nightfall. You don't want to be out here in the open at night.'

'Wait - you're just going to leave us here?' I said, my voice cracking in an unmanly way.

'The chopper came in heavy with barely enough fuel as it is,' said De Konig. 'Now, we're a few men lighter. We'll just about make it. Good luck.' De Konig jumped aboard the helicopter and went airborne. Within minutes, they were gone, and the sounds of the wilderness returned.

Collins cut Lucy's bonds and gave her the knife in silence. We could see the clouds in his face.

Lucy wasn't going to leave things as they were. 'What did he mean, he saved your life once?'

Collins spoke to her quietly. 'It's not important. The show's over. Let's go home.'

'You're giving up?'

Collins didn't answer, but strode purposefully back into the jungle. Lucy passed Roger the blade and ran after him.

Guide clambered down a nearby tree and joined our group. He had been watching the whole thing from a safe distance. 'Hi,' he said. The rest of us gave him dark looks.

When Lucy caught up to Collins, there were tears in his eyes. He tried to hide them. This was definitely not the Chuck of days gone by. He gestured to the Sat phone that she was holding. 'Please, I need to call my shwarmi.'

'Your shwarmi - he has a cell phone?'

'Yes. I need spiritual guidance,' he said, dialling. He waited for the call to connect.

I caught up to Lucy and tried to reason with her. 'Look, De Konig's got muscle. If he wants to work his way through the endangered species list - backed by a private army, I might add - we haven't got a snowball's hope in hell.' She ignored me and kept her eye on Collins. He was listening to someone on the other end with his eyes closed. I pressed my case. 'A couple of yahoos with a video camera aren't going to stop him.'

She turned on me. 'The fact that De Konig's involved in this is all the more reason for us to stick it out. Those species are the last of their kind. If you can't hack it, walk away. We'll do just fine without you.'

I was trying to figure out how I could walk away in the middle of the Amazon rainforest, but drew a blank. Plus, I didn't like being called a loser, which is damn well what she was suggesting.

Collins began to hum. His humming grew louder. He closed his eyes and hung up the phone. 'Ooouuummm...' The rest of us exchanged looks, unsure what to make of it. 'BaaaaaNaaaaaaNaaaaaaaaa' Collins grew calm. Centred. He opened his eyes slowly and blinked at us. 'Shwarmi thinks that this expedition is creating too much adverse energy for my manipura.'

Lucy was testy. 'So, what, that's it? You're just giving up, because of your manipura?'

'No, Lucy,' said Collins, 'I am not giving up. I am passing the responsibility onto you. This isn't my fight anymore. I have four more stages of healing ahead. This could undo months and months of tantra.'

'You need to snap out of it, Chuck. Get with the programme.' She was angry, hurt and, possibly, afraid. 'I - I can't do this without you.'

'Of course you can, Lucy. Have faith in yourself. You have great anahata.'

'Stop! Just stop! Enough with this yogi nonsense. What happened to you, Chuck? What the hell happened to you?' It was a mixture of anger and panic.

'I have discovered a higher plane of existence, Lucy. You must try it.'

'I'm sure the air is very nice up there, Chuck, but down here we can smell the bullshit.' She gathered strength and momentum by pacing around him. 'I'm damned if I'm going back to Percy with my tail between my legs! You have no idea what I had to go through to get you this commission. The sacrifices I've made. All these years. All for you, Chuck. For you!'

'When you are lying on your back,' said Collins, prophetically, 'you can only see the sky, but cannot touch it. When you stand on your feet, you can see and touch the world around you. It has much more to offer.'

This made Lucy angrier. 'Is that so? Fine.' She grabbed a plant and released it, then pinched Roger's arm. 'I'm touching.' She poked Bunny, then me. 'I'm touching the world around me. See.' She grabbed a clump of earth and let it fall through her fingers. 'What do I feel? What do you feel, Chuck? Feel this!' She punched Chuck in the face. 'I look at you and I see someone hiding. Avoiding. Letting down the team. Hiding from what? A curse? Look at yourself. You're alive! The curse is all in your head. It never existed! It's just an excuse.'

Collins considered her outburst, thoughtfully, but remained rooted to the spot. Then, he gestured with his arms outstretched. 'Come, everyone, let us form a happy circle.'

'I don't want to,' said Lucy. 'I am NOT happy!'

'That is why you must. Come.' He pulled us together - even Guide - but Lucy stood to the side, pouting. 'It has been an honour, my friends, to travel with you,' said Collins. 'But now, our journey has come to an end. Let us give thanks to this forest for bringing us together one last time. No regrets.'

'Dude,' added Bunny, 'I'd ride with you any day. You know that. No regrets.'

Roger chimed in. 'Same here, Chuck. No regrets' He handed him a carving. 'Here, I made you something to remember us by.' It was a group figurine - all of us - beautifully carved into an eagle bone.

'That's remarkable, Roger. You even have Marcus in there, without his arm. You have a rare talent.'

'Thank you,' smiled Roger, basking in the praise. There was

in a tear in his one, good eye.

'You've definitely given me fuel for my nightmares,' I said.

'Thank you, ghost. Hopefully, your pen will be mightier than your sword,' said Collins.

'Very scary,' said Guide, wanting to share. 'All you - crazy people. Very crazy people!' he laughed, nervously.

Lucy wasn't ready to join in. 'Why did you come, Chuck? Why did you come all this way, if you weren't going to see it through?'

Collins spoke to us first. 'You see, I told you - great anahata.' He turned to Lucy. 'You wanted another crocodile incident, no? For Percy. And why not? I owe you one. My lucky rabbit foot.' Lucy looked horribly conflicted at that. Collins trod on her silence. 'And, for a short while, it felt like old times.'

She pushed back her tears. 'You don't owe me anything, Chuck. You owe yourself. A second chance.'

'Lucy, Lucy. I know you. You like those pretty, shiny things. Medals. Awards. Emmy's, yes?'

'They are very shiny,' she conceded.

'I know you covet them, in your closet. Am I right? Come...' He held out his arm and brought her into our circle. 'Let us breathe in each other's essence.'

Lucy passed out and collapsed to the ground.

'It is a powerful essence, indeed,' remarked Collins.

Then, Roger collapsed, too.

'Hmm - my goodness, what an essence this is!'

I could see a dart sticking out of Roger's neck, but Collins was oblivious. He closed his eyes and began to hum. 'BaaaaaaaNaaaaaaNaaaaaa'

I hit the dirt, of my own accord, and lay as still as possible. Guide did the same. Bunny was struck by a volley of darts. He looked like a pin cushion. Unfazed, he batted them like mosquitos. It must have been all the chemicals in his system. Eventually, ten darts later, he went down like a sack of potatoes.

Collins opened his eyes to see scores of half-naked tribesmen, sporting dart blowers, step out of the jungle from all directions. There was nowhere to run, or hide. Resistance was futile. Guide and I stood up. We clustered together and faced the hunters.

'Mother of God,' exalted Collins, as he looked down at their flimsy loin cloths. They were hung like bulls. Not a single Cold Irishmen amongst them. He turned to Guide. 'Who are these people?'

'Unwanku tribesman,' said Guide. 'They are the most feared people in the jungle.'

'Can you speak their language?' I asked.

'A little,' said Guide. 'It's complicated. They have no vowels, no past tense, no future. I'm a little rusty.'

'Just ask them what they want with us,' ventured Collins.

Guide nodded and made a series of painful-sounding clicking noises, glottal stops, and fizzes. He sounded like he was communicating with a cricket, but the tribesman seemed to understand most of what he was saying. One of the them returned with a barrage of clacks, lip bounces, and a long sizzle. Then, he ended his monologue with a very exaggerated smile.

Guide turned to Collins, ashen-faced. 'They worship the Razor Eagle. They are very angry for what has happened.'

'They don't look angry,' said Collins. 'Look, they're smiling.' He beamed a toothy grin right back at them, but it set off a bunch of angry titters and aggressive gestures.

'No, no!' said Guide. 'Smiling is bad. To them it is an insult. An invitation to fight.'

Collins dropped his smile, but it was too late. The tribesmen tightened the circle around us with leering expressions and began a loud cacophony of rhythmic clicking. They stabbed their dart guns at us for good measure.

Collins took a step backwards to avoid being poked, but tripped on an outcropping, wrenching off his false leg. The tribesmen gasped. Collins quickly refastened his leg and stood up as tall as he could. Excited, the tribesman clicked and tittered amongst themselves, until one of them felt brave enough to run over and pinch Collins' prosthetic. He ran back and related the experience. Guide tried to eavesdrop on their conversation. Collins waited, expectantly.

Guide translated what he heard. 'They say you are like...' he faltered. 'I don't understand.'

Collins leaned in, 'What?'

'Like, the very expensive Peso Man. Mister Six? I'm sorry, I don't understand.'

'Peso Man?'

'Very expensive,' repeated Guide.

'Perhaps they mean the "Six Million Dollar Man",' I joked, not knowing what to make of this ridiculous situation.

'You mean Lee Majors?' laughed Collins.

That did it. Suddenly, the clicking stopped and the tribesmen looked at Collins in awe. They pointed up at the sky and begin click-clacking again.

'They say this Lee Majors you speak of is a God,' said Guide, quickly.

'Obviously, they never saw "The Fall Guy",' I said.

Collins turned to the tribesman and thumped on his chest. 'Me, Lee Majors!' The tribesman dropped onto their knees and bowed to the heavens. 'Finally, I get the recognition I deserve.' Collins was clearly enjoying this. He whipped off his leg again, waved it around for good measure, then re-attached it. His audience went into rapture, bent down on one knee and praised the heavens. They zip-zapped in awe. Just then, three of them grabbed Guide, and tried to twist off his arms and legs. Guide screamed.

'No,' shouted Collins. 'Only one, Lee Majors. Here. I am the special one.' On hearing this, they released Guide. 'Now,' commanded Collins. 'Take me to your leader.'

UNWANKU

The tribesman dragged Bunny, Lucy and Roger behind them by their feet, until they regained consciousness an hour later - whereupon, they were press-ganged into helping Guide and I carry Collins aloft, on a chariot of crossed-arms. Collins seemed to enjoy his new, God-like status. In fact, he milked it for all it was worth.

Lucy muttered obscenities under her breath. 'Don't get too comfortable.'

Collins reminded her to keep the pretence going, or we'd all be dead. She swallowed her pride for the good of the group.

'What can I say?' Collins chuckled. 'Maybe I'll stick around for awhile. Has its perks. Have you seen their shlongs? I'm gonna fit right in.'

'Ha!' laughed Lucy. The kind of laugh that suggested she knew better.

We entered a dense forest of tall trees, criss-crossed by rotting vines. Here, it became unusually quiet, save for the occasional shriek of a lone bird. It was spooky. Even the air felt cooler, sending a chill down my spine. Everything glistened, slick with dew. The earth was soft and fungal. It smelt of mushrooms, moss, and pu-erh tea - except for the occasional drip of condensation from above, which had the pong of raw sewage. One of them landed on my shoulder, like a large bird dropping. I was about to brush it away, when I saw that it was a human thumb.

I reacted violently, jumping and spasming in all directions, like a cheerleader on crystal meth. The others looked up and realised that the dark nests we'd seen above us were, in fact, human corpses in various stages of decomposition, rotting in the treetops.

'They offer their dead to the Razor Eagle,' said Guide. 'Food for the Gods.'

Apparently, when the thunderstorms came, it didn't rain "cats and dogs", but members of the family.

Once we passed through the garden of the dead, we came across a series of huts on stilts - a village. Naked children came to pinch our skin and tease us.

'Strange greeting,' I thought to myself, as they hurried alongside, clicking excitedly.

We approached a clearing in the centre and had attracted quite a crowd by now. There, we were met by a tribal elder, wrinkled as a prune, with breasts slung so low as to be mistaken for knee pads. The elder wore a loincloth with a noticeable bulge underneath. Hmmm. Perplexing. We called this person, "Pat", as we couldn't figure out if she was a he, or he was a she.

One of the welcoming committee - a woman with preternaturally bouncing breasts - ran over to Collins carrying an offering. He was about to break into a smile, until he remembered that this was incorrect behaviour. Instead, he nodded gravely, and bent down, as she draped a necklace around him, like a Lai. Then, before he could straighten, she batted his cheeks merrily from side to side with her mammaries.

'God thanks you, my child,' said Collins, hamming it up. It was then we noticed that Chuck's necklace was a string of human teeth.

Other tribes people stepped forward, cloaking Collins in a garment of rope and roots, rubbing mud on his face, and pinching his body, presumably for good luck. After all this fussing, he looked like something the cat dragged in on a bad and stormy night.

The tribes people began chanting with a feverish clucking, as they formed a human corridor, with Collins at one end and a weird looking, Medicine Man, covered in tattoos and piercings, on the other. Medicine Man looked a hundred years old, but was surprisingly spry, as he danced his way towards Collins carrying a wooden bowl. He did this with a furious clucking and jabbed gnarled roots at the sky to punctuate his song. Eventually, he stopped in front of Collins and poked him in the chest with the root. Collins tried to make the best of it by not laughing. It was an odd welcoming behaviour.

Medicine Man popped some of the root into his mouth and masticated, vigorously. We looked to Guide for an explanation of what was to come.

'It's an ancient ritual,' he said. 'We must eat the sacred root together. They say it will cure us of our evils and purify us.'

Lucy was uncomfortable. 'And if we don't eat it?'

Guide looked grave. 'Then, they eat us.'

Now, I realised what all the pinching was about. It was the standard greeting of cannibals. It was like squeezing the fruit at the grocery store to check its ripeness.

Bunny seemed oblivious to the implications. He was more interested in the herbals. 'What exactly does the root do?'

'It is said to reveal your inner self. It unlocks your most disturbing memories, so that you can confront them. The Unwanku do not have an awareness of time, so, for them, memories are sacred visions.'

'Load me up,' said Collins. 'I had peyote once and it blew my mind.' Bunny agreed. He was clearly looking forward to the experience. Collins reached for one of the roots in Medicine Man's bowl, but the wizened old geezer slapped his hand, as if admonishing a greedy child who'd reached into the cookie jar.

'It's not ready yet,' explained Guide.

Just then, Medicine Man hacked and hurled up the root from his throat, and yacked it into the bowl. Then, he snored, as if dislodging something from the furthest reaches of his oesophagus, and cacked up more frothy pulp into the bowl for good measure. He looked at Collins and gestured to the bowl.

Collins eyed the snotty meal with trepidation. 'He wants me to swallow that?'

'Only some. We must all share it,' said Guide.

Lucy enjoyed Collins' discomfort. 'God goes first.'

Stifling his gag reflex, Collins tipped the bowl and drank some of the Medicine Man's phlegm. He swallowed hard and winced.

'Not bad. A bit bitter. Tastes like aspirin, with a hint of asparagus.'

Roger was next. He sipped it and his face spasmed, but he kept it down.

When it was Lucy's turn, she clearly faked it. I could tell, because I was standing next to her. She sneezed to distract attention, tipped the bowl, wiped her lips, then said it was 'yummy'.

I wanted to do the same, but Medicine Man was watching me, closely. I did what I had to. I figured that previous girlfriends of mine had similarly "taken one for the team" and, now, it was my turn. No sooner had it entered my throat, than I felt the overwhelming urge to wretch and spew. I held fast and forced it down by imagining it to be a savoury smoothie, although the asparagus flavour made that difficult. It made my eyes water. Yuck! It was like swallowing an alka-seltzer slug.

Bunny eagerly gobbled up what was left.

Each of us were then led to what Guide later described as "contemplation huts" - spartan buildings made from a lattice of flimsy sticks, held together by mud and leaves. I could see Lucy in the hut opposite mine, peering through the slats.

'Do you feel anything?'

'Not yet,' I replied.

Then a few minutes later...

'What about now?'

'No, nothing.'

It was anti-climactic. I was expecting something mind-blowing. Instead, I felt a bit more clear-headed than usual. Perhaps, it was aspirin after all. Or, fear. These were cannibals. Friendly for the time being, sure, but cannibals nonetheless. We had just willingly eaten something we knew nothing about and allowed ourselves to be separated from one another in the middle of a jungle, many miles from civilisation.

Lucy was restless. 'How about now?'

I was going to say nothing, when it hit me.

My fingers elongated like silly putty, my face melting down my chin. The floor was sucked beneath me and I got tunnel vision. Everything circled downwards: my face, my hands, my feet. It was as if my body was melting down a drain that stretched to the very centre of the earth.

GAIA

Collins broke out in a cold sweat. It beaded off his nose and dropped into a giant pool of water that reached up to his ankle. Drip. Drip. Drip - drip - drip! The sweat water rapidly rose up above his torso and flooded the hut. He tried to swim to the surface and break for air, but it reached the ceiling and completely submerged him. He thrashed around, until he realised that he no longer needed to breathe - he had gills in his throat.

"Gnarly," he thought to himself.

The water was still and warm. He felt safe and secure, as if in-utero. The walls of the hut had disappeared. The space before him was now vast and limitless. From out of the shimmering light, a slow moving object glided into focus - an enormous manta ray. It hovered gracefully above him. He reached out to touch it, but it was too far away. Each time it rippled its wings, he swayed with the rhythm of its current.

He heard a voice, direct from the manta ray into his brain. 'I am Gaia,' it said.

'I am Chuck Collins,' he replied. It was all he could think to say.

'I know who you are,' said the manta ray. 'Follow me.' It turned around and glided back towards the light.

'Wait!' cried Chuck. He tried to follow, but felt himself swimming against a tide. He struggled, circled his arms, pushed harder and harder against the water, but went absolutely nowhere. 'Wait!' The current took hold of him, swirled, and spun him around like a top, away from the light. Around and around. He grew dizzy and blacked out.

The water abruptly rushed out in all directions and disappeared.

He was back in the contemplation hut, but the door was wide open. He walked through it and found himself in an African savannah.

'Dad?'

His adoptive father - a Zimbabwean ranger - stood waiting for him.

'Come quick, but come quietly,' he said. He held his rifle out to Chuck. Chuck hesitated. 'Quickly,' said his father.

Chuck looked around and saw De Konig a few paces off to the side, leaning on a walking stick, with a smirk on his face. De Konig was twelve years old and Chuck realised that he, too, was a boy once more. Chuck looked back at his father and followed his eyesight to a large elephant. The great beast was panting with laboured breath.

Chuck was afraid. 'Father, I - I can't.'

'You must. He is sick. He is suffering.'

'Please, you do it.' He tried to pass the rifle back.

His father refused to accept it. 'It is time you became a man.'

Chuck felt lost and alone. He gathered his courage, but he hadn't much. What little was left was too little, too late.

The elephant charged. It was angry and disoriented. Several tons of muscle and lard bore down on him, parting the bush before it, like an atomic shock wave.

The ranger shouted at Chuck, hoping to jar him into action. 'Quick, Chuck! Quick!'

The elephant moved at a sickening speed, its footsteps pounding the ground, quaking the earth towards them.

Chuck was all thumbs. The rifle slipped from his grip. He scrambled to catch it, then raised it awkwardly. It was heavy and his arms were trembling.

'Do it!' screamed his father.

Chuck fired off a shot into the trees by accident, splintering some branches. They fell onto the elephant's back. The elephant barely flinched. It came at them, huffing like a rabid locomotive.

De Konig leapt over, grabbed Chuck's gun, and snapped into position. He fired off several rounds with crisp precision, straight through the elephant's eye, into its brain.

The great beast crumpled onto its fore legs with a colossal grunt, wavered momentarily, then keeled over. It's breath, shallow. It's mouth, parched and frothy.

It had landed on Chuck's father. The poor man was crushed flat.

Chuck was dumbstruck. All he could see was his father's forearm, sticking out from beneath the elephant boulder, twitching involuntarily, then go still. The elephant's half-opened eye bored into him like a curse, as its life slipped away.

"An elephant never forgets… An elephant never forgets…" was all that Chuck could think of before the beast died - staring him straight in the eye. The curse. He would never escape it.

Chuck cried.

A baby pig - nestling in his arms - lapped up his tears. Chuck's sadness turned to joy. 'Piggy!' He hugged his old childhood friend. Piggy enjoyed the embrace, then wriggled free and ran off.

Chuck was now running through his Zimbabwean home. He chased Piggy through several rooms and out into the yard. Piggy was fast, hard to keep up with. Chuck managed to grab Piggy's hind legs, but it squealed, and slipped free again. Chuck laughed. Piggy snorted and darted into the barn.

The forbidden barn.

The door had been left open. Strange. It was meant to be locked. But, now, the lock hung open. Chuck followed cautiously after Piggy.

Inside, he was horrified by what he found. There were zebra skins, elephant tusks, and various trophy heads crudely scattered around a large and messy slaughterhouse, covered in flies. The stench was inhuman. It stuck to your nostrils like glue. There, on an empty table, was Piggy on a platter, roasted, with an apple in his mouth.

De Konig was busy skinning part of a giraffe. 'What are you

doing here?'

Chuck was horrified. 'You murderer! You killed piggy!'

De Konig was unrepentant. 'We needed the protein.'

Chuck grew faint from the taxidermist house of horrors. He bumped into a perfectly preserved zebra. It's eyes frozen wide, cold and heartless. "Marley?" He spun around, unable to escape the dead eyes of the animals surrounding him, eyes full of reproach and fear, frozen in time, friends from the past, judging him, hating him. It was suffocating. He felt as if he'd been buried alive. 'And all this?' His nausea turned to anger. 'Dad's going to kill you when he finds out!'

De Konig's words were icy cold. 'Who do you think taught me how to do it in the first place?' Chuck was speechless. 'You were always so bloody attached to them,' said De Konig, as he scraped at the hide. 'We can't survive on his ranger's salary alone, you know. If you weren't such a sissy, you could pull your weight for once and help out.'

Chuck noticed a stuffed warthog. 'Oh my God! Barnaby! What have you done to him?'

De Konig wiped his hands on his bloody apron. 'I thought he'd make a good footstool. It's part of a matching set,' he said, pointing to another warthog in the corner of the room. 'But I'm particularly proud of Daisy,' he said, walking over to a stuffed antelope. 'I hollowed out her insides to make a chest. Check it out.' He popped a latch on the side and pulled open the top of the beast's back, like a lid. Inside, was a fully stocked mini-bar. 'It's portable, too. A fellow commissioned it from me, to take on his hunting expeditions. He wanted to enjoy a tipple on safari. What do you think?'

'You're a psycho!' screamed Collins.

'I'm an artist,' said De Konig, annoyed and hurt. 'I just had to find my own self-expression, that's all. In a different way than you.'

Chuck wasn't ready for this. He stumbled backwards, in a daze, out of the barn, and back into the sunlight. He could see the Unwanku village huts, again. Now, he was confused - caught between the twilight of his memories and the present.

Where was he?

His head hurt. His heart pounded. The sun moved quickly in the sky towards the horizon, as nightfall approached. Suddenly, Guide crashed into him. He'd been running fast and was drenched, but not slick from sweat. He'd been basted in oil. There was a string of shrivelled vegetables and desiccated roots round his neck.

He grabbed Chuck's arm. 'Mister Collins! Please! Help me!'

Collins was still heavily inebriated by his trance. He tried to brush Guide off. 'Stop, you're buzz-killing my trip!'

Guide didn't care. He was freaking out. 'They want to eat me! They say I'm an offering to them, in return for their hospitality to you!'

Collins considered the situation. 'Hmm. Kind of like bringing a bottle of wine to a dinner party...'

'You must help. They think you're a God. They will listen to you.'

'But Guide, it's common courtesy to bring something for the host. Especially, if it's a housewarming. Don't you think?'

'Please, Mister Collins! I don't want to be put in the pot!'

'Why is it that you can't have red wine with fish?' Chuck pondered this conundrum. 'White is the convention, but doesn't salmon taste better with a nice claret?' Collins shook his head. It was all too confusing.

Guide's plaintive cries receded into the jetsam of Chuck's jumbled memories. Collins was plunged back into the darkness of his own personal history - back into dreamland.

He heard a voice. 'Chuck, it's me.' The voice was deep and authoritative. The voice of Morgan Freeman.

'Dad?'

'No, Mother,' said the voice. 'Mother Nature.'

Someone, who looked like Pat with a deer's head, appeared before him, as if from a flickering flame. 'Follow me.'

Chuck was led out into a garden paradise, full of strange beasts, and psychedelic colours. There was a large apple tree nearby with a serpent entwined around it. The apples were juicy red. Chuck stuck out his arm to pick one, but Mother batted his hand. 'Don't eat those. They'll give you the shits.'

They walked into a sun-drenched field full of poppies, where naked imps and idylls played hide-and-seek, beneath crystal waterfalls. 'Arms up,' said Mother. Chuck obliged, then ducked to avoid a safety-bar, which came down over his head. He found himself in an egg-sized carriage, sitting next to Mother, following a curvy track. 'I find it much easier to do the tour this way,' said Mother.

The carriage whooshed up, up, up to the stratosphere, until it broke free into the stillness of space. Once his stomach had returned back to its rightly place, Chuck looked down at planet earth and gasped. It was so beautiful. A kaleidoscopic marble of shimmering tetra-blue.

'It's a small world after all,' remarked Mother. Chuck nodded. Words couldn't do it justice. 'But she's dying Chuck. Our planet is dying.' Chuck shed more tears. He couldn't help himself. He felt unsettled by the visions he'd had from his childhood.

'Entire species are being wiped out,' continued Mother. 'Ice caps are melting. Forests burning. It's all turning into a crap-sandwich. Somebody needs to do something before it's too late. Do you get me?'

Chuck nodded. 'Someone must do something.'

'Not someone. You.'

'Me?'

Chuck measured the weight of this request. It was heavy. 'What about Jesus? Isn't he supposed to be our saviour?'

Mother was perturbed. 'He gave it a fair crack, but then he got his ass crucified. For awhile there, I thought Michael Jackson was going to get the job done -'

'And Bono?' interrupted Chuck.

Mother rolled her deer eyes. 'Don't get me started on him.' She put a hand on Chuck's shoulder. 'It's up to you now, Chuck. You are the one. The Only One.'

They shared a moment of understanding. Then, Mother punched him in the sola-plexus.

Chuck gasped for air.

'I have released you!' said the crazed deer. Mother's head

exploded into a millions stars and swirled into the Milky Way. 'We're relying on you Chuck. All of us....' Her voice faded into the cosmic wind. 'All of us...'

The carriage began its descent back to earth. A short while later, it jolted and stopped.

Mother's voice, only a whisper now - 'Shit, this always happens here. Arms up!'

Collins raised his arms to let the safety bar rise. He was unceremoniously chucked out of the carriage. Now, he was free-falling, but not afraid. The breeze was warm. Earth approached rapidly. He saw the Southern Hemisphere, the Amazon forest, then broke through the clouds and headed straight towards...

...a giant vagina.

He tried to avoid it, but he had no way of steering himself.

He flapped his arms. He flailed. Resistance was futile. He couldn't change course.

'Well', he thought to himself, 'there are worse ways to go.'

He plummeted straight into it and, then, found himself running along the ground. He was still inside the vagina, but it was made from hemp. Hands of the villagers poked him from the outside, as he ran through the rope orifice... pinching him... guiding him... towards a light at the end of the tunnel. Then, he broke free, and tumbled through the air, down, down, down... SPLASH... into a small clear lake.

The water was freezing and shocked his system back to reality. He burst to the surface and gulped in a lung-full of fresh-mint air. The effects of the root had worn off, jolted by the rush of cold water. He floated on the surface awhile, enjoying the sunshine, and let the feeling of his senses slowly return to him like a long lost memory.

It was a feeling of immense peace and tranquility.

'Dude, what a trip!' said Bunny, who was sunning himself on a rock, nearby.

Just then, Lucy tripped awkwardly through the opening of the hemp vagina, went head-over-heels, and plunged into the pool. 'Aaaarggghhhh!' She broke the surface with a scream. 'It's freezing!'

We were told later that the rope tunnel was meant to represent our rebirth. The true beginning of our journey.

Collins was in a lotus position, sitting on a rock in the sun, with his eyes closed, humming, "It's a Small World After-all". The rest of us were respectfully quiet. Eventually, he stopped and opened his eyes, blinking at each of us in turn, as if seeing us for the first time. He stood up, purposefully.

'Gaia has spoken to me!' He stretched his arms out, as if to embrace the sun. Pat stood on a boulder, opposite, eclipsed by the light, then dropped the loin cloth. It wasn't pretty.

Lucy thought Collins had lost his mind. 'Who?'

Collins turned back towards her, very pleased with himself. 'Didn't you have the vision, too?'

'Sure, loads of them. But tell us, what did Guy say?'

'Gaia has shown me the way. I must save the animals from extinction. All of them.' He squatted down to our level. 'I must stop De Konig. He is my brother, but he has been led astray. I know how he thinks. I know where he will go next.'

We all drew closer. Something prophetic was coming.

'My name is Chuck Collins and I'm on a mission from Gaia!'

He looked at Lucy in dead earnest. 'Pack your thermals.' Then, he smiled. 'We're going to save the Sabre-toothed Snow Goat.'

KUROMIZU

'That was Animal Channel,' said Lucy, snapping shut the satellite phone. 'Percy's pissing blood over the budget.'

She looked out across the vast expanse of snow and ice. We were high up in the Himalayas. But not yet above the clouds.

'He got compensation from Marcus' life insurance,' she said. 'Apparently, he'd inserted a clause about violent death from a feathered mammal, just before the deadline. However, he's annoyed we didn't get his demise on camera.'

'Alright,' said Collins to the crew, 'we'd better make tracks before nightfall. There's a storm coming in and we don't want to get caught out in the open with our pants around our ankles.' He led the way forward. We didn't have enough money to pay a sherpa, so we had our new boom operator, Curtis, humping most of our equipment. He was an eager beaver - only too happy to help.

'This is great,' he said. 'My first proper gig and I'm recording with Chuck Collins - THE Chuck Collins! In the Himalayas!'

The rest of us were far more sanguine. In fact, there was a wager on how long he'd last. At least one boom operator had died on every Collins expedition. Five had already been lost to date, excluding Marcus.

We donned our googles and cinched up our hoods. We'd have to climb higher to get above the storm, then dig in a shelter. Getting caught in a blizzard out here could literally mean the end of the line. Roger had replaced his usual glass eye with a rubber one, to combat the cold. Otherwise, he said it would give him a migraine. Now, he looked like a cyborg pirate.

Curtis cozied up to him. 'So, why did the last guy quit again?'

Roger fiddled with his equipment, avoiding eye contact. 'No one told you?'

'The agency said he was unreliable.'

'Yeah. He fell apart during an important take. We had to let him go after that.' He looked up at Curtis. Curtis looked over his left shoulder, but saw nobody there.

Roger took the lead, which wasn't hard considering Curtis was laden like a pack-mule. Nevertheless, Curtis chugged along like the little train that could. He wasn't going to be easy to shake free. 'Well, I won't let you down, Roger. No, Siree, Bob. I'll be right by your side.'

'Great,' said Roger. Then - 'Actually, you don't need to get that close to me. Give yourself plenty of room, you know? In case you need to react quickly to the situation.'

'Um, okay.'

'In fact, here, I've got some extra long cable in my pack. So, you don't have to feel like you need to stick close to me at all.' He held out the roll of cable. 'Even now.'

After an excruciating climb, we reached a ridge that gave us shelter from the icy wind. My goggles froze over. I removed them briefly to give them a wipe and got a blast of air so cold that it made my eyes water. My tears instantly turned to icicles. 'Christ, it's cold,' I said, to nobody in particular.

'That's why the Sabre-Toothed Snow Goat is attracted to heat,' said Collins. 'There isn't much of it around.'

Through my crystalline tears I saw a light bouncing in the distance. At first, I thought my eyes were playing tricks on me. 'Look - over there!'

In the relative shelter of the mountain, there was a base camp on the plateau.

'Looks like De Konig beat us to it,' said Collins. 'Here, pass me the binoculars.' Curtis dug deep into one of his many pouches and produced a super-duper pair of night-vision binoculars with an HD recording facility. Collins focused them on the base camp. 'I don't see him, or the Frenchie.' He scanned the area carefully. 'Nope. But it's a camp alright. They're sitting ducks down there.'

'Maybe, they're acting as bait to draw the goats out,' suggested Lucy.

'Nobody wants to attract a pack of Snow Goats, believe me. I'd rather go skinny dipping with a school of piranhas.' He pocketed the binoculars. 'I'd better go down there and scout the place out. The rest of you stay here and try to keep warm.'

'Bunny, go with Chuck,' said Lucy. 'At least you can wear the head cam and get some of it on tape.' Collins agreed.

As soon as the head-camera gear was secure, the two of them ventured forth.

Lucy looked down at the blackening sky. 'Storm's rising, getting closer. We'd better dig in now, just in case.'

I watched Collins and Bunny trudge through the knee-deep powder. 'Do you think Collins will be alright? He's been a bit manic, lately. He thinks he's superman, or something.'

'That's the *real* Chuck Collins,' said Lucy. 'I'm glad he finally came to his senses.'

Collins and Bunny fought against the snow, but found a rhythm. It was slow going. The wind blew horizontal sheets of ice, obscuring their way. It took them an hour to get to the base camp.

'The camp is bigger than I expected,' said Collins, when they reached the perimeter. He reached over and switched on Bunny's head camera. 'Why don't we split up and recce the area? We'll get more done in less time.'

Bunny nodded. 'Sure thing.'

Collins clapped him on the shoulder. 'Okay. I'll meet you back here in half an hour. Last one back is a rotten egg!'

'That's a stupid idea,' remarked Lucy, to the rest of us. She had a small video monitor strapped to her arm with an earpiece. Everything that Bunny was recording was being broadcast back to her. Unfortunately, she had no way to communicate with them. We clustered around the tiny screen, watching Bunny's point-of-view, as he stumbled around the perimeter of the camp, counting out the number of tents he could see. He got to "eight" - when a rifle-butt swung into view, smacking him in the face. The camera captured sky, then snow, then our screen went black. The transmission had been cut.

'Shit,' said Lucy. 'We have to warn Collins. He's walking into a trap!' She jumped up.

There was an audible click of a semi-automatic weapon behind us.

'Warn who?' De Konig, Fachon, and his mercenaries had us surrounded.

Collins slipped into the largest tent. It was cozy inside. There were gas heaters and lamps dotted about. He warmed his hands. Aahh, the simple pleasures in life. It was times like these that Collins appreciated most. He found a tin of unfinished food with a pair of chopsticks balancing on the rim. He helped himself. It tasted exquisite. Nothing like the freeze-dried rubbish that he had in his pack. He scarpered a few unopened tins and popped them into his pockets.

Despite the whistle of the wind outside, the tent was eerily quiet. As his eyes grew accustomed to the dim, he noticed a large number of cages chained together - big enough to hold snow goats. Also, there were maps and plans unfurled on a table nearby, so he made his way towards it.

Just then, he heard a flip-flop, flip-flop, flip-flopp-ing sound.

A shadow cartwheeled vigorously towards him then - CRASH! He was flung into a stack of hard-plastic Pelican cases, knocking the wind out of him.

He rebounded as fast he could to face his attacker, but they were gone.

Silence.

He looked around at the shadows flickering on the walls of the tent from the gas light. Any one of them could pounce.

He called out to them. 'Come out, come out - wherever you are!'

No answer.

'Humma humma, jum-mana! Humma humma, jum-mana!' Collins shifted his weight from foot to foot and shook his fingertips to get the blood flowing. He'd learnt a thing or two from fighting wild animals in the ring. He knew how to control his breathing and his circulation. He also knew how to take an unusual lot of punishment. He cracked his neck for good measure. Now, he was ready to tackle come what may.

Nothing.

'Hey! Stupid! Did you get lost, or something? I'm right here, waiting for you.' Collins thought that insults might speed things up, hasten an attack.

After a nerve-wracking lull, he heard a SWISH, and had his legs knocked from under him. He caught a glimpse of his attacker - a female figure. She was wearing black, skin-tight lycra. Possibly, a unitard.

Collins leapt up, surprising her with his speed. 'I've been boxing bears bigger than you, little lady,' he said. 'Let's dance!'

He put one hand up to his face like a boxer and other one down to cover his privates. He wasn't taking any chances. He'd learnt that from the bears. They fight dirty.

His attacker pulled back, giving him a better look at her.

Asian. Beautiful. Deadly.

She pounced again.

Collins held his fighter's stance, but she whirled around him easily, kicking him in the middle of his back.

'Ugh!' He crumpled and wheezed like a busted accordion, then picked himself up again. His attacker took advantage of the height differential to jump onto his shoulders from behind, pinning him in a head-lock with her legs. She held onto a steel strut supporting the roof of the tent for leverage, and squeezed her thighs together.

Collins felt as if his head was in a vice. 'Aaaarrggggghhh!'

His face went beet red. He couldn't breathe. Any moment now, he'd lose consciousness. He tried anything to buck her off - twisting, flapping, dropping to the ground, the Macarena - but she held him fast. Straining, he twisted, inch by inch, bit by bit, until he managed to wriggle his head around, and face her. She still had her legs around his neck but, now, he had a unique vantage point. With a terrific lunge, he bit her in the crotch.

She squealed and let go, dropping him to the floor. She looked down at herself. Collins had left a horrible, slobber stain on her suit.

'Sorry about that,' he said. 'But you were asking for it.' He gasped for breath. 'I've only ever done that once before, and it was to an incredibly volatile badger.'

The woman assassin limped over to one of the crates and grabbed a samurai sword. She unsheathed it slowly, letting the grind of metal on metal ring horribly in his ears - very likely, for dramatic effect.

Collins gulped. 'Hey - that's not fair. I'm unarmed.'

She didn't care.

She held the sword up in a striking stance, ready to attack, and waited.

Collins stood his ground.

They eyed each other without moving a muscle. Waiting. Sinews taut. Embedding their heels. Looking for an advantage. Any moment now, there would be a quick rush of the blade, and it would be all over in an instant.

Bang!

Collins got the drop on her - literally. He dropped to the floor and lay down on his back. She didn't know what to do. She hadn't started her charge, yet, but was thrown off by this highly irregular and unexpected manoeuvre. Collins propped his knees up, as might an up-ended turtle. Again, he covered his privates.

She tightened her grip on her sword. She was going to have to compensate, now that her target was below her, on the floor.

She lunged - terrifically fast. The blade, a mere wisp of wind.

She had intended to slice Collins from chin to navel, but he had anticipated this. He shot up his prosthetic leg and sacrificed it to the blade. It dug in deep - as he'd expected. His attacker was confounded. Not only had the blade not chopped the leg in half, but Collins seemed completely unfazed by it. He took advantage of her bewilderment and twisted his body around like a corkscrew, wrenching the sword from her hands. Then, he stood up - rather ungainly - with the sword still embedded in his leg. She was shocked to see him so cocky.

'Now we're even,' said Collins. 'Want to try that again?'

She was angry now and prepared to renew her attack - when a voice stopped her. 'Enough.'

A slender and compact Asian man in his late thirties had entered the tent. 'Excuse Chae. She can get a little - over excited.'

Chae backed off. Clearly the man was her superior. However, she gave Collins that look, as if to say, "We're not finished yet - you and I."

The man regarded Collins from a safe distance. 'Which team are you working for?'

'Mother Nature,' replied Chuck. 'And she kicks ass!'

He tried to wrest the sword from his leg with bravado, but couldn't - so, he left it in. Instead, he gave the man another warning. 'I'm on a mission from Gaia. You've messed with the wrong lady, my friend.'

The man chuckled. 'Mister Collins, you never cease to amuse me. I'm a big fan. I've seen all your shows.'

'Have you, now?' Chuck found this hard to believe. He thought for a moment. 'Did you see the one on the Mesocricetus Vampir Auratus?'

'Yes.'

'Impossible! It never aired!' Chuck punched the air with his fist. 'Boo-ya! Busted! Got you, mister Miyagi!'

The man kept his composure. 'The name is Kuromizu. And I bribed your post production house for a rough edit of that show.' He gestured calmly to a storage chest nearby. 'I can show it to you, if you like?'

Collins considered calling his bluff, but Kuromizu didn't seem the fibbing type. Everything about him reeked of ruthless efficiency. His movement was economised, his language precise and clipped, his demeanour impassive and calm. This was a man with a heart of ice.

Kuromizu smiled. 'I would have hired you myself had I found you in time.'

'I'm flattered.'

'But it seems I no longer need your services, now.' Kuromizu gestured to his female assassin. 'Chae is an excellent tracker.'

Chuck was still smarting from having nearly been choked to death by a woman half his weight. 'She's handy with a sword, I'll grant her that. But her reflexes are poor. I'd like to see her milk a Torpedo Squid at twelve hundred feet. That's what separates the men from the boys. No offence, missy.'

Chae gave Collins an icy look, pouting over the missed opportunity to slice and dice him.

Kuromizu fed off the tension. 'Chae grew up having to fight her village for food. Even against her own family. Food was very scarce where she comes from. It has made her very resourceful and a most excellent partner in hunting down these curious creatures.'

'Save your breath, Tiramisu,' replied Collins. 'I know what you're here for. I've heard it all before. Oh, what a cute, cuddly panda. He would make such a wonderful pet. Oh, I simply must have a platypus for my ornamental pond. Then, a week later - all dead from loss of habitat!'

Kuromizu shook his head. 'You misunderstand me. These creatures are not my playthings. I am their protector.'

'A likely story. Every poacher has his price.'

'No, mister Collins. You and I are very alike. We want to save this planet from destruction. Join me. We would make a formidable team.'

'I'm sticking with Gaia,' said Collins. 'She has a better health plan.'

'Suit yourself,' said Kuromizu, nodding to Chae. She was only too eager to finish the job.

But they were interrupted by an eery bleating. Chae stopped dead in her tracks. Kuromizu trained his ears. Collins grinned.

The goats were coming.

De Konig's men had silently infiltrated Kuromizu's camp.

They had stealthily taken down a few of Kuromizu's men when they, too, heard the horrible bleating.

Fachon's eyes lit up. 'They are here!'

De Konig handed out several, oversized cattle prods to his men and hefted a large tube that resembled a rocket launcher onto his shoulders. He turned to Lucy. 'Are you armed?' She shook her head. He handed her one of his pistols. 'Here, take this. Just make sure you point in the right direction.'

'That depends. Are you friend or foe?' she said, with a sly smile.

De Konig was about to answer, when he was cut short by Fachom.

'Vas-y Vas-y!' shouted Fachon, impatiently. He led the way forward.

Lucy wondered at Fachon's fearlessness. He was either very capable, or very foolish. She noticed that De Konig didn't share Fachon's excitement.

Kuromizu stepped out of his tent to find himself in the eye of a violent snow storm. It was too dark to see anything clearly, but he couldn't ignore the sound of erratic gunfire, and the screams of his unlucky men. It disgusted him, how they lacked discipline. He would have to go to a better supplier next time. Good henchman were hard to find. These ones kept dying on him, far too easily. Canon fodder. They had no backbone. They were more interested in their bodies and munitions than in the cause. Not like Chae. She was his prize protege, but he mustn't show it, not to her. He wanted her hard. Pristine. Incorruptible. It was time for him to take command. 'Light the torches! Prepare the crates!'

Chae carried out Kuromizu's orders with commendable ardour. She had clearly drunk the Kool-Aid. She disappeared into the maelstrom with an armful of tranquilliser guns.

Collins turned to Kuromizu. 'Are you ready for what's coming next?'

Kuromizu didn't answer, but peered out into the darkness.

There were a few more scattered bleats in different registers and, then - all hell broke loose.

Men fired from all directions on anything that moved. It didn't help that De Konig's team had entered into the fray. People were firing at their own shadows. Nobody had even *seen* the killer goats yet. But that was their way. The goats dragged off their kill, so all that was left were red puddles and pock marks in the snow. They fought like goat ninjas.

'They are a shy animal,' said Collins, trying to unsettle Kuromizu. 'Normally, they live alone in caves. But, when they hunt, they hunt together. It whips them up into a feeding frenzy.'

Kuromizu remained insouciant. 'Yes, I admire them. They have tremendous self-control. But know when to lose it at precisely the right moment.'

Collins pulled out his night-vision binoculars. 'Ah, I can see them now. Magnificent.'

Kuromizu stepped alongside him. 'May I?'

'My pleasure.' Collins handed over the binoculars. Someone screamed nearby, followed by a sloppy, slush-gurgle, then the airy song of blood whistling through their windpipe. When several throats were slit at once, they formed a macabre musical, like a satanic Zamfir on his panpipes, but without the cheesy background music. 'I expect he was gored by one of their tusks,' commented Collins. 'They can grow to over a four feet in length, you know.'

Kuromizu nodded in appreciation. Collins was right. There, in the green light of the night-vision goggles, he could see a mercenary, gored and spit by a tusk, being carted off into the darkness by a hairy quadruped. Kuromizu lowered the binoculars. 'Shall we step inside?' He held open the flap to his tent. 'I think that's enough fresh air for the moment.'

Inside the tent, it was relatively calm. Outside, torches had been lit around the perimeter, casting an eerie, flickering light on the canvas. Blood splatters on the fabric created an awful shadow-play of death.

Collins settled into a comfy arm chair, while Kuromizu liberated a bottle of Shochu that hadn't yet frozen. Then,

Kuromizu sat opposite him and poured. It was all very civilised, despite the toe-curling screams and gunfire that punctuated their conversation.

'This is one of my father's old recipes,' said Kuromizu, filling Collins' glass. 'He drank this every day and lived to one hundred and five, you know.'

Collins sniffed his glass. 'Interesting bouquet. Ginseng?'

'Correct. It's pickled in the bottle to smooth the aftertaste from the snake venom.'

Collins was unfazed. 'I drink snake venom for breakfast.' He knocked it back in one.

Kuromizu watched Collins closely, without touching his drink. There was a momentary lull, during which Collins tried to calm his lurching stomach and screaming nerve endings. He felt as if he'd swallowed an angry, baby octopus, which was now trying to claw its way up from deep within his bowels, back to the surface of his throat. Kuromizu smiled. He knew that feeling. His father had often tested him with the venom Shochu in the past. That feeling of having a whirling dervish in your gut.

To Kuromizu's surprise, Collins recomposed. He pushed his glass forward for another dram. 'So, what's the plan?' he said, nonchalantly, despite his intense desire to geyser his guts into Kuromizu's smug face.

Kuromizu filled both their glasses. 'We wait.'

'For what?'

'For the goats to get tired.'

SNOW GOAT

De Konig's team had been lucky so far and taken few casualties. They skirted the periphery of the camp and kept clear of the cross-fire. They hadn't been attacked by any goats - yet. Most of the opposition had come from Kuromizu's own men, who were paranoid and trigger-happy. When De Konig's team crept deeper into the camp, though, they got caught up in the pandemonium.

Lucy and the crew peeled away as soon as they spied Bunny, chained to the food stores.

He seemed fairly relaxed.

Lucy shouted above the fire-fight. 'Bunny, where's Chuck?'

'I haven't seen him since we split up,' he said, matter-of-fact.

'Alright, then. Let's get you out of here.' She looked at the padlocked chains around his hands. They looked pretty serious. She wondered if there was some way to shoot them off, like she'd seen in the movies.

'I wouldn't do that if I were you,' said Bunny. 'We might get hit by the ricochet.'

He had a point. Damn. They were going to have to find the keys.

Lucy got Curtis to help her search the area, while Roger filmed the firefight. She noticed that the equipment boxes lying around were all military grade and had "Kuromizu Enterprises" emblazoned on them. Eventually, she came across a bolt-cutter. 'This should do it.' Curtis gave it his best shot. After some fumbling, he managed to cut Bunny's shackles.

'Thanks.' Bunny was genuinely grateful, but remained where he was.

Lucy grabbed his arm. 'Come on.'

He refused to budge. He pointed at Curtis. 'I'm not going with him. I'm safer here.'

Curtis was dismayed. 'Why? What's going on?'

Lucy didn't want to explain the superstition to him. She pulled Bunny's arm. 'Forget about that now, we need to stick together. Let's go find Chuck.'

Bunny reluctantly fell in. Both he and Roger put Curtis on point and kept their distance. It was difficult to see what was going on in the storm, so we all held onto the boom cable and used it as a life-line, as might rock-climbers on an expedition.

When we finally found Kuromizu's tent, Collins and Kuromizu were in the middle of a drinking game. By the looks of it, both were losing.

'Nice to see you boys enjoying yourselves,' said Lucy, sarcastically.

Collins stood up. 'Hey, Luce! Come and join us.' He pulled up another chair for her, but fell on his face. 'Oopsey, daisy.' He recomposed himself. 'Luce, meet mister -'

'Kuromizu? Yes, I know. His name precedes him.'

Kuromizu stood, unsteadily. 'A pleasure, miss Keller. Can I offer you some poison?'

Collins laughed heartily at that, then fell over again. This time he didn't get up.

Lucy looked at his inert body. 'What have you done to him?'

Kuromizu held onto his armchair, as if it was the railing of a ship in a storm. 'He'll be alright. It's only a coma. If he wakes up, however, the hangover will make him wish he *had* died, believe me.' He swayed over to the entrance of the tent and vomited in the snow.

Lucy went to check on Collins. At first, she feared he was dead. But he opened his eyes, and put his finger to his lips.

Outside, Kuromizu was joined by Chae, who told him that they had captured and caged one of the goats. Kuromizu was pleased. 'We must leave quickly, before we lose more men. Call in the helicopters.' Chae ran off dutifully.

Kuromizu re-entered the tent and addressed Lucy and the others, while Collins pretended to be asleep. 'Sorry to leave you like this.' He slipped on a jacket that was loaded with equipment for killing people. 'Help yourself to anything you like.' He holstered a gun. 'I hope we don't -' he burped a wet one, as if something wanted to come up. Then, he swallowed. '- Meet again.' With that, he exited into the night.

Lucy pulled Collins to his feet. 'Are you alright?'

Collins sat up and cracked his neck like they were his knuckles. 'Sure. You're forgetting all the spider juice I had to drink that time in Madagascar! Snake venom is kid's play.'

'We better get out of here. I don't want to be here when the copters arrive. This storm is bad. We might end up rotor-fodder, if they get blown over.'

We ran out of there as fast as we could, but the snow was deep and the wind blew hard. We might as well have been running in slow motion, through a pool of molasses. Roger pushed Curtis ahead of him, or was using him as a shield from the elements - I couldn't quite tell which. Collins and I helped Lucy through the snow. We found ourselves tripping over corpses and equipment along the way. Eventually, we came upon De Konig and Fachon, who were having their own stand-off with one of the goats. They'd managed to hem it in between several men with their (extra) high-voltage, cattle prods.

'I must have him!' shouted Fachon, as if it wasn't obvious that they were trying their best.

Now that I saw a goat up close, I could see it was a hideous beast with mottled hair and a face like a shar-pei lion. It had huge, dripping fangs, long tusks, and smelt like an over-ripe Stilton - which was an achievement in itself, when you consider how cold the air was.

'Now!' shouted De Konig. His mercenaries fell back, as he shouldered his rocket tube and fired. A huge, weighted net spun out at high speed, like a frisbee, then enveloped the goat. This only made the goat more mad. It flung itself about under the net, knocking the men in all directions.

De Konig lunged forward and grabbed the ends of the net, ordering his men to do the same. They clung on for dear life, but the goat kept bucking to throw them off. De Konig ran up the net and jumped onto the goat's back. The goat tried desperately to gore him with its tusks, but De Konig was fast and athletic.

Just then, the goat barfed.

Nobody expected this.

A jet stream of vile smelling goop hit one of the mercenary's legs. The man screamed in agony.

'Their stomach's very acidic,' explained Collins. 'They do this when they're frightened.'

The mercenary buckled, as his hip collapsed, melting into a pool of blood-butter.

De Konig gave the goat a few, sharp bursts of his cattle prod. The goat shriek-bleeted. The sound made my hearing go out of register. My eardrums rang from the blast, as if they were receiving an off-the-air, TV test-signal. The goat bucked and ran, dragging the net with him. The shockwave disoriented De Konig, who lost his grip. He toppled backwards, rolling off the goat's back, and got his boot caught in the webbing. He was dragged along behind the goat, as it bolted into the night.

Fachon pushed his men forward. 'Don't let it get away!'

Collins watched De Konig disappear over the crest of a dune. He didn't hesitate, but ran after him. I guess he felt some sibling concern after all. The rest of us followed in hot pursuit.

De Konig's weight slowed the goat down, just enough for Collins to catch up. He leapt and caught the edge of the net, but got dragged along on his stomach. The goat was tough. It lifted its head high and shrieked at the moon, a shriek of pain and anger, while it sprinted forward. Not until Curtis, Roger, and I joined in by grabbing the net ourselves, did it show any sign of tiring. The five of us clung on tightly, as we tobogganed over the snow. I looked back and saw Lucy and Bunny disappear from view.

Collins shouted to De Konig. 'He's going to run us off the

cliff! They're like lemmings when they're desperate.'

'I know,' replied De Konig. 'Do something!'

Collins clawed his way up the net towards the goat. 'I'm going to try to cover his eyes!'

'What good will that do?' I said.

'It calms them down,' replied De Konig.

Curtis wrapped the netting around his wrist. 'This is just like a freakin' roller coaster ride!' He dug in like a rodeo rider. 'Yeeeehaaaaawwwwww!'

At least someone was enjoying themselves.

A helicopter crested the mountain ridge, rising up in front of us. Its front-mounted search-light picked us out. It hovered awkwardly in the gale. The light shone long enough for us to see that we weren't more than a hundred meters from the mountain edge.

'Crap!' I said. 'We're almost out of mountain.'

Collins had reached the beast's back. He hoisted himself up and ripped off his neck gator. Then, bit by bit, he pulled himself up onto the bucking goat.

I shouted out our range. 'Fifty meters to go!'

The helicopter flew overhead, towards the camp, plunging us back into darkness.

Collins reached his mark. He did his best to cover the goat's eyes. It began to slow.

'Not slow enough,' I thought. Maybe just enough to unhook De Konig. I wrestled with his boot. 'No use,' I apologised. 'We'll have to wait to get you out.'

De Konig wasn't taking no for an answer. He pulled himself into a tummy crunch and undid some of his laces. I tried to assist, but, suddenly, we went airborne over the cliff.

By the time Lucy and Bunny caught up to us, we were in a precarious position. Roger, Curtis, and I had managed to wedge ourselves against an outcropping of rock, gripping the net, while the goat, Collins, and De Konig hung over the precipice. De Konig was now hanging upside down, under the goat, his boot still wedged in the netting. The goat itself was wrapped in the net and breathing heavily, yet calm, on account of Collins, who still had his neck gator over its eyes. Collins embraced the goat and held on for dear life.

Collins shifted his weight to get a better foothold. 'I can't hold on for long!' Lucy and Bunny fell in, gripping the free edges of the net. Collins looked up at us. 'Somebody has to hold the neck gator, so I can help De Konig!'

'I'll do it!' offered Curtis, who climbed over the edge. 'I used to wrestle cattle back home on the ranch, when it was branding time. This'll be a piece of pie!'

'Better hurry!' shouted De Konig, not knowing how much longer his boot would hold.

As soon as Curtis drew near, Collins gave him instructions. 'It's probably better if you get below me. That way, De Konig and I can climb over you. Then, we'll pull you up last.'

'Okey-dokey,' said Curtis, nodding. He crabbed into position. 'Let it rip!'

Collins swapped places with Curtis, keeping the neck-gator in place. The goat hardly noticed the switch. 'Alright,' said Collins, 'I'm going down.' He climbed down to De Konig.

Meanwhile, my fingers were losing circulation. I looked to Roger and the others. 'How are you holding up?'

'Don't know. Difficult to say,' said Roger.

'Ditto,' said Lucy. I knew what she meant. The strings of the net were slicing through our gloves, digging into our fingers. It was only a matter of time before they dislocated them.

Just, then, Curtis slipped.

He was looking over his shoulder to see how Collins and De Konig were fairing, when the gator came off one of the goat's eyes. The goat swivelled its head, shuddered and belched, coating Curtis' face in acid-mucous.

There was a sickening scream, as Curtis lifted his hands to his melting face. 'Aaaaaaaaaaaaaaaaaaaaaaaaaaaaaa…' He plummeted down into the void.

Shit. I put my bet on him making it. Now, I was down a hundred bucks.

The goat writhed in the net. 'Can't hold it!' I cried.

Roger, Lucy, Bunny, and I redoubled our efforts, but the pain was excruciating. Collins looked at De Konig, calculating the odds.

De Konig panicked. 'Hurry up! You owe me!'

Some of the net slipped through my fingers. 'Too heavy! Can't hold it!'

By now, the goat was really pissed and belched again. The acid shower narrowly missed De Konig, passing within an inch of his shoulder. It ate through the rope of the net, instead. A few more of those and the net would disintegrate. De Konig screamed. 'Hurry up!'

Collins hesitated, then made his decision.

He began unlacing De Konig's boot.

De Konig was horrified. 'What the hell are you doing?'

'I have to do this. He's the last of his kind,' said Collins, as he popped the laces.

'So am I!' screamed De Konig. 'Chuck! Chuck! Have you gone insane?!'

Collins looked at De Konig for the last time. 'It's what Gaia wants of me.'

'Fuck Gaia! I'm your brother!' But further protest was futile. He knew that. He stopped shouting and looked at Collins. It was time to say good-bye. He looked Chuck sincerely in the eye. 'Asshole.'

De Konig's boot popped open and he, too, slipped down into the void.

The loss of weight gave us what we needed. We held fast, until Chuck had climbed back up onto the mountain. Then, he helped us hoist up the goat. When the goat was back safely on the mountain, Chuck let him go.

At first the goat hesitated, stood its ground. Then, it locked eyes with Chuck.

'You must go now,' said Chuck, magnanimously. We all knew what was coming next. The goat would spew on Collins and kill him. Roger didn't have his camera, so it would all be for nought. What a senseless waste.

But the goat didn't. Instead, it seemed to share a moment of understanding with Collins. Its breathing slowed.

Then, it turned and ran off into the night.

Collins felt as if his curse had been lifted. Gaia had come through. He was, indeed, the "Chosen One".

Fachon and the mercenaries caught up to us. Fachon was in a huff. 'Where's my goat?' He stomped over to Collins, who was staring out to the horizon, at the goat receding into the dying storm. 'Because of you, I've lost my goat AND my tracker! Do you know what that means?' Collins ignored him. 'All I have are the stupid eggs!' He flapped his arms and fumed. 'What am I going to do for my main? If I serve fish, I will be a laughing stock!'

Collins turned slowly to face him. 'You are a - a chef?'

'Am I a chef?' Fachon reeled with indignation. 'I am only the greatest chef in the world. Henri Fachon!'

Collins was catching on. 'And that, Tiramisu fellow. He's a chef, too?' He thought of the delicious rations he found in the tent.

Fachon spat towards Kuromizu's camp. 'He is a disgrace to his profession. The man is an abomination. All puffery and velouté! He is a monster that must be stopped at any cost! He will get his comeuppance from the judges! Or, my name is not Henri Fachon!'

'Judges? This is a competition?' Now, Collins was the indignant one. 'A cookery competition?'

Fachon stopped talking. The two men stared at one another without blinking.

'I tell you what,' said Fachon, changing tact. 'You are a tracker, no? I can use your help. Especially, as you just dropped mine off a cliff.'

'No offence,' said Collins, 'but I'd rather eat my own prairie oysters.'

'Wait a second,' said Lucy. She pulled Collins to one side, out of Fachon's earshot. 'Chuck, this is the scoop of the century. You've seen these guys. They aren't your average poachers. Someone is backing them and we should find out who.'

Collins wasn't buying. 'So, you want me to go against all my principles, everything I stand for, just for one lousy scoop?'

Lucy could see this would take more finesse. 'Listen, how do we know that there aren't other teams involved? If we end things right here, right now, with Fachon, then we're just cutting off our nose to spite our face. Try to see the bigger picture here. The planet is at stake. This could be the mission you were talking about. The one from Guy.'

'Gaia,' corrected Collins. 'What are you suggesting?'

'We go along with Fachon. Help him get what he wants. Then, when we get to the competition, we set the animals free. We can get it all on camera. You'll be a hero to millions. Of animals.'

It was a long shot, but Lucy was right. Fachon and Kuromizu could be just the tip of the iceberg. And there was some poetic irony in what she was suggesting. It appealed to the showman in him. If anything, it seemed to be the path that Gaia had put him on. He could see that now.

'Alright,' said Collins, returning to Fachon. 'We'll help you. On one condition.' Fachon smiled sweetly in anticipation. Collins wagged his finger at him. 'No killing. You keep the animals alive until the competition.'

'Of course,' agreed Fachon. 'They must be served fresh. Those are the rules.'

'And another thing,' continued Collins. 'I want full disclosure. Tell me everything about this competition.'

'We're losing time,' said Fachon, feigning concern. 'We must go.'

'We'll make it up. Just tell me what's going on.'

'Alright,' said Fachon. 'Let's do it over lunch.'

DINNER THEATRE

It was a summer's day in Brooklyn. Warm and prickly. But Darren Junior wasn't thinking about the weather. He was with his special friend.

He fed the deer everyday on his way home from school. It belonged to a small petting zoo, adjacent to the park. It was unusual to see an animal like this in the city. Sure, Darren had seen other animals there: dogs, cats… and, rats. Not a deer. The petting zoo even had a llama, some funny looking pigs, and a bunch of other animals he didn't recognise. The deer was his favourite. She was so pretty. He loved the feel of her soft fur through his fingers, the way she flicked her ears when she saw him. Her big, brown eyes.

He called her Gabby. The same name as his crush at school. He did it because the one at school was a one-sided affair. The other Gabby never noticed him, even though he primped himself every morning in front of the mirror. He started using hair gel, like he'd seen the older boys do. His mother teased him about it, so he applied it in the school bathroom in the mornings, then washed it out before he returned home.

Gabby the deer was as gentle and sweet as the Gabby the girl he liked at school. Petting the deer gave him a chance to soothe his unrequited love, yet fuelled it at the same time. It was a cruel feeling - to be in love. Whenever he came by, Gabby the deer would trot come over and take grass from his hand. He gathered it from the park over the weekend and saved it in plastic sandwich bags for her.

'It's Bambi! Look mommy, Bambi!' said a chubby little girl, who squeezed in next to him. She tried to pet Gabby, which irritated Darren. This was his special friend, not hers, and she was ruining their moment together.

An obese woman joined them. 'That's right, sugar lump, it is Bambi.' Her equally corpulent husband hoisted his daughter up over the railings for a better view.

An obsequious gentleman in a dark suit hovered nearby. 'Have you made your choice, madame.'

'Yes,' said the woman, 'we'll take this one.' She pointed at Gabby.

The deer swivelled its ears and watched the woman with its big, black doe eyes.

'Very well, madame,' said the man.

The father's attention had shifted to a family of bunny rabbits. 'Hey, why don't you chuck in a couple of thumpers, too, while you're at it.'

'Good choice, monsieur,' said the man. He snapped his fingers at several other fellows in uniform, who waited respectfully in the background. They led Gabby and the rabbits away.

The boy felt sad. Where was Gabby going?

'What is this place?' Collins had been watching the whole scene, nearby.

Fachon screwed his face up in disgust. 'It is Kuromizu's latest dining sensation, "Mange Zoo". He watched the head waiter and his lackeys lead the deer and rabbits into the rear of the restaurant. 'You get your pick of the petting zoo, plated in thirty minutes, or your money back. I ask you - how innovative is it to have a farm in your own backyard? They have even given him a Michelin Star for this nonsense. *Incroyable*!'

Fachon had reserved a table for Collins, Lucy, and I in order to make a point. Inside, the decor was faux pan-Asian. A fusion-style family restaurant. An attractive waitress in Burmese costume was parading a baby water buffalo around the dining room, as we were escorted to our table. This was meant to drum up business by allowing the diners to see what else was on the menu - an alternative to putting plastic food on display in the foyer.

'It's nose to tail,' said Fachon. 'The whole hog, as it were. He even serves the bits a Frenchman wouldn't eat.'

I looked at the menu. Today's special was a woodland owl and asparagus souflé, followed by a fricassée of beaver cheeks served on a bed of rocket leaves with molé sauce. Then came a carpaccio of line-caught, Hawaiian porpoise with argentinian gammon petit fours, garnished with gopher sweetbreads. The main course was a buffalo shank in a juniper and radicchio reduction, layered in a pastry of baked ostrich larynx. For dessert you had a choice of chilled antelope's brain in a coconut shell, or, for the less adventurous, a cheese plate made from reindeer milk. I guess they'd be running out of that soon enough.

'What do you reckon?' I asked Lucy. 'Shall we go for the "Super Yak"?'

She was visibly repulsed by everything she saw. 'What is it?'

'Every course is Yak, starting with Yak balls in a bechamel sauce made from Yak's milk with hoof shavings, Yak chops in a mesquite barbecue sauce, Yak tripe in sweet chili -'

'Enough,' gasped Lucy. She turned to Fachon. 'How can any of this be legal?'

Fachon shrugged. 'It's classified under a new city ordinance, promoting businesses that use sustainable produce and prepare slow food. None of these animals are in any danger. In fact, it is the common cow, pig, and chicken that are in danger from aggressive agro-farming.'

'I must admit,' I said, 'Kuromizu is clever. He's taken things that people would normally throw away and turned them into haute cuisine.' I looked at the prices. 'And fantastic margins to boot.'

'He is Japanese,' spat Fachon. 'They are used to living off roots and ugly things that they forage from the forrest. They have been doing it for generations. They didn't have meat until the twentieth century! And their vegetables, pah! Try getting an honest vegetable in a Japanese restaurant. *Impossible*! They only have tubers and slimy mushrooms.'

Collins surveyed the room. It was packed with punters. 'Whatever he's doing, he seems to be very successful at it.'

Fachon was not impressed. 'His food is not cuisine. It is chemistry. This is not art. It is dinner theatre. All these dishes - chicanery. He is not an artisan, like me. He does not let the natural flavours blend together, as they are meant to. Why? Because they would taste terrible. Terrible! No, my friends. He has a secret in the kitchen. Something to make anything irresistible.'

Collins looked at him. 'What is his secret?'

Fachon shrugged in his usual way. 'I do not know. It is a secret.' Then, he smiled. 'But I am determined to find out!'

I watched a young couple at the table next to us go into ecstasy over their chocolate oysters.

Fachon stood up. 'This kitchen has too much security. I know somewhere we can get a better look.'

We discreetly dodged the maitre d' - a man dressed as a rice farmer with a rope belt and kerchief round his head - and made for the exit. I shot a parting glance towards the kitchen, as a waiter sped through the swinging doors. I caught a glimpse of a poor penguin hanging over a pot of boiling oil.

Dinner theatre, indeed. This was animal cruelty.

'This is it.'

Fachon stopped in front of a nondescript metal door in the meat packing district of Manhattan. There was no signage. It looked like the entrance to a warehouse. You had to be "in the know" to even know about it. The name of it - I learned later - was "Chiarascuro".

Fachon paused before entering, contemplating it with a moment of sadness. 'I used to own the restaurant next door,' he lamented. 'I was at the top of my game. I had three Michelin Stars. Then, Kuromizu moved in, and I lost one of them. *Immediatement*.' He wiped his eyes. 'Thirty percent of my business vanished overnight. Poof! Poor Gascon, my sous-chef.

Such talent! He did not take the pressure well. He hanged himself with his apron strings two months later. *Tant pis.*' He smiled, wistfully. 'Well, pffft! What is it you say, your American expression? If life gives you lemons -'

'You make citron pressé,' finished Collins.

'Oui, c'est ca.' Fachon banished the memory and pushed open the heavy door.

We were greeted by the front of house - an attractive Asian woman in a cheongsam. I gathered from the decor that we were in a Chinese restaurant.

'Not just any Chinese restaurant,' explained Fachon. 'In Chiarascuro, all the chefs here are blind. Even the waiters are blind. Everybody is blind!' he laughed, breaking the tranquility of the place.

This drew a frown from the hostess. She greeted Fachon as "Monsieur Pinot" - a false name that Fachon had given to avoid detection. He was even wearing a false moustache for the occasion, which struck me as overkill. He looked like one of the Thomson detectives from Tin Tin. All he needed was a bowler hat to complete the fiction.

The hostess led us to another circular foyer with a fountain in the middle. At first she asked us if we had any dietary issues, or allergies. Once that was finished, we were met by a group of house staff - one person for each one of us. It was explained that they would take us to our table. Mine took my hand gingerly, as if guiding a child who'd only just learnt to walk, and led me into to the dining room.

We were plunged into darkness. Only then did I realise that our guides were blind.

'How in the world are we going to eat in darkness?' I wondered, out loud.

My guide had clearly heard this before. She explained - again, as if to a child - that we must banish the sense of sight, so that we could focus on our other senses, especially our taste, exactly as the chefs had intended. We wouldn't have to use cutlery, because our guides would be hand-feeding us throughout the meal. The whole thing sounded preposterous.

Collins stifled a giggle, as we entered the main dining room. His humour was infectious. Fachon began snickering, too. I bumped into something and they both burst into laughter. The guide hissed with disapproval at their childish behaviour, then brought me back on course. Their laughter subsided.

Unlike a normal restaurant, this one was unusually quiet. You didn't hear conversation, or even the clink of cutlery on china. Instead you heard chortles, small sounds of exhalation, swallows, slurps and chirps of delight. It made me think of a naughty massage parlour.

A moment later, I was seated at our table with a firm, yet considerate, pressure to my shoulders. Actually, there wasn't any table, as far as I could tell. I had a small stand to my right for my glass of water. My guide sat opposite me. She wiped my hands with a warm towel, presumably doing the same herself.

After a moment of anticipation, I felt something cold pressing against my lips. I was obliged to open them. A small parcel of food was deposited in my mouth. I felt like a baby bird. The taste was unremarkable at first and, then, it literally exploded into a rainbow of flavours: cherry, mahogany, some sort of earthy tobacco-like taste, followed by vanilla. There were rice kernels in it, but that's all I could discern. I felt as if I was eating again for the first time. It was unlike anything else I'd ever experienced.

I grew eager for my server's delicate hands and the delicious food they brought. It was very sensual. Her fingertips brushed against my cheek on occasion, almost like a caress. It was alarmingly intimate, yet, in a way, very remote. She sat out of reach, formal and impersonal, even. This was culinary foreplay. This went on for some time. It was a trance banquet. Within ten minutes, all of us had fallen into a silent, food funk.

Then, Fachon broke the serenity. 'I need to take a piss.'

His chair scraped backwards on the floor tile, making a shrill screeching sound. The waitresses were only too happy to get us away from the other guests, and into the restroom, where they left us to our own devices. Thankfully, it was dimly lit enough for us to see what we were doing. Fachon put his finger to his lips in a gesture to be quiet. He made us huddle together, afraid that there were security cameras in the loo. He reached under the sink and scrabbled around, until he felt something. He pulled out a small bag, unzipped it, and pulled out several pairs of night-vision goggles.

'I had a co-conspirator of mine plant these here earlier,' he said, passing them out to us. 'Suivez-moi.'

Wandering the corridors in the green, saturated light of the night vision goggles made me feel as if I was playing a stealth video game. Instead of shooting the waiters, we had to silently avoid them. This was difficult, as their blindness had given them a sixth sense. We left our shoes behind in the restroom to make it easier to creep along undetected. Whenever we came across someone, we crouched low and held our breath. Then we'd wait for them to pass by.

The retinas of their eyes reflected back the invisible light, like cats in the night. It was strangely terrifying. I mean, the worst that could happen is that we'd be found wandering the halls and taken back to our table. We could always feign ignorance and say we lost our way. Since they were blind, they'd never know that we were wearing goggles. Nevertheless, we really wanted to see where Fachon was leading us and that made the stakes higher and the game more exhilarating.

At last, we arrived at a ventilator grill. Confident that the coast was clear, Fachon pried it off, easily enough. Clearly, he had done this before. 'This is why I told you to wear comfortable clothing. We need to do a bit of climbing.'

Thankfully, the air shaft was fairly large. Still, it was hard to get a footing on the smooth metal walls inside. We had to squeeze ourselves upwards, help one another over the bend in the tubing, until we reached a horizontal part above, where we could crawl on all fours.

I wish I had thought about the order in which we entered, because I now had my face in Collins' corduroy-clad derrière, which smelled of musty elderberries. I would have preferred being behind Lucy. Collins had taken that spot already.

Eventually, we reached the end of the line - another

ventilator grill that overlooked the kitchen. Only three people could look at one time, squeezed shoulder-to-shoulder, so we took turns.

Below us was a food preparation area, cloaked in darkness. It was unlike any kitchen I'd ever seen. It had the usual food prep stations but, also, miles of tubes, bunsen burners, and other laboratory paraphernalia. The food itself arrived pre-packaged. It was unwrapped, doused in various liquids, and then garnished. The whole operation looked like a factory assembly line and there wasn't much culinary creativity involved. All the workers were blind.

Fachon whispered. 'You see, he is a chemist. Not a chef.'

Collins traced the tubes back to a row of metal canisters. 'What is he squirting on the food?'

'Aah,' replied Fachon. 'Quel grand mystère! Kuromizu keeps his ingredients more secret than Coca Cola, which is why he only employs the blind. He brings in his special preparation every day by armoured car. Any leftovers are incinerated each and every night. I have been trying to get a spy onto his staff for years. It has not been easy.'

'He manufactures it somewhere else?'

'He has laboratories all over the world. Industrial chemicals, mostly. I haven't yet discovered where he makes his culinary products.'

After our own private tour, we returned to our table to resume our meal. Now, that I had seen the man behind the curtain, so to speak, I was disinclined to appreciate it as much as I did before. Yet, Kuromizu's flavours were irresistible. They created a craving. A yearning. When each course ended, the rush of flavours gradually dampened, and depression set in. You didn't want the experience to end, but you knew that at some point it must. And that made me feel sad. Chemist or not, Kuromizu was a culinary alchemist of the highest order, no doubt about it.

After the meal, we gradually came down from our high. None of us spoke for the longest time. It was as if we were at the tail-end of a thoroughly exhausting, psychadelic experience, and we needed to retreat into our own inner worlds for awhile. Fachon led us through the streets like the Pied Piper, before stopping at a charming little, Italian cafe.

Without asking, he ordered us all cappuccinos. 'Cappuccinos are really a breakfast food. Very gauche in the afternoon, I know. But, here, they make them in a special way, using old hand pumps. It is one of my little vices.'

We all found them exquisitely delicious. In fact, the whole day had been such a sensory overload that the caffeine brought us back down to earth.

'The other essential ingredient,' lectured Fachon, 'is the milk. It comes from a very special cow that only eats high-altitude grass.'

'That's all very interesting, Fachon,' said Collins, who had clearly recovered his composure, 'but what exactly is all of this for? I asked you to tell me about the competition. Now is the time.'

Fachon's eyes quickly darted around the room, checking for eavesdroppers. He leaned in close and whispered. 'It is for the Steel Chef. The most important culinary competition in the world. For us, it is the highest badge of honour.'

Collins was surprised. 'From what I know of chefs, yourself included, bragging rights are good for business. So, why is this competition so secret?'

Fachon smiled a wicked little smile. 'For any chef in my profession, you need the finest of ingredients. The richest foie gras, the most exquisite truffles, essential oils, quality rice from the most sacred of steppes. Anything else is... McDonalds.' He spat this last word with disdain. 'The rarer the ingredients, the more likely you are to impress the critics. In the gourmand restaurant business, you live or die by the quality of the ingredients from your suppliers. This is more important than your coupons, or promotions, or theatricality. The common man is perfectly content with inferior things. But the critics who really matter - they are not beguiled by what can be easily bought at the supermarket. And their review is an important one. I should know.' His eyes took on the same distant look as when he told us of Gascon.

Lucy interrupted his trip down memory lane. 'So, the winner gets to have all these special ingredients?'

'It is more complicated than that, ma chérie. All of these precious things are jealously guarded by different family suppliers. They are like, how you say, OPEC?'

'A cartel?'

'Yes, a cartel. They only supply the greatest chefs. For a hefty fee, I might add. It is a mutually attractive arrangement. A cozy little club. They control the world's supply of fine dining. But, as you can imagine, they sometimes have cross-purposes. They do not always agree.' He sighed before continuing. 'Many years ago, there was much bloodshed within the cartel. Lives were lost in squabbles over turf and territory. The "Salad Wars" of ninety-three were particularly devastating. The Romaine clan killed practically all the Arugula family. For years, we were stuck with Iceberg, which is why it featured prominently on so many menus. American chefs even took desperate measures by tarting it up as something special, serving Iceberg to the public as a starter on its OWN. Can you imagine?' He chuckled at the thought. 'It is such a silly and inferior lettuce! We Europeans did not stoop to such ridiculous behaviour.' He could see that Collins was growing impatient with his digressions. 'Anyways, afraid that this violence would spread, the heads of all the major food families came together and devised a way of keeping the peace - by electing an outsider to a position of authority. A consiglieri, of sorts. They agreed to defer the management of their logistical operations to this person. He would have the authority to resolve disputes and keep everyone in line. They needed someone who was already inside the system. Someone who would command their respect, while understanding their business needs.'

'The Steel Chef.'

'Yes! The Steel Chef. He is the one with the ultimate authority, without question. And we, the chefs, devised the competition as a means of electing amongst ourselves who will have this tremendous honour and responsibility. The food families are not allowed to vote, or participate in the outcome. That is the agreement between us. Nevertheless, they must abide by our decision. The winner of the competition holds the position for four years, until the next competition.'

Collins mulled this over. 'Why, then, endangered species?'

'That was Kuromizu's idea,' replied Fachon. 'He has held the Steel Chef position for the past four years, but is fighting to remain in power. He is not popular within the chef community. We would all gladly see the back of him! If you ask me, it is the desperate act of a desperate man. He thinks that by choosing something almost impossible to obtain and, similarly, impossible to cook, he will be able to eliminate his enemies before the competition even begins. None of us have ever tasted these creatures, so we are all at a severe disadvantage. Except, Kuromizu. You have tasted his trickery. He does not need food to make a meal. He could make ground glass taste like crème brûlée, if he wanted to.'

'When and where will it be held?' Collins was fascinated. It was as if Fachon had opened the door to a whole other, secret world, full of conspiracy and intrigue. Dangerous. Accountable.

Fachon smiled enigmatically and simply laughed. 'That is more secret than the competition itself. It is Kuromizu's choice. All I know is that the time to assemble the ingredients ends in three weeks. After that, he will name the venue.' Fachon dropped the smile and spoke in earnest. 'Now,' he said, 'I have told you all what you need to know. I want your help in return. I have the eggs of the razor eagle, but Kuromizu has the sabre-toothed, himalayan snow goat. Which means I must have the upper hand when it comes to a main course. My sources tell me that he may also have the hemaphroditic boil worm. I suspect he will use it in an amuse-bouche, probably with parsley sauce, as is his signature. And, Romelly supposedly has the monkey spider - which, I suspect, he will smother in a beef reduction -'

'Wait, there are others?' said Collins.

'Mais, oui, there are others! As long as we are able to bring at least two of the most endangered species to the table, we can qualify. Any chef can challenge the incumbent, but only on his terms. This is exactly my point. I am without a second course. I need something to remain in the running. However, it must be spectacularly difficult to obtain! I do not want Kuromizu crushing my plans a second time. I want something that will blow the others away and impress the judges. Something that they will be talking about for years and years. Something worthy of the name of Henri Fachon!' His eyes were glazed over, drunk with ambition, like so many portraits of Napoleon.

Collins was pensive. He had something in mind, but needed to muster his conviction. 'I know what to do.'

'Tell me!' shrieked Fachon.

'It is the most dangerous creature on the planet. It is something that is not on any list.'

'I must have it!' Fachon's eyes were now ablaze.

Collins demurred. 'I can't vouch for its taste, however.'

'Leave that to me. I am Henri Fachon, remember!'

'But there is only one left. It would mean the end of a species.'

'If it means the end of Kuromizu, it is worth it!'

Collins paused. He could see the effect he was having on Fachon and enjoyed the tease. 'I will need at least two weeks to plan our expedition. And I will need a quarter of a million dollars for the equipment and transportation.'

'Money is no object,' said Fachon, proudly.

'And,' continued Collins, 'you must allow me to film everything. My priority is my program.'

'Yes, yes,' said Fachon impatiently, 'now, tell me what it is!'

Collins looked at Lucy, for he knew that she would understand the severity of what he was suggesting. 'The Iridescent Sea Possum.'

Lucy gasped and dropped her coffee cup.

It shattered on the floor.

It was a portend of what was to come.

COMMITMENT TO THE CAUSE

De Konig's body lay battered and half-buried in the snow, but he was still alive. He blinked at the sky, which was all he'd been looking at for what seemed an eternity. He had lost track of time. Now, day was breaking. At some point in the night, he had watched Fachon's helicopters - his copters - take off. That was hours ago. They hadn't even attempted a search and rescue!

So, this is what it came to. He never trusted Fachon. Not one bit. Now, he had proof. Now, he knew that - to Fachon - he was truly expendable. What did he expect? The man was an egomaniac, driven solely by revenge.

He never should have taken this job. But the money was good. Too good, in fact. That should have been the first alarm bell. And Chuck! That was the last straw. He had always been the cause of his misfortune. Why did he love those crazy animals so much? He loved them even more than his own brother!

Ahh! He fed off his anger. He would get back his own. Yes. True, he wasn't the best brother in the world either, but… that didn't matter. They were blood. Blood!

Betrayal. Anger. Stay alive. Stay alive!

He tried to move his body, but everything converged into extraordinary pain. He could feel the extremities of his limbs, so he hadn't broken his spine. That's what he feared most. He couldn't track anything from a wheelchair. Although, Collins had done pretty well with one leg. Could even run faster than before. Bastard! Still, this wasn't a sacrifice he was ready to make.

He felt something tugging at his foot.

He tried to roll over. Impossible.

He bent forward. Ahh, the agony!

What he saw gave him a terrible chill.

A big mother snow goat stood over him, huffing.

De Konig passed out from the pain.

Collins rented a small apartment with Fachon's advance and made it our base of operations. He later confided in Lucy and I the crux of his plan. He knew that we must infiltrate the competition, otherwise we had no chance of stopping it. For that reason alone, he was willing to put the sea possum at risk, if it meant a seat at the table. Fachon had to meet the criteria, or all was lost. However, the rest of his plan was hair-brained at best.

'We're going to swap out the endangered species for chicken?' Lucy was incredulous.

'Everything tastes like chicken,' suggested Collins.

'Not to the most refined of palates on the planet,' argued Lucy.

But Collins was undeterred. We knew now that the competition was to be a gala dinner. The guests were paying a fortune for the tickets - estimated to be at least ten million dollars per seat, on account of the rarity of the ingredients. But the guests, who were also the judges, were not chefs. They were heads of state, business leaders, and a rag tag assortment of dictators and billionaires.

'They may be self-proclaimed aesthetes,' conjectured Collins, 'but they are not chefs.'

He doubted they could tell the difference between an endangered species and an ordinary one. And why should they? Nobody had tasted any of these things before.

While Lucy and Collins argued over tactics, I was sent to do background research. I wondered how Fachon, in particular, was able to bankroll his operation. He had been a successful chef, yes, but that was once upon a time. In the interim, he had lost his restaurant empire, tarnished his good name, and pissed away his savings on drink. Somehow, this did not tally with the Fachon who we had come to know. Here was a man who was driven, maniacally, to seek revenge on a rival. Either he had a miraculous recovery, a reversal of fortune, or there was more to this story than met the eye.

Kuromizu was by far a more complex character. I had skimmed the outline of his operation at the docks in Vietnam. Now, it was time to dig for pay-dirt. His family was Japanese nobility, or had been when they were vassals of the Emperor. That was a long time ago. For many generations, they held a whaling business, but it was shuttered after international outcry made it impossible to hunt whales. The young Kuromizu, on the other hand, did not follow in his father's footsteps. Instead, he had embarked on an illustrious career in chemicals.

At first, he worked for the likes of Dow Corning, designing synthetic compounds for industrial purposes. Then, he was involved in cosmetics. At some point, however, he began working for the food industry. It was very difficult for me to get accurate details on what he did exactly, because his name would crop up on various clandestine, skunk works projects within large agri-chemical businesses. They guarded their secrets jealously.

It was as if Kuromizu lurked in the background of some of the food industries most closely guarded secrets. For instance, he was associated with the development of an "eleven secret herbs and spices" recipe for a prominent fried chicken franchise. More recently, he was rumoured to be behind the "Cispy Crack" donut sensation.

It was around this time that Kuromizu assembled his own restaurant empire. He began with a few themed restaurants, like the two that we had seen ourselves. They became instant media darlings. Despite the fact that the restaurant business is pretty cut-throat, with low margins, and even lower success rates, Kuromizu seemed to walk on air. He opened up a highly successful vietnamese-mexican restaurant in Tokyo, followed by a French Dim Sum restaurant in New York, and an

Ethiopian-Chinese restaurant in Los Angeles. All of his concoctions were praised for their innovative fusion of flavours. There was never a bad review. Profitability was assured. Shortly thereafter, he became the Steel Chef in the previous competition, no doubt buoyed by his phenomenal cult following. Perhaps, he had even cheated. Whatever the truth, he had come out of nowhere and conquered the world.

Winning the coveted prize seemed to slow him down, however. He appeared to do little after that, opening only a handful of restaurants in the subsequent four years. I didn't buy it. First, there was Fachon's personal anecdotes. Then, we had seen Kuromizu's restaurants from the inside. They didn't resemble standard culinary operations. Not to mention all the crates we saw on his expedition and his highly paid team of mercenaries. All of this indicated a supremely successful man, who stopped at nothing to vanquish his competition, even if he maintained a low profile in public. I expressed my reservations to Lucy.

'Keep digging,' was all she said.

It's not that she wasn't interested in my findings, but she had her own hands full, planning the logistics for the iridescent sea possum operation. Apparently, it was going to be the most ambitious expedition to date.

It saddened me, though, that Lucy and I hadn't grown closer. She clearly enjoyed working alongside Collins, more than me. They planned their adventures together. She was good at it, too. Over time, they slipped back into what I imagined to be a familiar pattern of behaviour. Laughing together, sharing jokes about past adventures... It made me feel like a third wheel again. My utility to the group was in question. My research was appreciated, but I wanted more responsibility. Was this presumptuous? Possibly. I wanted to be necessary.

Bunny caught me mooning one afternoon. I was watching Lucy and Collins from the other room, when he ambled up beside me. 'See something you like?'

I tried to cover my embarrassment. 'He's lucky to have her. She really looks after him.'

'Sure. He's the cow.'

I detected a hint of sarcasm. 'What do you mean?'

'Collins is a cash-cow, when he's firing on all cylinders. Who knows what happens when he runs out of milk? That's all I'm saying.' He offered me a reefer. 'Want something to take your mind off things?'

'No, thanks.'

I regarded Bunny anew. Rarely compos mentis, perhaps, but when he was - he was more lucid than most.

Roger had assembled an arsenal of aquatic equipment, as if we were planning an undersea takeover of Atlantis. I filled my spare time helping him to strip down, clean, and reassemble various bits and bobs. It gave me a chance to ask him why he always put his fake eye to camera. He explained that, because of his handicap, he had developed an excellent perception of distance. He didn't have to focus through the eyepiece, he simply judged the distance by eyeballing it.

This went against common sense. The guy had no depth perception at all, and, yet, he was able to do the most extraordinary things. It renewed my admiration of him. Ironically, he wasn't deep in other ways. Rarely philosophical or introspective, he preferred to talk about perfunctory things. For instance, he had shown me once how to disembowel a cricket before roasting it as a snack. His instructions were very methodical. This was important, evidently, as a failure to remove all the entrails would result in sickness.

He had also built all of our makeshift furniture. Fachon had rented us an unfurnished apartment. Rather than spend precious funds on dressing the place, Roger was quick to offer his carpentry skills. He made beds, tables, chairs - everything. I knew how adept he was at crafting things. I didn't realise, though, that it extended to military equipment.

'Here,' he said to me one day, 'check this out.' He popped out his eyeball and gave it to me. I wasn't entirely sure what to do with it. 'Do you feel it?'

I was a bit grossed out by the dampness of it. 'Feel what,

exactly?'

'Do you feel the button?'

I turned it around for a bit, until I felt a small nodule. 'Yeah.'

'Don't press it!' he warned.

'What is it?'

'Grenade. Push the button and it gives you ten seconds till detonation. I just had it made.'

He pulled out a box. 'See.' He flipped open the top and there were ten other eyeballs, lined up like candies in a chocolate box.

'You designed this yourself?'

'Sure.'

'Can it do much damage? I mean, it's pretty small.'

Don't get me wrong, I was very impressed all the same.

'It does enough, under the right circumstances,' he said, annoyed, before closing the box.

Clearly, old Roger had a few surprises up his... sleeve. I wondered what might happen if I got him together with Oz someday?

We spent the next week going over our plan of attack. This possum sounded formidable, yet Collins refused to tell us much about it. I couldn't help feeling that he held back a lot of things. He'd listen to you ask a question with a bemused expression, but rarely gave you a straight answer. It was hard to trust him completely.

When I finally had a private conversation with Lucy, I was in a punchy mood. I was cleaning some of Roger's equipment to relieve the pain of having watched her fawn over Collins more than usual lately.

'I have a name for your book,' she said, proudly. 'Chuck Collins, diary of an eco-warrior.'

'It's catchy,' I said without much enthusiasm. 'Are you going to write it?'

'Something wrong, Trevor?' It was less of a question and more of a challenge.

'I don't know Lucy. You seem to have things all figured out. I'm not entirely sure what I'm bringing to this party.'

'Are you feeling under-appreciated?' she spoke softly, now. I knew better. She had the maternal instincts of a preying mantis.

'I think you may need to revise my fees,' I said. It was spiteful, I know, but that's the mood I was in.

'I see,' she said, irritated. 'I forgot, you're only *paid* to care.' She put her hands on her hips. 'The fate of the planet means nothing to you?'

I shook my head. 'That may work on Chuck, but it doesn't work on me.'

Her face was black. 'I shouldn't be surprised. It's why I hired you in the first place. Money makes you more predictable. How much are we talking?'

I calculated my chances. 'How about you buy me dinner?'

She laughed, but it rang callous. 'Don't be so pathetic.'

'Maybe, I just want to get to know you better.'

'Listen, Trevor,' she said my name as if it tasted bad, 'I will be brutally honest, if that's what you want. I'm not interested in self-centred boys with a wounded ego, especially the ones who sit on the sidelines, preying on the girls who are easy targets. If this really was a party, you'd be that guy who waits until the end of the night to take home the girl whose too drunk to notice, in order to make himself feel better. Am I right?'

'No dinner, then?'

'No.' Her decision was final. 'And I'm not paying you a penny more, either. So, do me the courtesy of letting me know your decision before the week's out. I'll need to find a replacement.'

What she said cut deep. But I couldn't leave things there. I had to dig a little myself. 'Count me in,' I said, 'but I need your help with something.'

'What's that?'

'Clarification. For the book.'

'About what?'

'Why wasn't the crocodile asleep?'

She frowned.

'It had been darted,' I continued. 'It should have been asleep. Unless, there was something wrong with the darts that day?'

I had taken a stab in the dark, but it struck her in the heart.

'Who uploaded the video to YouTube?' I pressed. 'I believe it went live before the network ever received the footage.'

Lucy didn't answer.

'It's important,' I said. 'For the book.'

Finally, she came around. 'You're the ghostwriter, Trevor. You decide.'

'Are you committed to the cause, or to your career?' I couldn't help myself. She was asking for it.

'I'm committed to getting the job done,' she replied. 'By any means necessary.'

She left the room.

Despite the tension caused by our conversation, I had asserted myself. I felt better for it. Maybe, it had earned me some respect. Or, maybe it would cost me job security. It was difficult to tell. My feelings were getting in the way of better judgement. I had to let go of my fantasy. Lucy was devoted to the cause, alright. Hers and hers alone.

Meanwhile, Fachon had disappeared on a business trip of some kind - said he had some important things to attend to. He was due back the day before, but he didn't show. We buried ourselves in preparation for our next mission and tried not to openly acknowledge our concern.

TUBER MAGNATUM

The truffle weighed in at three kilograms - one of the largest ever discovered. It probably wished it was still deep down, in the soft peaty earth of the Italian countryside. Yet, here it was, half-way across the world, in a private viewing room at a Sotheby's auction house in Hong Kong.

Earlier in the day, it had been photographed with several attractive models wearing revealing outfits. It probably didn't like this either. It wasn't used to being gawked at. It wasn't exactly a sight for sore eyes. Even if it smelled shiitake-sweet, it looked like the Elephant Man's ball-sack. This didn't diminish anyone's excitement, however. The last time a giant truffle went up for auction, it fetched over three hundred thousand dollars. And that one had only been half its size.

Thankfully, when the press event was over, the lights were dimmed out of respect. Climate control was restored. The room was cleared of PR riff-raff, and only the most serious of bidders were allowed in.

The giant Tuber Magnatum was encased in a glass box that had a pair of velvet-lined, breathing apparatus attached at either end. This would allow visitors to sniff the heady aroma and gauge the quality for themselves. Normally, serious collectors and other headline seeking millionaires would send their minions in their place to do their bidding, but this was a extraordinary occasion. An extremely rare event. A tuber like this one came along once in a lifetime, if that. The punters in the room were the real deal. The stakes were high. Winning the prize would bring envy to its buyer, the world over.

They stood in awe of its presence. They spoke in hushed voices. At first, they kept a respectful distance, but the excitement zipped through the room like a live wire. One of the visitors stepped forward, hesitated, then put the plastic ventilator to his nose and mouth. He inhaled deeply - too deeply - because he was so overcome by the aroma that he passed out. Luckily, one of the many security guards dotted around the room had been prepared for such an event. He deftly swept in and caught the fellow, before he hit the ground and injured himself. Carefully dragging him to the side, he deposited him on a bank of soft, exercise mats to recover.

A few hours later, in the main auction room, the bidding began. Fachon had taken his place at the back, so he could survey the events. Bidding began at one hundred thousand dollars and escalated.

When it reached four hundred thousand, there was an audible gasp from the room.

This was followed by a lull in the bidding. That's when Fachon took his cue. He sprung into action and raised his hand. For a moment, it seemed that he was the winner. But then, another paddle went up, from someone sitting in the middle row.

Fachon shifted himself to get a better view. It was Chae. He smiled. Everything was going according to plan.

He kept in the game for as long as his nerves held out. He had no intention of winning the bid. No, he enjoyed forcing Kuromizu's hand. Fachon knew there was no way that he could ever afford the truffle himself. He was terribly overextended already from the preparations for the possum hunt. But he couldn't help it. He pushed the price higher and higher. He wanted to twist the knife in Kuromizu's back.

Chae retaliated at each tick, pushing the price past six hundred, seven hundred, eight hundred! Now the room was all aflutter. Everyone else had dropped out and were clearly enjoying the show.

At eight hundred and fifty thousand, Chae faltered. It was at that point Fachon realised that he may have overdone it. She was on the phone to someone - probably Kuromizu. She understood what Fachon was doing and it seemed she lacked the authority to go any higher. The auctioneer kept at her, but she remained silent.

'Merde,' thought Fachon. This would really shut him down.

As the auctioneer raised his gavel, Fachon felt his heart rise up into his mouth. This was not the ending he had in mind.

Another hand. 'Nine hundred thousand!'

It was Chae. She turned to look at Fachon for the first time. He could see pure hatred in her eyes. It wasn't the money. Of course not. Kuromizu was good for millions. It was the losing that she hated most. Fachon had banked on that.

Fachon wiped the sweat from his brow with his handkerchief and looked at the auctioneer. He shook his head.

Chae got the prize.

Fachon thought he saw a smirk at the corners of her mouth.

Outside the auction house, Fachon recomposed himself and waited for a taxi. He pulled out a fresh pack of cigarettes, broke the seal, and lit one with trembling fingers. He didn't smoke. But the event had rattled his nerves. He needed something to take the edge off. That had been a close call. Too close, in fact. As expected, the nicotine soothed him. A young gentleman asked him for a light, but, before he could oblige, a bag was put over his head, and he was trundled into a car that was idling nearby.

He spent the entire journey on tenterhooks. He had no idea where they were taking him. He tried to protest, but that only made his abductors more determined. In the end, they sat on top of him to stop him from squirming. For a man with such a refined sense of smell, it was an added insult to injury that his nose was wedged into a seat that wasn't even covered in real leather! For over an hour, he was forced to smell its cheapness.

A private jet was refuelling at Hong Kong airport. A blacked out sedan arrived with a large steamer-trunk, which the chauffeur and the pilots lifted awkwardly up the gangway, and onto the plane. It was eventually deposited on the floor of the cabin inside, in front of twelve elderly men who looked like the cast of Scarface at their thirty year reunion. They wore the expression of people who didn't care about other people. They were in it for themselves.

The pilot opened the trunk to reveal Fachon. He pulled the hood off his head.

Fachon was about to let rip a long list of expletives, until he saw that he was facing all twelve members of "The Council".

'Apologies for the dramatics monsieur Fachon,' said one of the men. 'We had to take precautions. No one must know of our association.'

'Of course,' replied Fachon, nervously. His mind was whirling from the implications. He had never met all twelve before. This was serious.

'We have called this emergency session, because we are concerned. It has come to our attention that you have experienced some trouble in your quest.'

'Yes, monsieur, but it is only a minor setback. I assure you that everything is back on track.'

'We certainly hope so, Fachon. We put our trust in you. We expect nothing less.'

'Why were you at the auction?' demanded one of the other men, perturbed. He was gaunt and sinewy, his neck shrunken in his collar, like a gravedigger in a suit.

'Forgive me, gentlemen, but I didn't want to make it easy for Kuromizu.'

'Now is not the time to be rash,' said the first elder. 'We have already taken the necessary precautions. The truffle has been injected by an adverse fungus. In less than twenty four hours, it will be nothing but a soggy mushroom.'

Fachon smiled at the thought.

'You must leave these details to us, monsieur Fachon,' the elder continued. 'We are not allowed to give you direct assistance, true, but there is nothing in the bylaws about refusing to help the incumbent. We suspect that Kuromizu may have become overextended by his recent acquisitions and ambitious restaurant expansion. This puts him in a precarious position. But, as you know, when an animal is backed into a corner, it becomes more dangerous. The Council has agreed to restrict supplies and sabotage itself in order to level the playing field for the competition. We are losing millions by the day. It will cripple Kuromizu in the short-term, but is a significant sacrifice, too, on our part. We want to know that you will keep up your end of the bargain. Otherwise, we are doing all of this in vain.'

'Please do not doubt my own commitment, gentlemen,' said Fachon, with pride. 'I have ruined my own business and my reputation, all to exact my revenge. I assure you that I will do everything to win this competition. I stake my life on it.'

'Nevertheless,' cautioned the first elder, 'do not underestimate Kuromizu. His high bid today may suggest some anxiety on his part, even if you are a fool in his eyes. And, he may come to suspect our culpability.'

All eyes were gravely on Fachon. The stakes were certainly about to get higher.

'Now, if you please,' suggested the first elder, as he gestured to the trunk.

Fachon took his cue and crawled back into it.

BEST FOR BUSINESS

De Konig awoke feeling warmer than before. He was somewhere dark. Was it night? He could hear the wind howling, but couldn't feel it on his skin. Damn. Maybe, he had lost feeling in his limbs. He moved a leg. Then, an arm. No - they were working. He managed to prop himself up on one arm and take in his surroundings.

He was in a cave. Somebody - or, something - must have dragged him in. His body, though, was in a bad way. It responded sluggishly to his will, as if it required an enormous effort just to contract the muscles. He could tell that his left shoulder had become dislocated. He pulled his limp arm towards him. The human arm is roughly ten percent of body weight. Wriggling it closer to himself was like wrestling with a twenty pound, daikon turnip. He slid it back to bend the elbow at a right angle to his body, then cradled it close. Slowly, he rotated his arm back into its socket.

The searing pain made him cry out in agony.

His cries were joined by a high-pitched bleating.

He held his breath and looked around. In the dim light, he made out a bunch of baby snow goats nearby. Their eyes were barely open. He must have woken them up, because now they were weeping for their mother.

He put his good hand down to draw his boot knife. In his mind, he mapped out how he would slam it into their skulls, one-by-one, but he was suddenly disoriented by a huff of halitosis. Through his watery eyes, he could see that the mother had come up from behind, and was breathing heavily over his shoulder. She stood guard, as he slowly replaced the knife in his boot. Then, she licked his face. A gentle, friendly lick.

De Konig didn't know how to respond. He involuntarily put up his good hand, and stroked her cheek. She grunted. A satisfied grunt. Then, she lay down with her young and let them suckle.

De Konig watched her. He felt an uncomfortable constriction in his chest - an unknown warmth in his heart. He had never known such kindness.

She nudged him with her hoof. He looked at her. She did it again.

Now he saw - there was one spare teat. She had made room for one more.

With a tear on his cheek, De Konig rolled into the warmth of his new family, and suckled his surrogate mother.

An array of black limousines blocked the entrance to Kuromizu's new, private Tokyo dining club, "Kurogane". The chauffeurs packed pistols, while a scary-looking, security detail stood vigil outside the building. Today the club was closed for a special function. A very special function. It was to be a formal meeting between all members of The Council and The Steel Chef.

Inside, the same twelve men who met Fachon on the jet, were seated around an oval table, drinking genmaicha. They didn't take orders from anyone and they hated to be kept waiting. Which they were, because Kuromizu wasn't there. Even worse, they had to sit on a hard tatami floor, which numbed their butts to sleep, in front of an unusually high lacquered table that made them feel like children at the adults' table.

Outside, a helicopter swooped down, drawing concern from the security detail in the parking lot, until they read the "Kuromizu Enterprises" logo on its side. It landed on an adjacent helipad.

A few minutes later, the dining room screen slid open to

reveal Kuromizu in traditional dress, flanked by Chae. He sat down at the head of the table, elegantly and at ease, in a seiza position. Chae served the elders fresh tea, but it didn't soothe their tempers.

One of them spoke his mind. 'Listen here, Kuromizu, what's the meaning of making us sit here and wait!'

Kuromizu took a moment to tuck back the sleeves of his kimono. 'Excuse my tardiness, gentlemen. I did some last minute shopping for our lunch. I wanted to make sure everything would be absolutely perfect for our meeting.' He clapped his hands. 'It seems that good ingredients are hard to come by these days.'

The twelve men wondered if this was a statement of fact, or a veiled threat. Despite his perfect English, Kuromizu was Japanese, which meant he was culturally poles apart from them. He had a passive aggressive habit of flattering you, while stabbing you in the back.

The entrance slid open again, revealing an array of pretty ladies in kimono. They streamed in, bearing platters of beautifully arranged kaiseki, which they gracefully placed in front of each guest.

This caught The Council off-guard, as the food was breathtakingly exquisite.

After the plates were served, the staff disappeared. Only Chae remained to help serve.

Kuromizu held court. 'I have brought you the finest delicacies from all over Japan. For you to enjoy. This, I did in a single day, gentlemen. Why is it that you cannot do the same for my chefs around the world in a single month?'

There was an awkward silence.

Kuromizu swivelled to face one of the Councilmen. 'Foie Gras, please report.'

The elder known as "Foie Gras" did not like being barked at, but Kuromizu was the head of The Council. For now. He couldn't wait to see the back of him. In fact, he had often fantasised of what he might do to Kuromizu once he lost the competition. Death by dogs was his favourite method of exacting revenge. He reserved it only for extreme cases of insubordinance from his most trusted suppliers. It gave him the satisfaction of a slow death, accompanied by lots of pleading, and bleeding. That way, he knew the victim was truly sorry for what they'd done. He had to banish this delicious thought from his mind, however, in case a smile should inadvertently flicker across his face.

'As you well know, we are experiencing a lot of trouble with our American supplier given the change in legislation,' said Foie Gras. 'The public consider our methods cruel to the animals and we are lobbying to lift their ban.'

Kuromizu held his look for a moment, then turned to the next person. 'Caviar?'

'We have been forced to halt all our shipments from the Caspian Sea, until we can satisfy the foreign governments that the sturgeon are sustainable,' said another Councilman.

One by one, the other members gave their grave reports.

"Water" complained of contamination to his supply of Kona Nigari, forcing a recall and health inspection.

"Salad Oil" was having issues with his unions.

Others had similar problems with quality control, production, legislation, or public opinion.

At last, Kuromizu turned to "Truffle". 'At least you had a very good auction. I am only sorry that I had to pay for it so dearly.'

Truffle was unrepentant. 'I run a business, mister Kuromizu. Times are tight. That was the find of the century. I did what was best for business.'

'Yes,' said Kuromizu, thoughtfully. 'Best for business.' He nodded his head. 'Well, let us celebrate,' he suggested. 'Please. Lift the lid of your soup. I have used the tuber magnatum to prepare you a special broth.'

Truffle hesitated.

'Please,' insisted Kuromizu, gesturing to the elegant crockery.

Truffle knew that all eyes were upon him. If he were to hesitate a moment longer, it might telegraph to Kuromizu that he knew something was wrong, and betray the Council. He had no choice. He raised the soup bowl to his lips with trepidation and drank.

Then, he drank some more.

'This is - this is fantastic!' he said.

He gulped the soup down. Then, after it was consumed, he began to lick his bowl, like a pig at a trough. His behaviour grew more insistent, desperate, even. Occasionally, he looked up at the others, apologetically, but could not stop himself. He stuck his fingers in the bowl to gather the last drops of soup. Then, he licked his fingers. But he couldn't stop. He was possessed by the flavour.

'Please, help me,' he said. 'My fingers, they taste just like truffles!'

With tears in his eyes, he began to eat the flesh off his fingers.

He begged Kuromizu. 'Please make it stop… the flavour… it is so good… too good!'

The other Council members were too disturbed to say anything.

Chae led the poor man out of the room. By then, he had gnawed several of his fingers to the bone - and still he couldn't stop himself.

Nobody touched any of their food.

Kuromizu broke the silence. 'I, too, run a business. And I must do what's best for business.'

He upended a box on the table, revealing the now-rotting, giant truffle that he had bought at the auction. It oozed black pus all over the table, the slick of disintegrated fungus gradually seeping towards the guests, fanning out, and running off the sides, onto the tatami mat.

He gestured towards the mushroom sick, 'When you knowingly sell inferior goods to the chef community, you must be punished. Our reputation is everything.'

There was an awkward silence, as Chae handed Kuromizu a small lacquer box. He put it on the table in front of him and propped open the lid. Inside, was a small chopping knife.

He placed the knife delicately to the side of the box, then picked up a napkin and wrapped it tightly around his pinkie finger. Then, he lay his left hand, palm down, with his fingers spread out, wide.

Without hesitation, he deftly picked up the knife, placed it below the knuckle of his pinkie, and chopped his digit off.

The Councilmen gasped.

Kuromizu tossed his dismembered pinkie to the floor in front of them, like a discarded carrot.

'That is for the loss of your colleague. I always repay my debts, gentleman.'

Kuromizu's ragged stump spurted blood onto the table. It was a messy distraction to him, so he wrapped the remaining part of the napkin around it to staunch the flow.

'As a chef, you will appreciate that the price of a finger is a serious cost to me in my profession. Nevertheless, it compares nothing to the loss of income I will experience if I should lose any of my Michelin Stars. Therefore, I would expect nothing less than the same from you.' He gave them a pointed look. 'I have twenty stars. You have ten fingers each. Let us hope, for your sake and mine, that I do not lose all of them.' Kuromizu lifted his chopsticks. 'Now, gentlemen, please. Eat.'

But everyone had lost their appetite.

KUMBAYA

All of us were crammed into a six-seater seaplane. Collins and Fachon in front, Lucy, Roger, Bunny, and myself in back. Plus, a new boom operator we'd picked up in Bermuda. We couldn't pronounce his name, so we called him, "Seven".

Not only was the plane excruciatingly small, but it was packed to the gills with boxes of Captain Munch cereal. According to Collins, we needed it as bait for the sea possum.

The tropical heat had turned the plane into an oven. Fachon sweated so much, he'd created a swimming pool beneath his feet. It had even soaked through his shoes.

Lucy fanned herself, while looking down at the wide expanse of sea below. She shouted to Collins above the drone of the propellers. 'You sure this is a good idea? Flying over the Bermuda Triangle?'

Fachon smirked. 'Not afraid of an old wive's tale, are you?' He was the one flying. Not the greatest pilot in the world, either. But it was his operation, so we couldn't complain.

'Looks like we've got company,' chirped Bunny, pointing at a ship down below.

Lucy shifted position. 'Kuromizu?'

'No,' said Fachon. 'It is mine - "Sail la Vie". I sent them ahead when you told me the coordinates. I didn't want to waste any time in getting the possum.'

'That wasn't wise,' said Collins, gravely. 'I hope they haven't made contact.'

'Don't be so dramatic,' laughed Fachon, as he fiddled with the knobs of the radio. He spoke into his headset mic. 'Come in Sail la vie.'

No answer.

'Come in Sail la vie.'

Again, nothing.

Lucy and I exchanged a knowing glance. This was a bad sign.

'I'm setting her down,' said Fachon, wiping the sweat from his brow.

Something caught Roger's eye. 'Incoming!'

We looked up to see a strange, v-shaped object streaming towards us.

'Merde!' cried Fachon. 'Geese!'

He took evasive measures. Too late. The flock went straight through the propellers - one after the other - spraying the windshield with gristle and bone, before conking out one of our engines.

'You were saying?' said Lucy, with irony.

Fachon twisted more knobs on his dashboard. 'It's alright, we still have the other engine.'

Collins shook his head. 'Geese are full of fat, Fachon. Now, the fat is in your engine.' We watched the last remaining engine splutter into flames. The geese oil had turned it into a torch, fanned ever stronger by the wind. Then, the smoke blew across the windscreen, obscuring the view.

Fachon hit the windshield wipers, but it was no use. 'We're going in blind,' he said. 'Put on your life-jackets!'

We all reached under our seats. Nothing. Maybe he shouldn't have hired such a cheap-ass plane.

Fachon blurted into his headset. 'Mayday! Mayday!'

We fastened our seat belts, as he pushed the stick down. He seemed confident at first, despite the circumstances. But, then, the plane went into a steep dive and it didn't feel right, even to a novice, like myself.

Fachon stared straight ahead. There was nothing for him to do now, except pray. Instead, he screamed in fear, like a little girl.

Then, Collins screamed, I screamed - we all screamed. Seven

was too terrified to scream, but his eyes bulged so badly, I thought they'd pop out of their sockets.

Except Bunny, who looked out the window. He drummed his fingers on his knee to a silent song. Then, gently at first, he began to sing. 'Kumbabya my Lord, Kumbaya. Oh, Lord, Kumbaya.'

I ogled him, but he continued, without apology.

It was strangely calming. Gradually, the rest of us joined in.

'Kumbaya, my Lord, Kumbaya…'

We weren't a bad choir, as it turned out.

Collins came in with a bit more baritone. 'Oh Lord, Kumbaya!'

Before long, we were all singing, as if our lives depended on it. Except, Seven. He was hyperventilating. And, Fachon, who might have been having a silent heart-attack. Nevertheless, he remained glued to the controls of the plane, pulling with all his might on the stick.

Collins turned to lock eyes with Lucy. He took her hand. They sang, and smiled at each other. Bunny smiled, too. Bunny took Collins' other hand. The rest of us followed suit, until we had made a human chain.

Roger broke the magic of the moment. 'Brace, brace, brace!'

Time slowed down at the moment of impact. Everything went queer, followed by quiet.

I became conscious of a powerful feeling in my chest. Bunny had united us before the oblivion. My fear was replaced by a feeling of warmth and release. A feeling of relief. I wondered if this is what it was like to face the light at the end of the tunnel?

Actually, no. I was mistaken. I had simply wet myself.

We hit the ocean hard, snapping off the landing gear. For an instant, I could see the depths below, through the windshield. The big blue. Then, there was a crack, as the windshield shattered inwards.

Collins still had his back to the front of the plane, facing Lucy, when he was enveloped in a torrent of water. For a moment, he looked like Moses parting the sea. Then, it hit the rest of us.

We held our breath.

The force knocked out all the seats, and threw us to the back of the plane. I couldn't see anything but cereal boxes. I tugged at my seat-belt. It didn't open. I could see Seven struggling with his. Finally, I pulled it with all my might and wrenched myself free. Luckily, the plane was only partially submerged, bobbing awkwardly, just below the surface. Roger had the presence of mind to start kicking at the cockpit door. It took him a few attempts but, with Collins' help, they smashed it open.

Fachon grabbed onto anything and anybody he could, in his struggle to get out the door first. He kicked me in the face. Then, he used other people's shoulders to propel himself forwards. He toppled through the open doorframe and splashed into the water.

The rest of us helped one another get free of our seats. Maybe, it was the result of living together the past couple of months. Maybe, it was the Kumbaya. Whatever the reason, we worked as a team for the first time. It was a glorious moment. And, then, it was gone, because we began to sink.

None of us wanted to join the plane at the bottom of the ocean. We grabbed the seat cushions, which appeared to have some buoyancy. The plane sank further and further, quickly gaining momentum. Collins was last out of the plane. He was determined to get the cereal boxes out. Lucy didn't want to leave without him, but there was no time to argue. I practically dragged her to the surface.

I looked back at the plane one last time. It was sinking fast, now. Collins was too pre-occupied with the cereal boxes to notice. In fact, we'd all been too pre-occupied with our own survival to realise - Seven was still in the plane. He hadn't been able to open his seat-belt.

He had his face pressed tightly against the glass. I'll never forget his bulging eyes, wide with fear, framed by the circular window, as he descended into the depths. He slipped into the murkiness, and was gone, forever.

I looked above me. The sky loomed tantalisingly close, but I struggled to get there. I could feel the oxygen leeching from my lungs. I wasn't going to make it. I kicked and kicked, begged my blood to give me more time, dragging Lucy along behind me, but the struggle was literally taking the life out of me. My nerve-endings screamed. My vision blurred. My limbs went limp. Just when I thought my lungs were going to collapse and burn, we broke the surface!

I gulped the sweet, humid, tropical air.

Lucy ripped to the surface and nearly choked.

I did a head-count. Bunny and Roger were bobbing nearby. Fachon was already swimming towards the boat.

Lucy spun around, frantically. 'Where's Chuck?' She saw a few cereal boxes bobbing on the surface - but no Chuck. 'Did he make it out?'

'Bunny, Roger - grab those boxes,' I said.

Lucy was flabbergasted. 'How can you think about the cereal at a time like this?'

'It's what we came to do, isn't it? It's what he would have wanted.' I felt myself take charge. I had the authority.

I grabbed the few boxes closest to me. They were soggy and had disintegrated, but inside the cereal was safely sealed in plastic bags puffed with air, which helped me to stay afloat. I corralled a few more over towards me, and clutched them tight. Lucy treaded water and waited.

'What are you guys doing?' Collins was behind us.

Lucy was relieved. 'Jesus, Chuck. I thought you were a goner.'

'Gaia won't allow it,' said Collins, in a messianic tone.

Lucy swam to him. '*I* won't allow it.' She held him close. The public show of affection seemed genuine. It made me jealous. My authority was gone.

Collins was unfazed. 'Alright everyone, swim to Frenchie's boat - before the sharks come.'

'Sharks?!' I was too thankful that I'd survived the crash that I hadn't thought of that.

'Sure,' said Collins. 'They got to eat sometime.'

Hopefully, not today.

Thankfully, we all made it to Fachon's boat in one piece.

It was a large vessel used mainly for salvaging, manned by a crew of roughly twenty. But, oddly, none of them were on board. We heard doors slamming, but it turned out to be Fachon searching for signs of life. He was exasperated by the time we caught up to him.

'Let's stick together,' said Collins. 'We have no idea what we're dealing with.'

'Pirates?' suggested Roger, in a not-to-unhappy way.

'Safety in numbers,' agreed Collins. 'Come on. Let's go below.'

The lights were out in the crew quarters, so we used flashlights to poke around. The only sound was the groan of the ship, gently rolling on the water. It was creepy. There was no evidence of a struggle. Everything was as it should be. Beds were made, bags of kit unpacked, food left half-eaten. It was a Marie Celeste. All that was missing were the crew themselves.

By the time we made it to the kitchen, we'd been through half the ship. The kitchen itself was a pig sty. Pots and pans were strewn everywhere. Something had clearly happened here, but what? Either a struggle, or someone had been hurriedly searching for something.

'This is messed up,' I said, to Fachon. 'When did you last hear from your crew?'

'Yesterday,' he replied. 'They were excited, because they thought they had found the possum.'

'They're all dead, then,' said Collins, solemnly.

Fachon got upset. He couldn't accept that possibility. He was tired of Collins' doom-and-gloom scenario. What he really wanted was to come back with a snappy retort, but was cut short by a tapping noise coming from one of the cupboards. It sounded as if someone - or, something - was inside. He grabbed a cleaver. The rest of us did the same, picking up whatever was to hand. I ended up with a sieve. Not the best option, I know, but better than going in empty handed.

We crept towards the cupboard. Fachon and Chuck shared a look, and with a quick nod they yanked it open on the count of "three".

There was a man squatting inside.

'Jean-Baptiste!' exclaimed Fachon. 'What's going on?'

Jean-Baptiste was too terrified to speak at first. He was shaking uncontrollably. Whatever he'd seen had put the fear of God into him. 'Monsieur le Chef! It is terrible!'

'What is terrible? What happened?' Fachon showed genuine concern for the first time since I'd met him.

Jean-Baptiste crossed his heart. 'I have been locked in the cupboard for nearly four hours.'

'What happened? What did you see?'

'I can't say.'

'You must,' urged Fachon.

'No, monsieur le chef, I honestly cannot say. I was locked in the cupboard entire time.' He rubbed his aching limbs to bring back the circulation.

Fachon grabbed his shoulders. 'Yes, Jean-Baptiste, but where are my crew?'

The poor man gathered his thoughts. 'I heard on the radio. They found the possum. They were excited. A celebration. They asked me to make a flan. You, know, from that recipe that you taught me with the special -'

'Yes, yes,' interrupted Fachon, 'what happened next?'

'Oh, monsieur, the screaming. It was horrible. They were all screaming. Over the radio. Such chaos. Then silence. Oh, such a horrible silence! I was scared. I looked for somewhere to hide. I did not expect the door to lock behind me.'

Fachon gave up his interrogation.

Collins and Fachon went to look for the submersibles. Originally, there had been two. Thankfully, one had been left behind - the back-up - which meant that the other was presumably still down in the depths.

'We have to hurry,' said Fachon, inspecting the vessel.

'It's no use,' said Collins. 'They're already dead.'

Fachon resisted the urge to explode in his face. Rather, he spoke in earnest. 'If they were your crew, would you take that chance?'

Collins considered for a moment. 'No, I wouldn't.'

'Then you must help me.'

Collins helped Fachon prep the submersible for launch. I had never seen Fachon so concerned for someone other than himself. It was his crew, after all. Maybe his heart had a silver lining? Assuming, he had a heart. However, I was more concerned with the dive we were about to make. The airplane debacle didn't predispose me to an undersea adventure. I'd had quite enough of the ocean, already. Also, the image of Seven sinking into oblivion still haunted me. And those eyes of his! Behind their fear, was there not a hint of reproach? That I might have helped him unbuckle his seat-belt? I'm not the superstitious sort, but I was scared of running into him down there, an aquatic apparition, getting his revenge on me. 'Perhaps I can stay behind? You'll probably need someone on deck in case something goes wrong.'

'Jean-Baptiste will stay behind,' said Fachon.

I pressed my case. 'Not exactly the best man in a crisis, don't you think?'

'Why - you scared?' Lucy framed it as a challenge.

'We need all hands on sub,' said Collins. 'The iridescent sea possum is a tricky creature. If we go in too light, we die.'

'That makes me feel so much better,' I said.

Bunny and I loaded the sub with the last of the Captain Munch. Collins had told us that the sea possum was an inherently curious creature, drawn to anything out of the ordinary. He had found the cereal to be quite effective in attracting other unusual species over the years - even those in the ocean - since nothing like it occurred in the natural world.

Once the equipment was loaded, the sub was hoisted over the side. We clambered awkwardly aboard and squeezed ourselves through the hatch. Collins was the last one in. We waved to Jean-Baptiste, before securing the lid. He pulled the levers on the crane and lowered us into the water. Fachon punched a button on the controls, releasing us from the winch cable.

We entered the ocean with a splash.

* * *

The sub appeared large from the outside, but was actually terribly cramped on the inside. I spent most of the time with my face in Roger's armpit, and my armpit in Bunny's face. We had to play a game of twister just to get around one another. I had been so concerned about what lay ahead that I'd forgotten to go to the loo before we embarked.

'Just go in the ocean, when we get outside,' said Lucy.

'We're going outside?' I hadn't planned on this. The sub suddenly became even smaller. My breathing became erratic. I felt claustrophobic. I had to shift my thoughts away from the obvious, focus on something positive. 'How long is it going to take us to get there?'

'Could be a half hour, or more,' said Fachon. 'The sea floor is a long way down.'

'We're going all the way to the sea floor? That could be miles!' I needed air. Fresh air. Not, armpit. Roger's armpit was clammy. I had to get out. I panicked.

'Don't worry,' said Collins. 'The floor is shallow here. We're only going down a few hundred feet.'

'Give or take,' added Fachon.

'Give or take what?' I said.

'Keep it together,' cooed Lucy. 'Take deep breaths. You're hyperventilating.'

'Damn right I am!' I clawed at the seal to the air lock. 'I have to get out of here! Now!'

Roger and Bunny grabbed me, pinning me down. 'You can't go out there,' said Bunny. 'We're already eighty feet below the surface.'

'Eighty feet? Eighty Feet! We're going to die! We're all going to die!' I screamed.

'Please, don't,' said Bunny. 'You're going to spoil my trip.' He shoved something into my mouth, but I spat it out.

'No, no. Don't sedate me. Please! I'm fine. I don't want to end up like Marcus.' Bunny ignored my pleas and crammed something into my mouth again. He held my mouth shut. I wanted to fight him, but what he gave me tasted good, really good.

'What is that? What did you give me?'

Bunny pointed to the cereal. 'Your blood sugar was low.'

Thank God. The memory of what happened to Marcus was sobering. And the cereal was really sweet. Pea-nutty. After a minute or so, my body began to cooperate. I felt embarrassed about my outburst before. 'I'm okay now. Please let me go.'

'Promise me you won't try to escape, otherwise I have to dope you.'

'I'm fine. Promise,' I said, weakly.

Bunny looked into my eyes. He seemed satisfied and released his grip. 'If you ever panic again, think of the jellyfish.'

'Jellyfish. Okay. Jellyfish. Why?'

'The jellyfish don't swim. Jellyfish *float*. Get my drift, man? Nobody sees the jellyfish in the water, because it flooooaaaats.'

'It floats. Jellyfish floats. Okay. Got it.' I had no idea what he was talking about, but I pretended to, so he'd release me.

'Just look out the window,' said Roger, brightly. 'There's a lot more space out there. I find it takes my mind off of thinking about being in this tiny tin can, far below the surface, thousands of miles away from shore.' He pointed to our glass observation bubble.

'That's not helping,' I said.

'What's that?' Lucy was distracted by the sonar, which was now pinging like crazy.

Collins flicked a switch. 'Here, let's put on the flood-lamps.' A beam of light cut through the darkness, spreading a wide cone of light. It picked up masses of huge, discarded objects, littering the sea floor. 'Wrecks.'

'Holy crap!' Even I had to marvel at the sight.

There were ships of all kinds scattered across the ocean floor, going back for centuries - a naval scrapyard.

'The sea possum likes wrecks,' said Collins. 'Lots of places to hide. Not too far from the surface. Good feeding opportunities.'

'Especially when divers come knocking,' I added.

We glided along in eerie silence. Floating above other boats at the bottom of the sea is a surreal experience, especially ones that came from another era. There was even a commercial aircraft. The logo was faded but we could just make it out - "Oceanic Airways". The irony was not lost on us.

Fachon pointed. 'I see it. Over there.'

The other submersible was grounded on the sea bed. It's lights were still on, illuminating a hole in the hull of an enormous wooden ship with four massive, broken masts. It was covered in moss and lichen, as if it had been resting there for hundreds of years.

'What do you reckon?' Collins directed the question to Roger.

Roger peered out into the gloom at the sleeping giant. 'Eighteenth century. Probably a cargo vessel. Could be American.'

'What would an American cargo vessel be doing all the way out here?' mused Lucy, out loud.

Fachon piloted the sub towards the other sub and set down beside it. Now that we had both lights trained on the ship, we could see a lot more of the terrain.

The cargo ship was huge. And so was the hole in its hull. Had it been hit by a cannon ball? Wrecked by a reef? Or, had something burst itself out from the inside? I began to wonder about those old fishermans tales of giant squid - Kracken. Hadn't they actually discovered one recently? It didn't bear thinking about.

Fachon peered through our observation window, trying to see if there were signs of life in the other sub. BAM! Something collided with the observation bubble and disappeared. Fachon instinctively flinched and fell back.

'What the hell was that?!' I was still thinking about the hole in the hull. 'Is it the possum?'

'That's not their way,' said Collins, collected.

Something flashed in our peripheral vision. BAM! It had launched itself, again, at the glass, and was gone.

We stepped back and huddled together, as if we might be safer further inside the sub.

Then, It struck again.

BAM!

It was a five foot penis with teeth and a tail fin.

I spasmed. 'What the hell is that thing?'

Collins went up to the glass to examine it. 'Relax. It's a frilled shark. Nothing to worry about.' Was he kidding? Something like that was the stuff of nightmares. 'Probably attracted to the light. I wonder what he's doing in such shallow water?'

Fachon opened the door to another compartment of the sub that I didn't realise existed. 'We must suit up and find the others.' Inside, I saw a row of deep-diving suits with yellow, metal helmets.

'I don't want to go outside,' I said. Being in the sub was bad enough, but out there - with the angry penis and the possum - God only knew what would happen to us.

Collins agreed. 'You stay here with Lucy.'

Lucy wasn't happy. 'No - I'm coming with you.'

'Negative. That would make us an odd number. We should dive in pairs. In case one of us goes loopy,' said Collins.

'Goes Loopy?' Lucy thought it was an excuse.

'We're using a helium blend,' explained Collins. 'It should give us twenty minutes. But, if we over-exert ourselves, or stay too long, our blood goes toxic. Not a good place to be. Plus, we'll need someone to man the sub.' He looked over at me. 'And he's acting like a spooked, girly-man, which isn't going to help us in a crisis.'

Lucy looked at me wearily. 'Great. Babysitting duty.'

The other four suited up, while Lucy and I helped transfer the cereal into special sacks.

'Why don't you just keep it in the plastic bags?' I wondered, out loud.

'Because they'll explode during the compression,' chided Collins.

Mr Smartypants had an answer for everything.

When they were ready to go, we closed the compression

chamber on them. Collins gave the thumbs up and Lucy turned a valve. We'd both been given a crash-course in the sub controls. It was a bit too rushed for my liking, but the clock was ticking.

After a few turns of the wheel, water began to fill the chamber. The divers sat in silence, while the water rose to their midriff, then to their necks, and, finally, they were submerged.

Roger turned the wheel at his end and their hatch opened to the deep, dark sea.

SEA POSSUM

Fachon was the first to speak. 'Let's check our radios.' He sounded like a French, Donald Duck.

'It's the helium,' explained Lucy.

Back in the sub, we kept our eyes on a bank of dark video monitors. The divers switched on their headlamps. One by one, the video monitors flickered to life, giving Lucy and I a camera feed of what the divers were seeing, themselves.

Lucy counted them out. 'Camera one, two, three, and four - all online. Recorder's running. You're good to go.'

'Collins, you and I will check the trap,' said Fachon, with as much authority as he could muster through the helium. 'The others will go inspect the sub.'

'Roger that,' said Roger, in a Mickey Mouse voice.

Bunny laughed at Roger's pun with a chipmunk giggle. The ridiculous sound he made set them both off giggling like miniature hyenas on speed.

'Knock it off boys,' said Lucy. 'Keep your focus. You haven't much time.'

Bunny and Roger swam over to the other sub, while Collins and Fachon swam towards a large metal box, sitting on the ocean floor, about ten feet from the hole in the hull.

'The trap was built to your specification,' said Fachon, to Collins, pointing at the metal box. 'We'll need to trigger it manually,' he said, gently tapping a big red button on the side.

'Alright,' said Collins, as he placed cereal baskets with

weights around the trap. Fachon copied him. The cereal slowly leaked out the sides like a bird-feeder. Hopefully, it would attract the possum.

Roger and Bunny peered into the other sub's observation hatch, using their headlamps to illuminate the inside.

'No sign of life in the other sub,' said Roger.

'Come back,' said Collins. 'We're going in.'

The four divers regrouped, then entered the hole in the hull, single file. Inside, they peered around a large cargo hold.

There were manacles and barnacled chains attached to the walls, threaded through eyelets in the floor.

Collins called to Lucy over the radio. 'Are you getting all this?'

'Jesus,' she gasped. 'It's a slave ship.'

'Time is short, gentlemen,' said Collins. 'Bunny. Roger. You go aft. Frog and I will go to the fore.'

Fachon bristled. 'Please stop calling me that.'

'Sure thing, Frenchie.'

They split up and went in pairs, in opposite directions.

Monitors one and two showed Roger's team floating through a corridor, full of bolted doors. Bunny tested one of them. It gave way after a sharp tug, revealing a small cabin. Inside, it was smothered in algae.

Something, however, reflected light from one of the shelves.

Roger fished it out. It was a metal cup. He turned it over in the light of his lamp. 'There's a crest of some kind.'

Lucy was dismissive. 'Keep moving, Roger. We've got the shot. We'll analyse it later. This isn't the History Channel.'

Roger put the cup down.

Meanwhile, on monitors three and four, Collins and Fachon had come across a trap door in the floor. The door to the trap itself had long gone, but they scoped out the area carefully, before venturing forward, in case something lurked beneath.

'I'm going in,' said Collins. He pulled himself down through the hole.

Inside, there was another room with more shackles, but this one was packed more tightly together, and had a lower-slung ceiling.

'What torture it must have been,' said Lucy, to me. 'They were prisoners on these ships for months.'

It made me wonder if the ship had gone down full of cargo and, if so, whether they were all tethered at the time. I can't imagine a more horrible way to die. Come to think of it, where were they now? Wouldn't there be something, left behind?

Bunny and Roger opened another cabin door.

This time they were greeted by something unexpected - a diver sat at a table, with his back to them.

'I think we found one of your crew,' said Roger.

Fachon chirped over the radio. 'Is he alright?'

Roger regarded him a moment. 'Well, I don't see any sign of trauma. He's just sitting here.' He reached out his hand and tapped the fellow on the shoulder. The diver didn't move.

Bunny and Roger grabbed the diver and pulled him towards them. The diver flopped upside down, and that's when they saw - his face was contorted in an unholy expression of fear.

Roger let go. 'Shit me!'

Fachon hollered from his helmet. 'What is it? What's going on?'

'He's dead,' said Bunny. 'Scared to death by the looks of it.'

'Then the myth is true,' said Collins, ominously, despite his chipmunk voice. 'They say that the possum has Medusa's Eye. Its looks can kill.'

'Ridiculous,' said Fachon. 'Medusa's Eye! Pffft!' he rasberried in a high register, like a kazoo. 'Keep searching.' He pushed forward towards another door. He needed Collins' help to pry it open. It broke away into several pieces.

The two of them floated into another room, but it was too murky to see much. Sea grass grew from a hole in the floor, where something had punctured it from beneath. Fachon managed to get tangled up in the grass. He tried to wrestle himself free, but it only made matters worse.

'Wait a minute,' said Collins, swimming over.

Fachon's headlamp flickered, then died. His monitor went dark, too. 'Merde!'

Collins inspected his helmet. 'Stop moving for a minute, will you?' He couldn't find anything out of the ordinary.

Bunny and Roger had found another room - a much larger one this time.

At the opposite end, they saw three divers, huddled together on their knees. No bubbles coming from their respirators.

'Hmmm,' said Bunny. 'This doesn't look good.'

On closer inspection, it was as anticipated - all the divers had faces frozen in fear. Their limbs were as stiff as a board.

'You getting this Lucy?' Roger held his video camera up to each one in turn.

'I see it,' she said.

Bunny was creeped out. 'This is whacked, dude. They definitely saw something they weren't supposed to.'

'It must be close,' said Collins over the radio, fiddling with Fachon's helmet. 'Whatever you do, don't look at it. It scares its food to death in order to keep it in its larder. That way there's no blood to attract other scavengers.'

'How are they supposed to find it, if they can't look at it?' I didn't see the point.

Roger scanned the area with his camera. Being a keen amateur historian, he was fascinated by the ship's construction and artefacts.

'It reminds me of this time off the coast of Australia,' said Bunny. 'I was surfing with my friend, Chip, when he got his foot taken off by a shark. You should have seen the look on his face! Just like our poor amigos here.'

'Bummer,' said Roger, as he traced his camera across a line of wood carvings.

'Total bummer! We were just about to ride this killer wave. We'd been waiting for it for hours and then it suddenly appeared.'

'What did you do?'

'Got on our boards, man. Foot or no foot, there was no way Chip was going to miss that wave! He surfed it right onto the shore. It was awesome.'

'I see it! I see it!' cried Roger, suddenly.

His camera had picked out a small, fluffy, glowing object, about four feet in circumference, floating at the other end of the room.

'Don't go near it,' said Collins. 'We're on our way.'

He gave up fussing with Fachon's helmet and gave it a sharp blow.

Fachon shouted like an angry gerbil. 'Alors! What are you doing?'

'It's kinda cute,' said Bunny, eyeing the fluffly globe.

He and Roger swam warily towards it. They could see that it had two eyes, which were tightly shut.

'Do you think it's dead?'

'No,' shouted Collins. 'That's what it does. It's only playing possum!'

Fearing the worst for Bunny and Roger, Collins hit Fachon's helmet again. The headlamp flickered back on, but not before Fachon retaliated. He hit Collins in the chest, knocking him backwards into some shelving. The shelves disintegrated on impact. They fell apart in slow-motion, followed by a low, groaning noise. Then, the ceiling collapsed, raining down debris on top of them.

As the silt began to settle, they found themselves engulfed by hundreds of floating, white globes.

'Merde,' exclaimed Fachon.

When he finally stopped thrashing around, Lucy and I got a glimpse - they were swimming in a sea of skulls.

Collins was surrounded by them. He tried to bat them gently out of the way, but there were too many. 'This must be the possum's trophy room.'

Fachon was twisting angrily in the sea grass, his torch beam glancing off the creepy skulls, which were now bobbing around him in all directions. His agitation was knocking heads together, literally. The skulls collided and bounced off one another, making a pleasant but peculiar music, like a kalimba. There wasn't anywhere else for them to go.

'Goddammnit, stop moving!' shouted Collins, at Fachon. 'You're only making it worse.' He pushed the skulls aside in an effort to get closer to him, but whatever vacuum he created was simply filled in by more skulls.

Roger laughed. Not a nervous laugh, exactly. It sounded sloppy.

He stuck out his hand and stroked the possum. 'My blossom,' he said, in childish voice.

Bunny laughed, too. 'Blossom the possum!'

They both laughed.

'Shit,' said Collins. 'They've entered the loopy zone.'

His fight to get through the skulls became more frantic now. They were everywhere - staring ghastly into space from empty eye-sockets. Their gaping jaws frozen in time, a rictus of alarm. Presumably, these poor souls were the original cargo that went down with the ship. Collins batted a bunch aside, but more kept coming.

'This is ridiculous,' said Fachon. 'I can't see anything!' He punched one to pieces. Then, another. And another. It created a small clearing, allowing Collins to get closer to him.

Collins drew his knife. 'Stop moving, or I'll end up cutting you!'

Fachon held still long enough for Collins to cut him a way out.

'Come on!' said Collins, leading the way.

* * *

Roger slapped Bunny's hand away. 'He's mine. Go get your own.'

'Come on, man,' said Bunny. 'We can share.'

Roger tried to cradle the possum protectively. 'I saw him first!'

'No, you don't understand. He needs me.'

Roger wafted next to the possum. 'Here - film us together.'

Bunny took the camera and got the shot.

'Hurry,' said Collins to Fachon, as they smashed their way through the skulls.

One of the jawbones had locked itself around Fachon's hand. He waved it about, trying to dislodge it. 'Get it off of me!'

Collins tried to calm him. 'You're using up too much air. You've got to relax.'

'Okay, now it's my turn.' Bunny took his place, passed the camera back to Roger.

Just then, the possum opened its eyes.

'Get out of there Roger!' crackled Lucy, over the radio.

Bunny pulled away, his back to the possum. 'Listen - mommy has spoken!'

He and Roger began laughing. But it grew infectious, more raucous. They couldn't stop themselves, as they were so incredibly high by now. Their laughter grew so bad that they began to choke. But this made them laugh even more. It was a vicious circle.

'Great,' said Lucy to me, 'they're going to laugh themselves to death!'

The possum turned to Roger, who was in its eye-line. Roger raised his arm, pointed at it, and began laughing even more, but this time in fear.

Bunny thought it was hysterical. 'What are you doing, man? Dude - you look like Roger Rabbit!'

By now, Fachon and Collins had escaped the trophy room and made it to the first level. Their heavy suits, although neutrally buoyant in the water, made it more difficult to cover ground at speed, especially on board the wreck. They used a combination of running, swimming, and hauling themselves along the corridors. They moved as fast as they could towards the room where Roger and Bunny faced imminent death.

Without warning, the possum popped open.

In an elegant flourish, rather like a sea anemone, the small furry orb spread out like a giant reflector, unfurling itself to over ten times its previous size, revealing endless row-upon-row of hideous, razor-sharp teeth, set in a spiral configuration. It was a marvel of biology - a marine version of a Buckminster Fuller design - that was both one of the most beautiful and one of the most terrifying visions I'd ever seen.

Lucy watched the monitors in horror. 'Mother of God!'

Roger's face contorted. Bunny tried to see what was going on, but Roger had clamped his arms around him in a vice grip, so he couldn't turn around. Nevertheless, Bunny could see what was happening in the reflection of the glass from Roger's helmet. It snapped him out of the loopy zone.

He wrestled Roger towards the exit. 'Don't look at it, man. Close your good eye!'

But Roger didn't, or couldn't - although, his end may have been prolonged on account of him having only one, good eye. Perhaps, he got only half the Medusa affect. Even so, he was mesmerised by the sight of what had now become a giant balloon of death.

Bunny pulled with all his might. He could see the possum tracking them, almost teasing, like it was playing with its food.

Collins and Fachon burst into the room, and grabbed Bunny, careful not to look directly at the possum.

Collins tried to separate Bunny from Roger. 'Let him go, Bunny, - he's gone.' It was true. Roger had been frozen by fear.

'I can't,' said Bunny. 'He's locked onto me.'

The three of them scrambled towards the exit in slow motion. Running scared underwater was like escaping from a nightmare - one where you want to scream, but no sound comes; and you try to run, but your legs refuse to cooperate.

They were possum bait.

Lucy raced into the airlock and suited up.

'What are you doing?' I said.

'I've got to help them spring the trap.'

There was no point in arguing. I slammed the door and spun the wheel, following the protocol I'd seen earlier.

'Hurry!' she cried. She hadn't even put her helmet on.

'I'm hurrying!'

I filled the chamber with seawater as fast as the pumps would allow. She secured her helmet just as the water reached her shoulders, and was out the door like a shot.

I checked her monitor. All systems were working.

She went straight for the trap.'How far are they?'

Judging from what I could see on their monitors, they were getting close. But so was the possum.

Collins was madly dumping cereal. It seemed to be working. He closed his eyes and spun around, so I could confirm it to him.

'Yep! He's eating it,' I said. 'Keep it coming, though. I think he likes it a little too much.'

But Collins had run out. He grabbed some of Fachon's cereal and dumped it all at once, in a cloud behind them. The three of them broke through the hole in the hull, grabbing the sides and catapulting themselves forward.

'Lucy, remove the safety lock!' shouted Collins.

Lucy ran her fingers over the button and found it covered by a metal flap. She pulled it back. 'Primed!'

The possum burst through the hull. Then, hesitated. There were several targets. It considered who to follow first, who to devour. It settled on Collins.

'It's after you, Collins!' I said.

For some reason, I could watch the possum on a video monitor without being affected by the Medusa Stare, but the others had to avoid eye-contact.

Lucy shut her eyes and swivelled her head-camera towards the possum. 'Tell me when to fire the trap.'

Collins reached the trap and hovered over it. The possum stopped. It could sense something was wrong. 'What's happening?'

'I think he's spooked,' I said. 'He isn't taking the bait.'

Collins emptied the cereal bags that he'd weighted to the trap, earlier. The cereal surrounded him in a mist. The possum undulated its teeth. I presume the cereal had whet its appetite. It looked like it wanted more, but was unsettled by the trap, below. He was a shrewd one, this possum.

Collins was desperate. 'We've got to drive him into the trap!'

We had run out of options.

I suddenly remembered. 'The grenade! Roger's eyeball. It's a grenade!'

Bunny knew what he had to do. It was a horrible thing to ask. He looked down at his poor, dead friend. If it had been anyone other than Bunny, we'd be toast.

'Sorry, bud,' said Bunny, as he unlocked Roger's helmet. He had trouble digging out the eyeball with his glove. 'Wait a minute.' He pulled out his knife.

Collins didn't think the possum would hold his position much longer. 'Hurry!'

'Sorry about this man,' said Bunny, again to the corpse, as he pried out Roger's eyeball. After an agonising few seconds, the eyeball popped out. Bunny tried to catch it, but the gloves made him clumsy, and he missed. He managed to bounce the eyeball on his knee and knock it back upwards, giving him a second chance. This time he caught it.

'There's a button,' I said, 'On the back. Press it. You've got 10 seconds!'

Bunny searched for the button. He could barely see what he was doing and he couldn't feel it through his gloves.

The possum's undulating teeth grew more frenzied. It turned itself around in Bunny's direction.

'Hurry!' shouted Lucy.

'I'm trying!' said Bunny. 'Jellyfish, jellyfish, jellyfish, jellyfish…' He fiddled with it, pressing wildly, until he felt something 'click'. The eyeball was primed. 'Got it!'

Now what? There was no way he was going to swim up to the possum with a loaded grenade.

Bunny shrugged. 'And, I'm *really* sorry about this, dude!' He popped the eyeball back in Roger's socket and gave the corpse a hard shove.

Roger's body floated for awhile towards the rear of the possum. Thankfully, he was neutrally buoyant and kept on course.

The possum was distracted by Roger's corpse, as it floated towards him. It gnashed its teeth in anticipation.

That's when the eyeball exploded.

It didn't make any noise. We just saw a small flash. Then, Roger's body burst outwards in all directions, like raspberry chum, in a sea of glass bubbles.

Bunny was knocked downwards, hitting his helmet, sharply, on a piece of timber from the boat.

The shockwave did the trick, however. The possum was blown towards Collins.

'Now!' I cried.

Lucy pulled Collins downwards and hit the button. The possum was engulfed in a flood of bubbles. None of us could see what was going on.

'Did it work?' shouted Collins.

'I can't see anything. Wait a minute,' I said.

The bubbles gradually cleared, followed by a stillness. A red haze refracted the light, creating a rainbow of colours. Roger's rainbow. It cast a kaleidoscope lighting effect on everything around us. Sadly, it was beautiful. But now was not the time to reflect on it.

The trap had sprung a giant net via charges, but the net hung flaccid in the water.

The possum was gone.

I didn't want to relay the bad news, but there was be a clear and present danger.

Then, I noticed something very small, something fluffy, at the bottom of the trap. The possum had shrunk to its original size.

'It's there!' I cried. 'We got it!'

Collins grabbed the ends of the netting and pulled them together, snapping them in place with small, metal anchors.

Bunny was hurt. Perhaps, a minor concussion. He was also quieter than usual, which is saying something, given he was a man of few words. I think Roger's death had affected him more than he cared to admit. They had been close. From what I understand, they'd even joined Collins' crew at the same time, all those years ago. Perhaps the death was too fresh to register. There would be time enough to dwell on it later. That's when the hurt comes.

Fachon decompressed alongside Bunny in the sub's ante-chamber. Fachon had suggested that Lucy and Collins bring the possum to the surface in the other sub, after they secured their catch, since their sub was equipped with a tank expressly for that purpose.

Fachon told me to surface ours in the meantime.

I didn't feel comfortable leaving Lucy and Collins behind - especially, alone with the sea possum. 'Shouldn't we wait for the others?'

'Bunny's in a bad way,' said Fachon, from the decompression chamber. 'He might need medical attention. We can decompress here in the meantime. Just get us topside.'

I did as I was told. But it didn't feel right. What if there was something wrong with the other sub? We might not be able to make it back down in time.

Fachon peered through the decompression window and talked me through the controls.

I lifted us out of there.

LOST AT SEA

We had another surprise waiting for us topside.

The rest of Fachon's crew. They weren't dead, after all.

And they were armed.

When the first sortie had failed to get the possum, Fachon had ordered the rest of them into hiding. His plan was to use Collins to get the possum and, then, leave us in the lurch.

Which, he did.

He didn't want us crashing his party at the big event dinner and scuppering his chance to become the next Steel Chef. Kuromizu's rendezvous was in forty-eight hours and he wasn't taking any chances.

Collins, Lucy, Bunny, and I were left overboard to fend for ourselves in one of the subs - sans power, I might add. Two of Fachon's crew smashed the controls, just to be sure.

'I'm sorry that it must be this way,' said Fachon, unapologetically. 'I must win the competition. That means *cooking* the animals, mister Collins.' He was clearly lording it up, now that he had the upper hand. 'You,' he said directly to Collins, 'are a not on the guest list.' He cut loose our safety wire. 'Bonne chance.'

We watched Fachon's ship merge with the horizon. We were all exhausted from our near-death experience. Roger was dead. Bunny was recovering, but emotionally listless. And, now, we were adrift in the middle of the Bermuda Triangle.

It couldn't possibly get any worse.

'Don't worry,' said Collins. 'Gaia will help us.'

I was tired of hearing his same old mantra. 'How will Gaia help us?'

'She said so.'

'No, Collins. You had a dream. A bloody dream in which a friggin' deer head told you to save the planet.' I was desperate. Overwhelmed. And I felt seasick from the rollicking waves. Our sub was bobbing on the surface like a cork in a swell. I no longer had the strength to argue.

Collins smiled like a buddha. 'I don't expect you to understand. She didn't call on you. You are not the Chosen One.'

I wanted to wring Collins' neck.

'Let's focus first on staying alive as long as possible,' said Lucy, pragmatically. 'Bunny, what supplies have we got?'

'We still have some boxes of Captain Munch. If we ration it, maybe two, three days, tops.'

Great. So, we'd spend the next couple of days eating cereal. And, then, after that, probably eating one another.

I saw a bar of soap that Roger had carved into a manta ray during our descent. It made me feel an immense sense of loss. We hadn't been emotionally close, but I had gotten to know him better than most of my so-called friends. We had been through hell and back - and, now, he was fish food at the bottom of the ocean. I wanted to hide his sculpture somewhere where Bunny wouldn't find it, but it was no good. We were too close together. In the end, I dropped it in a puddle of water and watched it slowly disintegrate. I felt bad doing this. It was our last connection to Roger, but I thought it was for the best.

'Thanks,' said Lucy, after a few hours at sea, 'for the grenade. You really came through.'

'Sure,' I said, without much conviction. 'But thank Bunny. He's the hero.'

It was nice to have her praise, but what good would that do now? Besides, I wasn't in a mood to make up. She had wounded my pride on a number of occasions. It was better to play hard to get. Not that it mattered much now. We weren't going anywhere.

Bunny was listening to his iPod, sharing one of his earbuds with Collins, who was lying back with his eyes closed. Lucy was dividing up the cereal into equal amounts. She liked to keep herself busy.

I was agitated. The sub was tiny. We had the access hatch open for some air, but otherwise it was terribly close quarters. I didn't want to just sit and wait. Instead, I mulled over the events of the past few months.

'What's with the rabbit foot?' I said. Lucy looked up at me. 'Back in the jungle. Collins called you his lucky rabbit foot?'

'Not me,' said Lucy. 'His prosthetic. He thinks it brings him luck.'

'Then why did he say he owed you one? Back in the jungle.'

'I gave it to him.'

'Gave him what?'

'His leg. It was a birthday present.'

'You gave him a prosthetic leg for his birthday?'

'I felt responsible for what had happened to him that day.' She stopped what she was doing and looked at me sincerely. 'I know what you think. But I didn't do it. Not on purpose. It *was* my responsibility to check that everything was safe and ready. I didn't.'

'Why not?'

'We had an argument.' It sounded like she wanted to get something off her chest. Perhaps, she figured that this was the end. If so, it was better to make peace before facing the abyss. 'He asked me to marry him.'

So, she fed him to the croc. Christ! Remind me never to make the same mistake.

'Was the thought of marriage to Chuck that bad?' I said, looking for an opening.

'I didn't want to be tied down. I had a career. I wanted to prove myself. I had a plan.' She smiled, wistfully. 'But nothing with Chuck goes according to plan. It's exhilarating. Exciting.

Terrifying. Everything happens whenever he's around. You can't help getting sucked in.'

'I know what you mean.'

'Except, he's a terrible force of nature. It's all about himself, his cause - his ego. He didn't complete me.' She thought for words. 'He consumed me. Do you understand?'

I believe I did. In some ways, he was similar to my friend Roger, from school. He lived at high speed. The rest of us were just along for the ride. It was hard to get off. But, if you didn't, you'd end up in a car crash. 'I understand,' I said, sincerely.

I left Lucy alone with her thoughts and looked out the window. We'd probably last a week without food and water. It was going to be a very slow and excruciating crash, indeed.

The first few hours were doleful. The next twelve, we spent in a funk. Some of us tried to sleep. Collins sat meditating. And humming. He told me he had to conserve his essence. What a ponce!

His humming grew louder and more irritating.

'Please,' I snapped, 'you're driving me bonkers!'

Collins didn't stop.

I grabbed him by the neck. 'Right, that's it!'

'Wait!' Lucy grabbed my hands. 'Listen!'

The humming was now very loud. It couldn't be coming from Collins. I knew this, because I had cut off his air supply. His face was now blue. I released my grip. It was unmistakable. It was an aircraft of some kind. I eagerly popped my head up through the hatch and scanned the skies.

'I see it! A helicopter!' I waved my arms frantically in the air. I ripped off my shirt and used it as a flag. The helicopter circled around, then spotted me. 'It's coming! It's coming!'

The blast of the rotor blades hit me like an air cannon. I could see a life-line with a harness dropping down from a winch. It swung tantalisingly close, but too far to grab.

I leapt and missed, splashing down in the water. The harness bobbed nearby. I wrestled it around me and was lifted skyward. I looked down at the sub and felt a pang of regret. It was an unexpected sensation. In my eagerness to save my own skin, I had left the others behind. I realised, then, that I'd been selfish. No matter how badly I wanted to kill them sometimes, they were the only friends I'd got.

In the helicopter, I was met by De Konig.

He wasn't happy. 'Where's Fachon?'

'He abandoned us.'

'And Chuck?'

'He's on the sub.'

De Konig nodded and dropped the line back down towards the sub. Someone gave me a blanket. I realised then how cold I was.

Lucy was next. She was given a blanket, too.

After Bunny came aboard, De Konig secured the life-line.

Lucy looked down. 'What about Chuck?'

Collins waited patiently, below. From up high, he looked small and precarious, standing on the sub, reaching out to us with outstretched arms.

De Konig was unrepentant. 'Let Gaia save him.'

Lucy was horrified. 'How can you be so cruel?'

'Why? He did the same to me.'

'That was different,' said Lucy. 'He had to make a choice.'

'Well, now I'm making mine.'

De Konig ordered the pilot to head home.

Lucy was spitting mad. 'How can you be so heartless? He did what he had to do to save us. All of us. It was a difficult decision for him to make.'

'How difficult?' De Konig seemed genuinely curious.

'Why don't you ask him yourself!'

De Konig was pensive. He looked at Lucy, then at the sky. After a moment, he tapped the pilot on the shoulder, and made a circular motion with his finger in the air. The pilot banked the copter back around.

'I wanted to see him squirm a little,' he said.

Collins was dragged aboard like a wet sponge. He looked at De Konig in silence. De Konig refused to look at him once, the entire ride.

We landed on the helipad of a large, well-equipped, military boat.

'I see you're doing well,' said Collins, finally.

'It's not mine,' said De Konig. 'It belongs to the boss.'

Collins poked a finger at him. 'Ha Ha! Made you talk!'

De Konig shook his head and walked away. He didn't care for such childish games.

We weren't exactly treated like regular guests. Instead, we were escorted at gunpoint in pairs to separate cabins, which were locked behind us. Bunny and I were bunking together by the looks of it. I showered and changed into the fatigues that had been laid out on my bunk. After an hour, or so, someone rapped on our door. We were greeted by two mercenaries with automatic weapons. 'Time to go,' said one of them.

They escorted us to a larger room inside the ship. Lucy and Collins were already there, waiting, when we arrived. The soldiers didn't leave us, but sat on the side, guns in their laps, pointing in our direction.

De Konig entered crisply, making the men stand to attention. 'Leave us,' he ordered. They did as they were told.

De Konig took his time. We waited in anticipation.

Finally, he spoke.

'I've always hated you Chuck. Not because you caused the death of father. I was angry at you for a long time after that. It was because you were always his favourite. No matter what I did, I never earned his praise. Unlike you. I did everything he asked of me. I dealt in his dirty side business… the poaching, gutting, stuffing, trading with criminals. I have a lot of blood on my hands, thanks to you. I hate you because you always thought you were better.'

'I'm on a mission from Gaia,' said Collins, without irony.

Lucy swatted him. 'Now is not the time, Chuck.'

'No,' said De Konig, 'now IS the time. You are too bloody proud, brother. It is always the animals. Nothing but the animals. They hate you, brother. But you treat them with more respect than your own kin. People die around you everyday, yet here you remain. Stubborn to the last.'

The two men looked into each others eyes. A quiet stand off.

The penny dropped.

'It was you,' said Lucy, suddenly. Something had clicked for her, but - whatever it was - the rest of us weren't up to speed.

De Konig ignored her and addressed the rest of us. 'Do you hear what I am saying? He will lead you to your ruin. You are all marked for death.'

'It was you, who burned down Animal Land!' Lucy was certain of it.

De Konig considered his response. 'Yes.'

'Why?' said Collins, stunned.

De Konig shook his head. 'I was paid to do it.'

'By whom? Fachon?'

'No,' said De Konig, 'Kuromizu.'

We were all stunned. Nobody said a word.

De Konig sat on the edge of a table, resigned to tell all. 'He knew you were a liability when it came to the competition. You were the wildcard, the idealist. You were investigating him at the time. He also wanted your animals.'

'My animals?'

'Yes. Animal Land was like a giant supermarket to him. Lots of exotic species, ripe for the poaching. We started the fire to cover our tracks.'

'So, you're working for Kuromizu,' said Lucy. 'Not Fachon? You're a double-agent!'

'I have always been working for Kuromizu. This is his ship. These are his men. He never intended for Fachon to get to the finish line. He knew he would pose the fiercest competition. I was meant to frustrate his plans, so I kept him close, and informed Kuromizu of his movements. Made sure that he would be beaten every time. But then, somebody dropped me off the side of a mountain.' He looked angrily at Collins.

Collins was ready for action. 'We must stop the competition. Join me in my cause, brother! You owe me.'

'I owe you nothing,' said De Konig angrily. 'I did what I did gladly. I was good at what I did. Dad never appreciated my talents. All he ever spoke about was you. When Kuromizu asked me to destroy your fantasy, I did it gladly. I was angry at your success. And, because no matter what I did, father loved you more.' De Konig seemed deflated by his confession.

Collins laid a hand gently on his shoulder. 'I forgive you, brother.'

De Konig cracked. 'I - I worked for six whole weeks… six weeks on a gazelle portmanteau. It had horn drawers with French dovetail joins. Hand-stitched hide. I lovingly crafted every inch. Sanded the bone to make handles for the drawers. It was my masterpiece. It was a present for Dad. But he never appreciated my gift. He gave it to an exporter the very next day, as a bribe for future business.' De Konig had tears in his eyes. 'He would never have done that to you. Never to you!'

I've rarely seen a grown man cry except, perhaps, during a body waxing, but I saw it now. De Konig sobbed, while he enveloped Collins in a bear hug. It was uncomfortable to watch.

De Konig wiped his tears. 'Sorry. Something happened to me. Out there. On the mountain.'

'What happened?'

'I -' De Konig looked like he was about to start the waterworks again. 'I discovered love.' Collins patted him, gently.

'A pure act of selflessness,' continued De Konig. A memory worked itself to the surface of his brain. He was back on the mountain, in the Himalayan cave, carving up the meat of the dead snow goat mother and her calves, eating their meat, scraping their skins. He stood framed in the doorway, wearing their pelts to keep warm, before setting out onto the mountain, back to civilisation.

'A sacrifice,' said De Konig, wistfully. 'I have never experienced anything like it before.'

'Now you understand,' said Collins. 'You are one with Gaia.'

'I will help you, Chuck,' said De Konig. 'Kuromizu is not what he seems. This competition is only the beginning. He has something planned that is far worse than you can imagine.'

'What is it?' implored Collins.

'I don't know. It is far worse than I can imagine. But I have seen his organisation up close. It is evil. Pure evil. And well organised. He has vast resources and he has been using his position as the head of the Council to feed his evil empire. This is why he protects it at all cost.'

'What now?' said Lucy.

'You must escape,' said De Konig.

'Escape?' You must be joking, I thought.   We were on a military boat full of mercenaries, out at sea.

'I will help you,' continued De Konig. 'I know where they are rounding up the animals for the competition. At a secret airbase. You will meet me there and I will smuggle you onboard the aircraft.'

KUROMIZU AIRWAYS

De Konig had the whole thing figured out.

When we were within cruising distance of the shore, he deposited us in a dinghy with an outboard motor, which we were instructed not to start until we were well out of earshot. He'd tell the others he'd executed us, and thrown us overboard.

We were cast back into the sea - for the second time in one day. We watched ourselves get left behind by Kuromizu's ship. When the sun sank, we figured it was safe under cover of nightfall, and we motored to shore.

It took us a few hours to reach Turks and Caicos. And, then, another day to reach Cuba - our final destination. We had to pay off a dodgy pilot to smuggle us in. Thankfully, De Konig had given us money. We were reamed by all the go-betweens, however, on account of our clandestine entrance - without passports, or legitimate purpose. In the end, we spent everything we had to get to the airbase.

The airfield was not well-secured, otherwise we'd have trouble getting in. There was a lot of activity, though, the night we arrived. Private jets, helicopters, and a bevy of Bentleys, Maybachs, and other assorted high-end vehicles, were dotted about the largest hangar. We got lucky when one of the guests took a detour to seduce his date, without taking his security detail along with him. We planned to steal his tickets and their clothes.

When I struck the fellow on the back of the neck, he turned to look at me as if he'd just been stung by a bee.

Lucy decked him with a spanner.

The date turned out to be a prostitute, who was happy to be tied up, so long as we gave her the contents of the man's wallet. There was enough cash in there to keep her off the streets for awhile. She planned to take her daughter on a vacation to Florida.

The man's dinner suit was a decent fit. Lucy looked amazing in the prostitute's clothes. Her skirt was exceedingly short.

'I approve,' I said, cheekily.

'Wipe that smirk off your face,' she said. 'We've got work to do.'

Once inside, we mingled with the other guests, until we found an emergency exit to sneak in Bunny and Collins. That's when we found out where all the security was. They were dotted around the inner periphery of the hangar, with automatic weapons slung low, swapping cigarettes and smalltalk.

The hangar had various exotic animals on display. Here, the diners could see what they were paying to eat. It reminded me of a black-tie version of "Mange Zoo".

The iridescent sea possum was in an enormous fish tank. Special, dark glasses were on hand to allow it to be inspected without it killing anyone. Fachon paraded nearby, in full chef regalia, like a proud parent. His razor eagle eggs were in a gold bowl, kissed by black velvet. Two other chefs displayed their catch. Even Chae was in on the act - now dressed as Kuromizu's sous-chef.

Collins was perturbed by what he saw. 'Two Velocarabbits, a snaggle-toothed platypus, a vulture penguin, albino air leeches, and an Anaerobic Tiger-tailed Viper! And those are just the starters. This is a disaster!'

'They're goose isn't cooked yet,' placated Lucy. She saw De Konig and some men crating up the critters. They were having trouble with a Scorpion Leopard. It wasn't happy to be incarcerated and it swung its barbed tail at them, but they had come prepared with riot shields and cattle prods. They forced it back into its cage. 'We've got to let De Konig know we're here,' said Lucy, slipping in amongst the crowd. I had no choice but to join her.

All of the dinner guests were wearing black tie. Like a box of Quality Street, they came in all sorts: Russian gangsters, African dictators, Latin American industrialists, Chinese ministers, investment bankers, and the last host of American Idol. Basically, anyone with ten million on hand to dine at the culinary equivalent of the Olympics. Their taste was dubious and their wealth comfortably overstated. They were busy inspecting one another about as much as the ingredients on the menu. Whenever I came under scrutiny, I pretended to be from New Zealand. That way, nobody would care enough to ask questions.

To get to De Konig, we'd risk being seen by Kuromizu. I didn't think he'd recognise me, as he'd had a lot going on last time we met. But he and Lucy had traded words, which made her harder to hide. We took our time, perusing the exotic and endangered species at leisure.

I stopped at one of the cages. 'What's with the hamster?'

'The Mesocricetus Vampir Auratus,' said Lucy.

'What's that in English?'

'Vampire teddy-bear hamster. Very vicious.'

I looked at them afresh. Cute and cuddly, until they go for the jugular.

I stole a look over at Kuromizu and noticed that Chae was staring right at me. I gripped Lucy's arm and spoke under my breath. 'Don't look now, but I think we've been rumbled.' Lucy bent down to examine the cage, letting her hair fall to obscure her face. Chae leant into Kuromizu and whispered something in his ear. Whatever it was, he straightened up and clapped his hands for attention.

'Esteemed ladies and gentlemen. Now that you've had a good look at our fresh ingredients, it's time to prepare for the evening's main event.'

I could see Bunny and Collins break cover from behind a cargo box, so I looked over at Chae. She was still staring straight at me.

Kuromizu continued. 'I realise that some of you have had a long journey, but our final destination is still some hours away. I have taken the liberty of providing a suitable aircraft, which will take us all to dinner.' He let his eyes fall on each and every guest in turn, finally resting on me. 'Please have your tickets ready to show security. There will be plenty of refreshments and canapés aboard. My staff are only too happy to service your every request during the journey.'

With that, a beauty pageant of women in fashionable, flight uniforms appeared. They dispersed amongst us and led us towards the waiting plane.

'This way, please,' said one of them, to Lucy and I, as she took my elbow.

Kuromizu was already on his way to the plane. I looked back at Collins and shrugged. We had no choice but to follow.

Collins managed to make contact with De Konig, who had spiked two of his men with a doped syringe, and hid them inside one of the cargo boxes. 'Quick, take their clothes,' he said.

Dressed like mercenaries, Collins and Bunny helped De Konig load the crate aboard the rear of the plane. I saw them go in, as I mounted the gangway of the large aircraft with the rest of the guests.

'Feels like we're walking the plank,' I said, to Lucy, who shushed me. 'You do realise,' I continued, 'that now we have to make small talk with some of the worst men in the world?'

'You'll be in your element, then.'

'And what about Fachon?' I said. 'What happens when we run into him?'

Lucy didn't answer.

'Tickets, please,' said a cute stewardess, before handing mine over to an ugly goon behind her. He scrutinised them carefully, then gave Lucy and I the twice over, before handing them back, as if they were a fresh turd. Another fellow waved a metal detecting wand over us. I could see a silver platter laden with firearms that had been confiscated from the other guests for safe keeping. It was quite an assortment of handguns and automatic weapons. There was even a grenade. The fellow seemed somewhat crestfallen that we hadn't anything interesting on us.

'I left my grenades at home,' I said, apologetically.

We entered the plane. The seats were set very far apart. More so than first class. No luxury had been spared. There was a proper silver service and the finest champagne. Lucky for us, Fachon, Kuromizu and the rest of the chefs were in the upper deck. Apparently, they took the canapé preparations very seriously.

I tried to avoid the food I was given for as long as I could, not knowing what was in them, but Lucy forced my hand. 'They'll get suspicious.'

I picked up a puffed-pastry filled with something that looked like pâté, capers, and snot.

'Cream of Albino Air Leech,' explained the hostess.

'Oh, wonderful! I hear the air leech is very good for your complexion,' said a man opposite us, with an enormous scar across his face.

'Here, have mine,' I offered. He was only too thankful.

'Yummy,' exclaimed Lucy, as she deposited it surreptitiously into the barf bag in the seat pocket in-front of her.

Down in the hold, Collins stuck close to De Konig and tried not to make small talk with the other wranglers, animal handlers, and assorted mercenaries that kept vigil over their catches. Bunny, however, bummed a tranquilliser dart off another tracker and shot himself up. 'I get airsick on long flights - especially, when they crash-land into the ocean,' he said. It wasn't long before he was sleeping like a baby.

Collins took the opportunity to do a head-count of the animals. How in the world was he supposed to get all of them to safety? And without anyone else knowing? He hoped they were going somewhere with a good exit opportunity, because he had no idea how to fly a Boeing 747.

THE MAIN EVENT

The flight was an estimated sixteen hours.

Lucy and I had watched every in-flight movie. We started off with the latest hits, then the classics. By the end, she was left watching "Rambo 2", while I saw, "Dirty Dancing".

It had come to this.

I had gotten to know a few of the other guests during the flight. Dictators can be very charming, when they're not busy killing people. Naturally, we didn't have much in common. I don't have ten wives, sixty-carat rings, or a hundred million dollar estate in the Caymans. Nor do I have a staffing problem post-genocide. But I did my best to come across as if I was meant to be here. Truth be told, I was enjoying myself.

I remembered Lucy's words back in the Silver Spoon, when she said that my neighbourhood invasion wasn't the real rich, I understood now what she meant. These were the real rich, part of the super-elite. Far above the one-percenters, these were the shadow-class, the ones who pulled the strings of power. They were the ones that controlled the flow of global capital and kept if for themselves.

The only odd man out was a Russian banker and his wife who'd received their tickets as a gift from Putin - a thank you for helping him make forty billion in assets disappear throughout Europe and the Far East. They thought the affair was exceedingly glamorous and got themselves a bit too tipsy. So much so, that they were cut off at one point, after drawing disapproving looks from the others. The wife went to the loo first and failed to come back. Her husband went in search of her, but didn't return, either. I never saw either of them again.

I could see that I'd need to tread carefully. This was an exclusive members-only club of the highest order. Discretion was mandatory. I needed to understand them in order to blend in and stay alive. Ironically, they didn't look significantly different from the general population, which made the invasion more insidious. Their clothes and accessories were more expensive, sure, but they had no distinguishing features. They had come from different backgrounds, different countries, had different accents - but their outlook was the same. They belonged to an international elite that transcended geographical boundaries.

There was a time when people had security in the class system. You knew where you stood in society. The upper classes wore different clothes, funny hats, and spoke with peculiar accents. They attended silly sporting events and interbred with their cousins. They kept things close and in the family. Their world was unobtainable. You may not have liked it, but your life was already mapped out for you. If you weren't born of nobility, you'd never be a member of the ruling class - and you probably wouldn't want to be, either. You were made to feel like an outsider. You couldn't buy your way up the social ladder, even though many tried. You followed in your father's footsteps, or took an apprenticeship somewhere - and settled. The hierarchy was understood. It gave people purpose. The underclass adjusted their dreams accordingly, and got on with their lives.

But not any more. Now, it's a free-for-all. The nobility are asset rich, but cash poor. Their parties and social gatherings seem quaint and shabby. Davos is the new power-party of the future, and it's not patroned by toffs. They aren't allowed in anymore. This is the Age of the Uber-class.

Many of the Uber-class aren't privileged by birth. They come from all walks of life. They worked hard and feel entitled to it. And they look down on anyone else who hasn't achieved what they have. They believe that opportunity is open to all and there for the taking. This type of thinking puts enormous pressure on the rest of us. If you don't succeed, you must be retarded, right? After all, anyone can do it. Unfortunately, for many of us, the belief in social mobility has only brought infinite choice and endless anxiety. Paralysed by choice. A deer caught in the headlights, before it gets hit by a truck.

After contemplating the "Happiness Quotient", I learnt that the wealth gap is widening at an alarming rate. Across the planet, this highly-mobile, transglobal group of industrious men and women, pocketed the lion share of every nation's gross domestic product. In America, for example, the one-percenters captured close to ninety percent of all income growth throughout the first decade of the millenium.

The bankers were the most conspicous. Barrow boys who'd worked they way up from the East End to the City. They didn't need to apologise for their wealth. They enjoyed rubbing people's noses in it. I don't hate bankers, mind you, although some of them make it easy. I'd met some decent ones over the years. But good people can do bad things. It doesn't take a predisposition towards evil. It just takes the right conditions.

The problem was they belonged to a odious fraternity. At the top were the merchant bankers - the ones with the least amount of scruples. They enjoyed the game of musical chairs and made sure that they had somewhere to sit when the music stopped, while the rest of us fell on our butts. But to feed their insatiable appetite, they needed an army of yes-men. They hired the hungry and gave them obscene paycheques - a prevention against moral conscience. But, every once and awhile, they couldn't help snagging one with a backbone. An occupational hazard. So, they devised a system of authority and punishment that demanded allegiance by permitting bad behaviour. Eventually, it broke people down and moulded them to their mission. They encouraged their ranks to treat one another badly and, by extension, the rest of the population.

The only fly in the ointment is that you might actually know the person you're hurting. If you cared about them, it could mess with your brainwashing, and undo years of submission training, upsetting the hierarchy. So, to improve the rate of rape, they made sure that there was absolutely no connection between the related parties. They divvied up debt, sliced it, diced it, diversified it, then spread it to the far corners of the globe. No relationship, no culpability. If you didn't know who you were screwing, it was easier to screw them. It was an orgy of greed. What is a derivative, if nothing more than a complex way of obfuscating who's screwing whom?

You may wonder how good people can be made to do bad things. We've seen it often enough in wartime. But it doesn't take war to test the wills of better men. It simply takes a persistent culture of obedience to bad-behaviour that you ratchet up, little-by-little. If you want to boil a frog, you do it gradually and by degrees. It doesn't realise it's cooked, until it's too late. It's the same with people. Take a look at the Milgram experiment of the nineteen-sixties. Ordinary people can be made to do unconscionable things. All you need is someone telling them that greed is good.

Bankers are lobsters. But, then again, they are merely the footsoldiers of the super-elite. In fact, the gap between the top one-percent of the one-percenters is greater than that between the one-percenters and the rest of the population. In other words, there is a greater divide between the super-rich and the merely wealthy. It's sobering to consider that the combined incomes of two men - Buffett and Gates - is greater than the earnings of half the US population.

There are an estimated thirty million millionaires in the world, but only eighty-five thousand of whom have more than one hundred million in assets. These are the top one percent of the one-percenters. The ones who run the globe. They live in a bubble, divorced from common existence. They have no idea what real life is like anymore for anyone else. Their wealth and power give them permission to behave as badly as they want. They can do anything to anyone without repercussion. They encourage bad behaviour in others. Their ignorance is trumped only by arrogance. Their crime against humanity is their indifference.

They don't have to worry about getting a seat when the music stops. They make the music.

And this is where they came for dinner and a bit of light entertainment.

In the meantime, Lucy and I were stuffed, having succumbed to the endless canapés.

'Don't tell Chuck,' she said, finally. 'He most definitely would not approve.'

'Look around and remember these people,' I said, to her. 'These are your future donors, for Animal Land Two. Do you think they'd write you a cheque, no questions asked?'

'I suppose you're right,' she admitted. 'It was a dangerous idea.'

'I think we'll need a back-up plan.'

'We?' she smiled. 'Does this mean what I think it does?'

'Either it was a figure of speech, or I might have had a change of heart,' I said, smiling back. 'Or, it could be indigestion.'

The cabin lights were dimmed to allow the guests to snooze for the remaining five hours. I took Lucy's hand. She was startled by the gesture.

'You know,' I said, 'I think I'm going to be sad when this is all over.'

She went mock-serious. 'And why is that, Trevor?'

'Because I consider you a friend.'

'You're not going to get progressively weird on me, are you?'

'I'm trying to be sincere.'

'Don't try too hard, or it doesn't work.'

'I will miss you. Bunny, too. Even, Collins - although he's clinically insane. All of you.'

'Are you planning on going somewhere? It's not over yet, you know.'

'We might not make it out alive.'

'Is this when you talk like a condemned man and then ask me to join you in the mile-high club?'

'Why, are you game?'

'No. I'm scared shitless. Aren't you?'

'Yes - but sometimes that makes me horny.'

'Trevor,' she said seriously, 'there you go again.'

'Yes, I know. Taking advantage of the last girl at the dance.' I looked around at the other women. They looked as if they'd eat you alive. 'You're worth it,' I said. 'You're by far the prize.'

'You're selfish, yet sentimental. A conflicting combination.'

'So I've been told.' I let go of her hand. 'You're a pretty smooth operator, yourself. You say you're scared, but you've won everyone over without even breaking a sweat.'

'I've known people like this all my life,' she said, thoughtfully. 'They used to come to parties and stay at the house. I had to blend in to survive. It wasn't easy. My mother was the cook and my father the butler, but he died when I was too young to remember. Our employer was very generous. He paid for my boarding school education. It wasn't until I was a teenager that I learnt that he was my biological father.'

'Mr Keller.'

'Yes. He had many wives, but many more mistresses.'

'An insatiable appetite. But, then again, your mother was a cook, so that must have been a good match. They say that the way to a man's heart is through his stomach.'

'He had no heart, only a stomach. When I returned home before heading off to university, it was the worst four months of my life. He wanted to play daddy. I didn't like it. I may have been born into privilege, but only by force. It wasn't earned. As for my mother, she stopped talking to me as her own, addressed me as her employer's daughter. She had used my time away to cement her emotional distance. I was very upset about this, for the longest time. She believed that there was a natural order to things, that she had been given a gift, but now it was time let it go and allow me to fulfil my own destiny. She died while I was at Uni.'

'It sounds very Dickensian.'

'Yes, I suppose it was. It made me very angry. I was terrible to my mother and even worse to mister Keller. I can forgive my mother. She was probably heart-broken, but lacked ambition. She was a simple woman. She thought it for the best. But Keller, I can't forgive. He toyed with her affection, then went back to treating her as a servant. He believed that by virtue of his fortune, he could do as he pleased. He had made a lot of money in construction, often by destroying breathtaking beauty, in order to build shopping malls and other monstrosities in developing countries. He had to wine and dine many politically important, but morally bankrupt people. He probably imagined himself doing it in the name of progress. I knew better. He did it for the money.' She had been speaking to the air before, but turned to face me when she said this. The subtext was not lost on me and I regretted what I had said in the past. The truth was, I liked the company of crazy people more than the normal ones. I could fit in their company. They reminded me of my old neighbourhood. I preferred them much more to the smug, self-righteous wankers who replaced them. She was tarnishing me, now, with the same brush.

'Look, Lucy,' I pleaded, 'I know how it sounds, but I'm actually very grateful that you found me when you did.'

'Is that so?' she wasn't convinced.

'It's true. I was angry, myself. That's the only way I can explain it. I was doing everything I could to screw the establishment.'

'Literally.'

'Okay,' I laughed, 'I deserved that. Francesca was a phase. I didn't believe in anything, or anybody. I liked taking the piss. It's going to sound schmaltzy, but I feel as if I finally have family now.'

She reached out in front of her. 'Where's my barf bag!'

'Stop. Please. I mean it. I have never really been a part of anything, because I never really believed in anything. Until now. Thank you for including me in this.'

'You're welcome. Although, you said it yourself, our chances of survival are slim.'

'It was worth it in the end.'

Okay, maybe that was laying it on a bit thick, but I meant what I said. She smiled, patted my arm, then grabbed her pillow and nestled into her seat.

We took turns sleeping. We didn't want to be completely

wiped when we landed.

When the pre-landing announcement was made, I looked out the window to see where we were, but it was too dark and foggy to figure anything out. Wherever it was, there weren't many lights on the ground. By the time we disembarked, most of the guests were getting their second wind. There was a renewed, frisson of excitement. I stepped out onto the mobile stairs that met the plane. We were greeted by an enormous military parade. It took me a moment to recognise the uniforms, but, when I did, it filled me with dread.

'Lucy,' I said, 'this isn't good. We're in North Korea.'

It was just as much a shock to De Konig and Collins, as it was to Lucy and I. Planning an escape was going to be infinitely harder under the circumstances. The nearest neighbour was to the South, but it was separated by a field of barbed wire 250 kilometres long and 4 kilometres wide, not to mention land mines and trigger happy guards. We would need to escape by air, or by sea. Neither of which had been good to us, lately.

After the military parade, the guests were treated to a short and unremarkable speech by supreme leader, Kim Jung-On - son of late Kim Jung Il. I could see the family resemblance, except this one was fatter. Perhaps he, too, had an exotic palate. I seem to recall his father was partial to donkey meat and more unusual species.

The guests boarded a tour bus, while the animals were led from the plane - a perverse inversion of Noah's Ark. After all, they were not being saved; they were going to be eaten. Thankfully, the venue wasn't far from the airport. I'd had enough travelling for one day.

It was an army barracks - nondescript on the outside and full of cold linoleum corridors on the inside. After winding our way through the building for a few minutes, we arrived at an opulent ballroom, lavishly decorated for the event. It was like stepping onto a movie set - in another universe.

A camera crew from the State news channel captured our

red-carpet arrival. Normally, the guests would be press-shy, but we were in North Korea. Nobody from the outside world would ever see this. Most of them mugged for the cameras. Inside the ballroom, there were twelve circular tables of six seats each, meticulously set with polished silver, and five sets of drinking glasses. At the end of the room was a raised platform with a long table set for twelve. This, I learned later, was for The Council. They were honorary guests. Then, at the other end of the room was a glass wall that separated us from the kitchen.

There were large, LCD television screens dotted around the ballroom to help us see close-up what the four chefs were doing in the competition. We could already see Kuromizu and Fachon prepping their courses. There was an emcee standing at a lectern, talking excitedly to camera.

One of the waiters showed us to our table, and I took my seat between Lucy and an Argentinean cattle magnate. He turned out to be a valuable source of information, since he had attended the previous Steel Chef competition and had paid over fifteen million dollars for his ticket - a huge price increase from the last one on account of the rarity of the ingredients. He explained to me each of the four chefs could use their own endangered species catch for their signature dishes. Otherwise, they were forced to use the same raw materials from the pantry and had to make everything from scratch, so that there would be no unfair advantages. At the conclusion of the meal, the diners would then fill out score cards. The Council was forbidden from voting. Whoever was declared the winner by the end of the evening would become the Steel Chef for the next four year term. I wondered if this was why Kuromizu was taking no chances? I had already seen his predilection for chemistry. Now, he'd have to leave his chemistry set at home and rely on his raw talent. The only advantage each chef had was their skill in preparing the endangered species that they, themselves, had caught.

What we didn't realise at the time was that Collins and the others were not going to get the five star treatment. When they stepped off the plane, they were taken into custody by the North Korean military on Kuromizu's orders. De Konig thought it pertinent that Kuromizu had chosen not to do this in Cuba, but didn't know why. He'd have plenty of time to ruminate on this while being tortured in a jail cell, explained one of the soldiers, who turned out to be their interpreter.

They were taken to the same army barracks as Lucy and myself, but not to the ballroom. Instead, they were deposited downstairs, in an abattoir.

The room was chilly, the walls tiled, and there were several large and foreboding drains in the floor. Two thirty-foot long rollers ran the length of the room. They were covered in a thick blanket of sharp, steel spikes, spattered in dried blood stains. Collins' team wasn't keen to find out why.

'This is our meat processor,' began the North Korean interpreter, as he dismissed all but one of the guards. 'Not as advanced as yours, perhaps, but very effective.' He pulled up the only chair in the room and sat down to light a cigarette. 'We lead our cows to where you are standing now.' He reached over and tugged on a metal box with an array of buttons, that hung down from the ceiling. 'Then, we adjust the height of the roller,' which he did by pressing a button. The rollers were on hydraulics and split apart, until one was too high to jump over and the other to low to crawl beneath. He pressed another button and the rollers began spinning at a sickening speed. It made a racket, so he spoke louder. 'When I press this red button, the rollers move towards the cow and pulverises the meat in seven seconds.'

Collins was more interested in the contraption than he should have been. 'Doesn't the cow end up all over the room?'

'Yes,' said the interpreter. 'We scrape it off the walls and into the drains below, where it is prepared by the cooks. Messy, but efficient. We can process a herd of cattle in about five minutes. And we don't waste anything.'

'Nose to tail,' offered Collins.

'Precisely.'

A guard handed the interpreter a long rubber apron, goggles, rubber gloves, and a shower cap, which he proceeded to put on.

'Now,' said the interpreter, pushing the red button and closing the gap between his captives and the rollers, 'what, exactly, are you doing here?'

After praising the supreme leader for his generosity in hosting the event, the emcee launched into a blow-by-blow analysis of what the chefs were doing. He spoke in a very animated fashion, which was brightly translated into English by the perky young lady next to him, who had a high-pitched, munchkin voice. She was about twenty-something and was dressed in a very revealing, French school uniform, for some reason. A four-man camera crew covered the kitchen itself. Kuromizu worked calmly and methodically. Fachon, on the other hand, was dripping with sweat and looked terribly harassed. The British chef, Romelly, was no better. He cursed his staff in a colourful fashion, his temper hotter than his stoves. And, the italian chef, Insarda, was giving an equally good performance by showing off his knife skills with intermittent juggling.

I pretended that I needed to go to the bathroom. I wanted to see if there was a way out, so we could team back up with Collins. Unfortunately, I discovered that each of the doors into the hall were protected by a pair of soldiers with automatic weapons. They showed me to the restroom, then waited outside for me to finish.

'It's a no-go,' I said to Lucy, when I joined her back at the table. 'This place is sewn up tight.'

The animal meat arrived by trolley into the kitchen and was divided according to who caught it. It had already been slaughtered and cleaned. Fachon retrieved his razor eagle eggs and passed them to his sous chef for mixing. Lucy and I were glued to the monitors.

'I hope Collins managed to switch out the real thing,' whispered Lucy, anxiously.

'Those eggs look pretty familiar. And the meat doesn't look like chicken,' I said, solemnly.

She patted my hand. 'Don't give up yet. Chuck is very resourceful.' I suspected she did this more for her own benefit, than for mine. The fact is, we didn't want to contemplate otherwise. If those were, indeed, the endangered species that had been caught, then we were witnessing the extinction and last rites of several animal species. And here we were, drinking fine champagne, while the waiters decanted the Chateau Lafite Rothchild, so it could breathe before the main course.

The Council had arrived. They took their seats. They were serious and glum, as if they were attending an insurance seminar. A large digital clock showed us the count-down towards the first plating. Only four minutes to go. The pressure in the kitchen was building. Fachon was scolding one of his team. Romelly went into overdrive and was now assaulting his. Insarda threw things up over his head and plated them, mid-air. Kuromizu, as per usual, was as cool as a cucumber.

The guests enjoyed the spectacle. They clapped at Insarda's buffoonery and thrived off the tension created by Fachon and Romelly. When the clock reached the last ten seconds, the emcee led everyone in a communal countdown.

'Ten… Nine… Eight… Seven… Six…'

Back in the abattoir, the rollers were only a few feet from Collins, Bunny, and De Konig. They had instinctively huddled together, as might cattle.

The interpreter was on his third cigarette. 'Unfortunately, you have not told me anything I don't already know.' He looked at his pack. Only two cigarettes left. He sighed. 'We need to pick up the pace.'

He pressed the red button and closed the gap another six inches.

'I know that two of your friends are in the dining room right now. What I don't know is - what is your plan?'

'Plan?' Collins was sweating now. 'We have no plan!'

'Yes,' concurred De Konig. 'There was no time. We made it up as we went along!'

'You expect me to believe that you came <u>here</u> without a plan?' said the Interpreter.

'That's how we roll, isn't it Bunny?' Collins looked to Bunny, who was still under the influence of the tranquilliser.

'Dude,' said Bunny, to the interpreter, 'can you turn off those roller things? They're making me dizzy and ruining my buzz. Plus, the lighting in here is terrible. It's really bumming me out. This room has seriously bad karma.'

'Look,' said Collins, taking back the conversation, 'we came here to save the animals. We were going to swap them for chicken.'

'So,' said the interpreter, 'where are your chickens?'

'We don't have any.' Collins knew it sounded lame. 'We were hoping to find some... along the way...?'

The interpreter rubbed his temples. 'Either you are extremely clever, or incredibly stupid. Both of which are good reason enough for me to kill you now, and do us all a favour.'

Lucy poked her first course with concern. 'Sod it,' she said and popped a fork-full in her mouth. She chewed briefly, then looked at me with tears in her eyes. I already knew. 'It doesn't taste like chicken,' she said sobbing, 'and it's bloody delicious!'

'Are you alright, my dear?' asked scarface, who was sitting across from her.

'Yes,' I covered, 'it's because of it's sublime beauty. She always gets this way around good food, don't you dear?' I patted her arm. 'She has unusually sensitive tastebuds. They give her the most extraordinary food-gasm.'

Everything was lost, now. The chefs were already onto their second course and Collins had failed to make the switch. It felt as if Lucy and I were dining on the deck of the Titanic. We'd just hit the ecological equivalent of a giant iceberg, the end of at least ten species - maybe more - and the band was still playing on the decks, while the billionaires of this world were enjoying their meal. Now, I began to see why Lucy had been so angry when I first met her. These people weren't evil because of some calculated plan to destroy the world. No. They were evil in their indifference. They were no longer part of the human race. Their apathy would destroy us all. They didn't care about the consequences. They had no compassion. They simply wanted to have a good time, something to brag about to their friends. The world was their oyster, but only for themselves. They had no humility, whatsoever. For the first time, I was angry, too.

Lucy and I felt numb. We watched the second plating without enthusiasm. Kuromizu had prepared snow goat curry. Fachon had made the sea possum into a quiche. The chefs were given five minutes to leave the kitchen and work the dining room by shaking hands and signing autographs, while the waiters garnished and plated their next course.

The monitors showed photos from the endangered species hunt, as if they were holiday snaps. Insarda hammed it up for the camera, while holding up a rare bird that he'd slaughtered, which, incidentally, wasn't on the menu. Not everything caught, apparently, had been used in the cooking. The chefs had made some cuts in their selection, after seeing the creatures up close. It was a senseless waste. There were even photos of Fachon, holding up the two eagle eggs to his chest, as if they were bosoms, while one of the mercenaries held up his fingers in a v-shape above his head, like bunny ears. It was grotesque. It was maddening.

The chefs took a break from their hot stoves and joined the diners in the ballroom. It was time for them to network, shake hands, and sign autographs. We were at the half-way point of the evening and they lost no opportunity in pressing any influence they could upon the voters. I watched Fachon mop the sweat from his brow and let the punters take their photos with him. He had finally got what he wanted. A shot at the title. Eventually, he reached our table. I didn't bother to hide. I sat back leisurely in my seat, holding a glass of champagne.

He was startled when he saw us. He didn't know what to do. At first, I think he wanted to alert security, but, then, recomposed himself and grinned. 'Are you enjoying your evening?'

'Congratulations, Fachon.' I said, raising my glass. 'We wouldn't be here, if not for you.'

'I hope it was worth it,' snarled Lucy, under her breath.

'Oh, oui, ma chérie. It was worth everything. Tout le monde.'

The rollers were inches from their flesh. Collins, Bunny, and De Konig were now hugging each other in a last embrace. The end was near.

Suddenly, the rollers stopped, then receded.

The interpreter sighed. 'I believe you have told me everything you know. Come.' He stripped off his gloves and apron.

Collins was too relieved to say anything, but let himself be led out into the corridor. Bunny, however, was nonchalant, as if everything had simply been a bad trip. 'You forgot to take off your shower cap,' he said. The interpreter thanked him and removed it.

Collins clapped Bunny around the shoulder. 'You know, Bunny, you've always been my lucky charm. My true rabbit's foot!' He laughed at his own joke, but Bunny was nonplussed.

'I'm starving, Chuck. Isn't there supposed to be a dinner or something? Do you think we can score some chow?'

JUST DESERTS

After being escorted through the endless, Escher-like corridors of the barracks, Collins, Bunny, and De Konig were finally led into a darkened room. Inside, they encountered Kim Jung-On, who paid them no attention. His full concentration was on his work. He was hunched over a bank of television monitors. From his headset, he directed the cameras that were covering the evening's event. In front of him was a huge glass wall. Collins looked at the interpreter for permission to approach it.

'Be my guest.'

Collins went up to the window and saw that it looked down onto the dining room, roughly thirty feet below. He picked out Lucy, before he was interrupted by a new visitor.

Kuromizu slipped into the room. 'The main course is about to be served,' he said, gently shutting the door. 'I wanted you to be here to see it.'

'I thought you wanted me dead,' said Collins.

'No. I wanted you out of the way. You have been so determined to interfere with my plans that I had to bring the schedule forwards. Soon, you will see that we are on the same side.'

The monitors in the dining hall flickered momentarily, followed by a pre-recorded video of Kuromizu.

"Ladies and gentlemen, esteemed members of The Council, please take your seats. We are about to serve the main course. I would like to take this opportunity to thank you for your continued support and patronage, and for attending our Steel Chef competition. As you know, I have been fortunate enough to preside over The Council for the last four years. As to whether or not I preside over the next four, well, my fate will be determined here today."

The waiters began placing the main course in front of the guests. The dishes were covered by a silver dome with a handle, in order to keep them warm.

"Heading up such a historical organisation as this has been both a privilege and an education. As a young boy, growing up in Taiji, Japan, I never dreamt that one day I would be standing here before you, blessed with so many opportunities and good fortune. Taiji is a small town. Most of the people I grew up with spent their entire lives there. In fact, I was the first of my family ever to leave in search of my own fortune. Nevertheless, I have not forgotten the humble lessons that I learnt. My father was a strict man. He believed in discipline, austerity, and harmony with nature. He hunted the whale, as did his forefathers and their forefathers. It was a family tradition. Tradition mattered a great deal to my family. Their methods were the same for hundreds of years and he had enormous respect for the animals that he killed. He prayed to them in the Shinto tradition. He asked them for their forgiveness and for providing his family with their livelihood. He took only what he needed and he had tremendous respect for the ocean. Of course, all of this ended when whale hunting was banned. The international community did not approve of it, even though it was not part of their culture. Nevertheless, they stood in judgement, and a thousand year tradition was destroyed. Our community was destroyed. Western modernisation swept through Japan and the old ways were lost. Our family fell on hard times. I was forced to seek my destiny elsewhere. It is a sad irony that the whales are now dying, dying because they have been allowed to overrun their habitat. There is no one to protect them from themselves. For you see, there was a profound symbiosis between the whale and the whale hunter."

The waiters stood by each table in attendance, waiting

patiently for the presentation to finish, so they could pull off the domed lids.

"I would like to begin our next course with a prayer. Let us pray for harmony to be restored. As we eat the flesh of these noble creatures, the last of their kind, let us remember their sacrifice. Let us respect their magnificence and fortitude. Their achievements in the face of adversity. And ask their forgiveness for doing what must be done to ensure our own preservation for many generations to come."

The broadcast ended. The diners who had bowed their heads in respect now looked up, keen to sample the delicacies that the miracle workers had laid before them.

But the waiters had disappeared.

Lucy was about to open domed lid and look inside, when I stopped her. 'Don't. Something isn't right.'

Growing impatient, the other diners eagerly lifted their own covers. That's when everything went terrible wrong.

Nothing was cooked.

It began with the vampire hamsters. Angry at being stuck in a confined space for so long, they leapt from the plate, and plunged themselves into people's necks. Then the screaming started, as others tried to get out of the way. They fell over their chairs and bumped into tables, upsetting other plates, knocking them to the floor.

The albino air leeches went airborne. A woman in an evening dress, stumbled towards us, covered from head to toe, as if they were sequins. She collapsed onto our table, sending our plates skyward. Lucy and I ducked for cover.

Someone had let in the scorpion leopard and the emesis sun bear, which took turns mauling the guests.

I grabbed Lucy's arm. 'We've got to get out of here now!'

The doors were locked from the outside. I could see the soldiers on the other side, watching us through the glass with vacant eyes, while the guests were ripped apart in the dining room. The victims clawed at the door handles, pleaded for their lives, rammed themselves against the doors, but it was no good. The exit was barricaded. There was no way out. We were in a human slaughterhouse.

Collins watched the wretched scene from the observation room above with a strange fascination. He flinched whenever fluids sprayed the glass, but, otherwise, couldn't take his eyes off what was happening. Kim Jung-On was visibly aroused. He cued his cameras by remote control. On his main monitor was a close-up of the komodo soup dragon gnawing on someone's leg, while on another screen, a face-sucking blobfish was giving the African dictator's wife a second face-lift.

Kuromizu watched Collins closely. 'I wanted them to have a good meal before their journey. You see, mister Collins, I never intended to hurt the animals. Quite the opposite, they are very important to me.' Down below, a snow goat sprayed Fachon in stomach acid - the same goat he had nearly caught in the Himalayas. 'Poetic irony, don't you think?'

Collins spoke without emotion. He was fascinated, yet repulsed, by what he saw. 'What did you serve to them at dinner?'

'Prejudice can be persuasive,' said Kuromizu, avoiding the question. 'People see what they want to believe, based on what little they know.' He sighed. 'I could have given them chicken and they'd be none the wiser.'

'I knew chicken would work, but Lucy shot me down. Was it chicken?'

'No. Emu, catfish, and twenty kilos of preserved donkey-meat. Left over from the late Mr Kim. '

'And the razor eagle eggs?'

'Ostrich.'

Chae entered the room and put down a bowl of hot water and a nail brush in front of Kuromizu. He proceeded to clean his nails, while addressing Collins. 'When you face an insurmountable force, you must use that force against itself. Greed is the force that now drives our economy and threatens our existence.' He examined his nails. 'Western society has created a toxic culture and exported it around the world. Survival of the fittest, they call it. Social Darwinism, democracy, capitalism - all of these ideologies have been used to justify slavery. Only a handful of people, including those down there, control the world's resources, while the rest of the world lives forever in their debt. They consider themselves the fittest of the species when, in fact, they are simply the most mercenary.'

'And this is the solution?'

'It is just the beginning.'

Collins watched as the head of the world's largest investment bank was eviscerated by the scorpion leopard, while his dinner partner - a beautiful woman, now pale from loss of blood - dragged herself painfully across the floor.

Kuromizu lifted his hands and let Chae replace the nail cleaning tools with a small bento box. 'This is what I believe the banking establishment calls, "a market correction".' Inside the box was a modest rice ball wrapped in seaweed. He was famished from the competition and hadn't yet eaten.

'Then why all this? Why the competition?'

'The medicine may be bitter, mister Collins, but it is far preferable to the death of the patient,' he said, picking up the rice ball. 'I needed to collect the animals as quickly as I could. The competition seemed an efficient way of doing so. Four teams, four weeks - twelve of the most endangered species. And fully paid for by the contestants and the diners themselves. I believe the Americans call this a win-win scenario.' He had finished his rice ball. Chae handed him a moist towel. 'And, I needed to eliminate a few people - people who would not appreciate my plan.' He was thinking of the blood-soaked table of The Council, now experiencing their last supper. 'It was time for a change in management.' He turned and gestured to Kim Jung-On. 'His late father was a shareholder in my company and shared my vision. Sadly, his son doesn't have the same culinary interests, but he is a very keen filmmaker, as you can see.'

With his eyes glued to the screen, Kim Jung-On pawed the edge of his table, until his fingers found his pile of puffed cheese crisps. He took a handful and popped the whole thing in his mouth.

'I am told that he has the finest snuff film collection in the world, which is why he was only too eager to lend a hand, so long as he could direct it himself. Tonight's fundraiser brought in three hundred and forty million dollars, which should be enough to care for the animals and further my research.'

'Research?'

'Yes. These creatures have rare qualities that can help us. Despite their endangered status, they have unusual survival skills. In the right hands, these can be weaponised.' Kuromizu was surprisingly candid, like a friendly professor. 'As you well know, animals in the wild have modest requirements. They only eat what they require to survive. They maintain a balanced habitat. They support the preservation of their group. It is only when they are brought into captivity that they lose all self-constraint and their sense of community. They become gluttonous. Their actions... self-serving.'

He had fastidiously wiped his fingers clean. He handed the used towel back to Chae.

'Millions of species have gone extinct since the beginning of time, mister Collins. It happens when there is a radical change in the environment, or when there is extreme competition for scarce resources. At the present time, mankind is experiencing both, simultaneously. Ironically, these circumstances are of his own making. We are no longer fighting for survival against the elements, but against one another. The self-proclaimed elite have created a coliseum for their own amusement by putting everyone else into the ring. They have become our predators. What they don't realise is that their own moral degradation has precipitated a feeding-frenzy that will consume them, too. What the world needs right now is more balance and less competition. If we value the preservation of our species, we must remove those who have only their own self-interest at heart, the gluttonous ones, and recalibrate society.' He approached Collins. 'What do you do with a species that has overrun it's environment, mister Collins?'

'You cull it,' said Collins, regretfully.

'Exactly. We must cull our species in order to save it,' he said, putting his hand on Chuck's shoulder. 'You said that Gaia called upon you.'

'Yes. She asked me to save the planet.'

'The planet does not need saving. It will take care of itself. It will shed itself of this human infestation and start again. That would be most regrettable, don't you agree? Gaia does not distinguish between man or beast. We are all beasts in her eyes. No, Gaia called upon you to save us - all of us, mankind included. Gaia has given us a second chance by calling upon you. You are her soldier of fortune. Together, we must smite this infestation and cut out the cancer. Unless we do something soon, we will go extinct. That is why we must restore harmony, before it's too late. That is why we must eliminate the members of our species who are taking more than their fair share.' He looked Collins straight in the eye. 'Survival of the fittest, mister Collins, will lead to the destruction of mankind.'

Lucy and I hid under a table. She plugged her ears to blot out the screams. All we could see were feet running in circles, skidding on puddles of blood. One man collapsed nearby, covered in velocerabbits. They nibbled off his flesh at high speed with their razor sharp teeth.

'What the hell are we going to do?' I said. Lucy had her hands around her ears. I pulled them down. 'Lucy - think!' She looked at me in shock. 'What do we do?' I repeated.

She thought for a second. 'Play dead,' she said. 'They attack because they are scared and they attack anything that moves.'

We both lay down on the floor as still as we could. I took her blood-soaked hand in mine. This was not a good way to die.

Is there ever a good way to die? Probably not. But going in my sleep at a ripe old age was kind of what I had in mind. Not this.

I drifted off for awhile. It was nice to hold her hand. It was small and warm. It kept death away - just a little longer. Love comes when you least expect it. And when you most regret it. But without love we are alone and forever in competition with ourselves and with everyone else. It's much better to be connected. Even if we lost ourselves in the process.

'Where are you taking them - the animals?' Collins had seen enough.

'I am taking them somewhere safe. A safari and ocean park where they will be well looked after. You would approve. It's ten times larger than Animal Land and completely self-sufficient. I learnt from your mistakes and built something better.'

'You burned down my dreams,' said Collins, feeling hurt.

'I fuelled them,' said Kuromizu. 'I was your anonymous investor. The one who provided the gap financing to see Animal Land come to fruition.'

'And, then, you burnt it down!'

'I am sorry. The animals were more important to me than your career. You see, I have most of them at my own facility already. They are safe and sound in their natural habitat, sheltered far from the maddening crowd.' Kuromizu looked at Collins, deadly serious. 'Hasn't that always been your dream? To protect the animals and to be respected by them in return?' Collins nodded, sadly. 'Mister Collins, you are the finest animal handler the world has ever known, as demonstrated by your remarkable recovery of the iridescent sea possum. I'd like you to be my chief park ranger at Kuromizu Park. There are no tourists. No concessions. Only endangered animals. And it's our only hope for the future. Will you join me?'

Collins was caught off guard by the invitation. There was so much to take in. He thought of Lucy and felt despondent.

Kuromizu considered this. 'Your friends in the dining room are already dead. Regrettable, but they were warned. As for De Konig, he betrayed me and I cannot set a precedence. He must be punished.'

'Wait a minute,' said De Konig, from the back of the room. 'I'm ten times better than he is, mister Kuromizu. Give me a second chance and I'll prove it.'

'There are no margins for error,' said Kuromizu, to De Konig. 'No second chances. You have made your bed. Now, lie in it.'

De Konig switched tack and pleaded to his brother. 'Chuck -

don't do this. You know what this man is capable of!'

The only real regret that Collins felt was for Lucy. He had loved her. Even told her so, once upon a time. But she had never said it back. She deserved this, then. She thought only of her career. Not of his cause. Not of him. It made him angry. She may have tried to atone for it since, but it was too little, too late. It was only the guilt eating away at her that made her stay. He said nothing to her about any of this, of course, because it had been useful to him. Now, however, he was forced to face the facts. She was a victim of her own ambition. She didn't love him and she didn't love Gaia. She didn't even call Gaia by its proper name! He felt like crying, but there was no point. It was messing with his chakra. He had a higher purpose to attend to.

Collins spoke patiently to De Konig, as gently as he could. 'It's not about what I want, brother. It's what Gaia wants.' Then, he looked at Bunny. 'Are you in?'

'Sure, 'ol buddy. But I need to get something to eat. My blood sugar's getting low.'

B-TEAM

Lucy and I lay as still as possible, long after the screams had stopped. It had been touch and go for awhile but, as Lucy said, the animals only wanted the screamers. They had a lot of food in the room, so they were soon sated, and ignored us. After what seemed like an eternity, a clean-up crew came in. The animals were dopey from gorging on the dinner guests and were easy targets. The crew darted them with tranquillisers, and put them back into their cages.

Lucy and I crept towards the door. We had to keep up the pretence, though, of being dead. Nobody seemed to notice two, slow-moving corpses. They didn't expect anyone to be alive. To help sell the subterfuge, we smeared ourselves in blood and giblets. Little by little, we made it to one of the open doors, and waited patiently for the moment to make a run for it.

I squeezed Lucy's hand. 'Ready?' She squeezed mine back. 'Now!'

We darted through the door with no idea where we were going, or what we would find on the other side.

We made it halfway down the corridor, before we heard someone approaching. Thankfully, there was an open door that we ducked into. It was an empty dishwashing room. We were in a large complex devoted to food preparation. Lucy and I caught our breath.

'You look like Carrie on prom night,' I said.

'Funny, so do you.'

We wiped the blood from our faces and prepared to make

another go of it, when we heard whoever it was pass by us. We held our breath, until it was safe again to talk.

'If I ever take you out to dinner, let me chose the venue, okay?' I said. Lucy laughed nervously. 'Ready?'

Ducking and diving through doorways, we managed to avoid the other staff and make our way from one corridor to the next. We were grateful that only a skeleton crew remained; most of the evening's staff had apparently gone home.

Unfortunately, in the fourth hallway we ran into a couple of guards who were escorting De Konig. They were startled by us, which gave De Konig the upper hand. He kicked one in the back of the knee and went for the other one's gun. None of us were martial artists, so we weighed in with clumsy blows, kicks, and scratches. I managed to bring one of them down by the earlobes. Eventually, De Konig got the gun and dispatched the guards. However, we'd made far too much noise in the process and could now hear a commotion coming towards us.

'Time to fly,' said De Konig, who led the way.

Luckily, we made it out to the airfield alive, just in time to see Kuromizu, Collins, and Bunny board the plane that would take them out of North Korea. De Konig explained that they were headed for Kumomizu's safari park.

Lucy was spitting mad. 'How could he just leave us like this?'

'He thought you were dead,' said De Konig.

'I don't care. Kuromizu's a monster. You saw what happened back there!'

'I agree but something's happened to Chuck. He thinks he's on some kind of mission from God.'

'Not God - Gaia,' I said.

Lucy was flustered, tired and upset. 'I thought he'd become a better man when we found him and brought him back from the brink. Back from insignificance. I thought he was more at peace with himself.'

'Listen,' I said, 'we've got bigger problems to deal with, here. We're on a military airbase in North Korea. None of us speak the language, or look remotely asian. And they will soon realise that we've escaped. You couldn't ask for a bigger shit storm if you blew up a city sewer.'

That focused everyone's attention.

'What's the plan, then?' De Konig was asking me. Me! Things were really that bad.

'We're going to make it out of here alive. We must. And I'll tell you why. Kuromizu's cooking something and it isn't yesterday's leftovers. He's up to something big. We're going to find out what and blow it wide open. We're taking him down and everyone with him!'

I was roused by my own speech and running on a high, now that I'd become responsible for the lives of two other people, besides my own. The odds weren't good. But I had hope. What other choice was there? We were three very different people with conflicting agendas. But now we had a common purpose - to get out alive. Hopefully, we could stay the course. Something much bigger than ourselves was about to threaten our very existence - and everyone else's. And, after the slaughter in the ballroom, we were the only people who knew anything about it.

I pulled out the bracelet I'd stolen from a severed hand at the dinner table - plus, an array of other jewellery that I'd pilfered during my slow crawl across the dining room during our escape. 'Here, all of this must count for something. At least we can try to bribe our way out of here.'

This made Lucy laugh. De Konig thought her outburst crazy. He shook his head and looked out across the airfield.

'Plus,' I said, 'I still have the Sat phone.' I checked the battery level. 'Just enough for a couple of calls, I reckon.'

We were a motley crew, no doubt about it. Sometimes, the most unlikely teams can make the biggest difference. We hadn't been handpicked. We'd been chosen by fate. Kept together by circumstance. And now, responsible for saving the world.

De Konig was a tracker and a paramilitary. That would come in handy.

Lucy was resourceful, intelligent, and beautiful. Good qualities on any expedition.

And, I?

I punched in a number on the Sat phone. A moment later, it connected.

'Oz, it's me. I need your help.'

I was a survivor.

Chuck Collins and his crew will return in, **Endangered Species: Book 2, "The Last Supper"**

To keep in touch with the latest ES developments, talk to the author and other fans, please go to:

http://www.seam.tv/groups/endangered-species/

If you enjoyed this book, then please give your feedback:

http://www.seam.tv/endangered-species-intro/

ABOUT SEAM

Shared Experience Art Machine is a community of artists and audience who collaborate to create meaningful entertainment with a positive social impact. Together, we create **Social Science Fiction** stories. These are stories that explore topical issues and radical technology that have profound social consequences.

Endangered Species is an eco-thriller, action-comedy series that examines our most pressing ecological disaster scenarios. It is written collaboratively by the SEAM Writers Room. This book is the first in a number of series that we are producing to fulfil our mission to produce engaging entertainment that offers something much more than escapism. We are hoping to make a positive impact on the world by framing the debate around the inconvenient truths that threaten our existence.

If you like what we are doing, then we welcome your support by visiting our website (www.seam.tv) and getting involved in our development process. We welcome both writers and members of the public. In fact, we feel that it's important for artists and their audience to have direct communication in order to make meaningful and relevant entertainment. On our website, you'll be able to chat to our writers, our producers, other audience members, and to help us plan what stories to tell next.

In addition, if you are a storyteller yourself, we have other books and forums devoted to transmedia entertainment that we hope you will explore with us. A lot of our content is free, but there is some content that we charge a subscription for. All of the proceeds from our subscriptions goes to help us employ writers and build entertainment franchises to make the world a better place. Stories can save lives. And stories build community. We sincerely hope that you will come and join us on our journey.

Thank you for your continued interest and support!

SEAM LTD

www.ingramcontent.com/pod-product-compliance
Lightning Source LLC
Chambersburg PA
CBHW071146170626
46809CB00002B/789